Knight Fall

The Reminiscent Exile: Book Three

Joe Ducie

Cedar Sky Publishing

Knight Fall

The Reminiscent Exile: Book Three

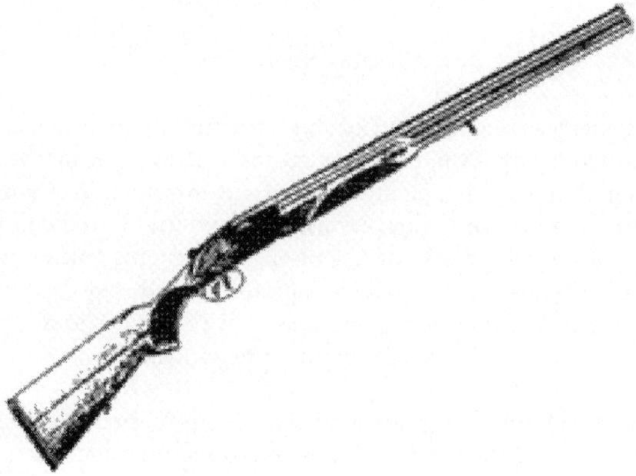

Joe Ducie

Cedar Sky Publishing

Cedar Sky Publishing was founded in Perth, Western Australia.
This book also available as an e-book for Kindle.

First printed in the United States of America, 2013

Written by Joe Ducie: www.joeducie.net
Cover artwork by Vincent Chong: www.vincentchong-art.co.uk

ISBN-13: 9780987329448

For CHARLOTTE,
who is not a pigeon

CONTENTS

ACKNOWLEDGMENTS

Time are changin' on the writing front. I'm becoming a bit noisy, much like Declan. Heh. But this story and all my others wouldn't be here without the considerable help of a select group of folks.

To Finola Richardson, my primary editor, who continues to keep these pages from becoming too soaked in scotch. So lovely.

To Brian Alder, who can't get no satisfaction.

To Elisha Rooney, who can read between the lines far too well!

To the editors and proofreaders at Red Adept, who turn this word medley into pie.

And to Vincent Chong, who always designs such kickass covers for these tales.

OPENING SALVO – WORLD-WEARY ENOUGH TO FALL ASLEEP IN A NIGHTCLUB

Life is a dream for the wise,
a game for the fool, a comedy for the rich,
a tragedy for the poor.

— Sholom Aleichem

CHAPTER ONE

Broken Reason

Battered, bloody, and drenched from the rain, Emily Grace, the Immortal Queen of the Renegades, stood at my shop door. A white dress, speckled with crimson drops, clung to her body, and a sodden dark blue shawl covered her shoulders, strangling her neck like a scarf.

She offered me a pained smile, her sapphire eyes fighting tears, and took a single step over the threshold before collapsing into my arms. I caught her, mindful of her baby bump. The scent wafting up from her neck reminded me of ancient forests and creeks. A little river of blood ran down her throat, leaking from a cut hidden by the shawl.

"My life in your hands, Declan Hale," she whispered, still smiling, and her eyelids fluttered closed.

"Em," I said. "Can you hear me?"

Nope. She'd passed out.

I glanced out at Riverwood Plaza, but the small group of shops and apartments was dark and awash with fierce black raindrops the size of poker chips. I couldn't see more of the plaza than drenched silhouettes.

Anyone—or anything—could have been hiding in the shadows. Renegade soldiers, Voidlings, assassins with a grudge… A sense of hooded eyes and unseen malice weighed on my shoulders. I slammed the door and flipped over the 'Closed' sign, which activated a bunch of invisible wards and enchantments against the night.

Using a quick invocation, I levitated Emily through the warren of towering books under gently glowing chandeliers, to my small writing alcove built into a window box overlooking Riverwood Plaza. Her perfume mingled with the heady scent of vanilla and old leather books. I laid her down on the couch there and cast a few diagnostic enchantments. White light, the fires at the heart of creation, danced within and around my fingertips.

She was alive—hurt, but alive.

A vicious crack of thunder punctured the world outside, and a flash of lightning shocked the plaza. In the shadows and rain, I thought I glimpsed elongated and tortured faces, screaming or laughing.

Just in your head… I told myself but didn't quite believe.

I picked up my phone, checked the time—just after two in the morning—and called Sophie, because I sure couldn't patch Em up. The phone rang a half dozen times before she answered, mumbling a sleepy hello.

"'Phie, it's Declan. I need you at the shop right now. Someone you need to heal."

She yawned down the line. *"Should I bring Ethan?"*

"Sure, bring him along. And before you ask, no, I

don't know what's going on. Just be quick, okay? And careful. Use the back door. Bye."

I ended the call and tossed the phone aside. Sophie was one of the best healers I'd ever known, and she was only getting better. I wasn't even close to her skill level, but there were still one or two tricks I could play with until she arrived. I got down on my knees in front of Emily, between her and the coffee table, and gently placed my hand on her neck. Her skin was chilled, wet from the rain and the blood, but I could feel her breathing.

Smoky, ethereal light spun from my palm and between my fingers. I used a minor healing enchantment to seal the cut on her throat. Then I set to work on the bruises on her face, her split lip, her blackened eye, and the myriad shallow cuts covering her arms and hands.

Someone had carved a deliberate and wicked crescent moon into her left breast.

Anger began to swirl in my gut, making my heart race. *Whoever did this has made an enemy tonight.* I would spend considerable effort tracking them down and making them suffer. That kind of travesty could only be justly repaid in kind, and I was never averse to a bit of late-night wet work.

I was mindful not to use Willful enchantments around the swell of Emily's belly and the baby. The kid was about ready to pop out of her any day now, but soaking him or her in Willful light, however well intentioned, could lead to complications.

I simply wasn't skilled enough in healing to handle that. I needed Sophie.

As I worked, I couldn't help but let out a wry chuckle at the thought of saving Emily's life, not even half a year since she had stabbed me, cast me from a tower a mile above the old lost city of Atlantis, and killed me among the shards of the Infernal Clock. Funny old life, but it just wasn't in me to let her suffer—the fact that she had shown up on my door in this state made me guess she knew that much about me, and probably a great deal more. For as long as I'd known her, Emily had always been a half-dozen steps ahead of the game. Something in her resonated in me, and I was drawn, circling ever closer to a flame she surely fanned often.

"Declan…" she muttered, eyes closed and a small frown creasing her brow. She gasped but didn't wake, and then smiled. "A scar on my heart… to keep the Everlasting apart."

With most of her cuts and bruises healed to the best of my Willful ability, I sat back on the coffee table, knocking aside a stack of pages from my endless, never-finished novel. Staring down at Emily, I rested my elbows on my knees and held my hands, soaked in her blood, over the dark jarrah wood floor. Small drops dripped from the tips of my fingers.

"What are you doing here, Em?" I asked softly.

It felt like the first move in a new game. Broken quill, but I was far too tired and far too *sober* for any such nonsense.

~~*~*

Sophie and her boyfriend, Ethan, arrived not a quarter of an hour later, letting themselves in through the back with their key—a heavy, ornate key tuned to bypass the wards and enchantments protecting my shop and what little shreds of sanity I had left against the Void. Broken quill, but I hated the Void, the dark, empty space between universes. After being pulled from bed at hours far too untoward, my friends looked tired in their hastily assembled jeans and T-shirts, which were sodden from the storm.

Emily was still unconscious, and I hadn't moved from the coffee table. Her blood had dried on my hands, and Sophie—after a moment of sheer shock at seeing just who her patient was—shoved me aside, her hands already alight with silver smoke, and delved into the Immortal Queen.

I moved around the table and stood next to Ethan Reilly, my wayward apprentice.

"Boss," he said, stifling a yawn. "What kind of time you call this?"

"Do you know who she is?" I gestured to Emily. Her feet, encased in a pair of thin leather sandals, pressed against the arm of my couch. The toenail on her big toe had been torn away—a wound I had missed.

Tortured, most definitely. By someone or some*thing* rather adept.

Ethan shrugged. "She's from the realms of Forget, I take it?"

"Yes." I chucked. "Oh yes. Her name—what I know her by, at least—is Emily Grace. She's the leader of the Renegades. Their Immortal Queen."

"Oh dear," Ethan said. "The one that knifed you good and proper and booted you from Atlantis. Shouldn't you be, you know, arresting her?"

I ran a bloody hand back through my hair and sighed. As of two and a half months ago, my exile of five years had been rescinded for services rendered to the crown, and I was officially a Knight Infernal again—in name, at least, at the lowly rank of Guardian.

None of the ruling class or my old comrades had seen fit to welcome me back to Ascension City just yet. For good reason, I suppose. I was loved and hated by the populations of a hundred worlds. Mostly hated. Perhaps more so than the Renegades during the height of the Tome Wars.

The Knights and the Renegades did not get along,

but we hadn't really been in a state of open war for the best part of six years. My doing, my *fault*… mostly. Although I hadn't been back to Forget and Ascension City since my reinstatement, I'd heard rumors that my pardon had stirred a lot of resentment among the Renegades, even caused a few minor conflicts in the outer territories. Understandable, given the sordid reasons for my exile in the first place and the manner in which I'd been dragged back into action twice this last year.

Oh, yes, and perhaps because you killed their king not too long ago, nattered an annoying voice in the back of my mind. *Emily's husband.*

"Arrest her? I'd much rather go for a drink," I told Ethan, fiddling with the strap of the patch I wore over my blind left eye. "How is she, Sophie?"

Sophie frowned and flicked her auburn ponytail over her shoulder. The glow of her hands, pressed against Emily's baby bump, flickered and died. "Well enough, as far as I can tell. I think she's just exhausted. There's no internal damage that I could find. And I think…" She bit her lip. "I think the baby's okay. I've never really delved into someone who's pregnant before. It's… intense. Two heartbeats."

"Thank you for coming." I released a long sigh and held up my bloodstained hands. "Can you hang around while I go clean up?"

"Sure. Did she say anything to you about why she's here?" 'Phie licked her lips. "This feels dangerous."

Already walking over to the spiral staircase that led up to the second floor and the washroom, I cast a quick look over my shoulder. "Nothing that made any sense. I'll be down in a minute."

CHAPTER TWO

Storm Sense

When I went back downstairs, the wind howling through Riverwood Plaza shook the storefront of my shop and rattled the windows. Rain slammed into the glass, and thunder rumbled overhead.

Ethan was staring out of the window in my writing alcove, an arm resting lightly around Sophie's shoulders. Worry masked his face by the light of the chandeliers.

"Everything okay, sunshine?" I asked.

"Thought I… saw something." He shook his head. "Wild storm out there."

I moved behind the counter, past the dusty ill-used cash register, and rested my arms on the old mahogany. "What did you see?"

Ethan shrugged and offered me a sheepish grin. "Faces… faces in the rain."

I nodded, reached below the counter, and retrieved my sleek single-barreled shotgun. The metal of the silver barrel gleamed in the half-light, reflecting the evanescent glow from above. The heavy weapon carried a strong, reassuring aroma of gun oil.

"Mate, what the hell?" Ethan spluttered.

Sophie looked at me and raised a single eyebrow. "You've gone robust."

I gave them both a wink and punched the sale key on the old register. The cash drawer sprang open on rusty hinges, and where the notes and coins belonged were a variety of colorful and, in some cases, otherworldly shotgun shells. I settled on the cache of clear crystal shells, loaded with a mix of star iron, magnesium, and tiny rune-inscribed ball bearings. The fancy shells cost a pretty penny in raw materials, but damned if they didn't punch a hole the size of a basketball in anything unfortunate enough to stray in front of the gun's business end.

Once the gun was loaded with eight rounds, I pumped one into the chamber and loaded the pockets of my waistcoat with a few extra shells, three on each side, standing to attention like good little soldiers.

"So what's out there?" Sophie asked calmly. She looked down at Emily, still unconscious but frowning, as if she were having bad dreams. "Is it whatever did this?"

"Maybe," I said. "Faces in the rain… Stinks of the Void, doesn't it?" I chuckled and held up one of the clear shells. "Nasty mix of alien elements and Infernal rune-encrusted bearings. Vrail sent me the design a few months ago, after what happened with Scion. Thought maybe Detective Brie would like something with a bit more kick to it than her service firearm, seeing how she's insisting on hanging around."

A not altogether unpleasant situation, as Annie Brie was all kinds of lovely, but it was hard to smile when our current friendship was based on a rather significant… omission of truth. Annie had died mere months ago, facing down Scion with me on Diablo Beach, and I'd brought her back to life with a petal of the Infernal Clock. A method of resurrection that offered certain protections and, in ways I didn't understand, immortality. Not invulnerability, however.

Funnily enough, I had Emily to thank for that petal.

I had not yet told Annie I'd brought her back to life—she assumed she was just knocked out. Yet by doing so, I had tied her harder to the realms of Forget and the malevolent old gods, the Everlasting, than ever. Fair to say, I sensed such a revelation would not go over too well.

Thinking on Annie made something in my mind spin toward Joondalup, about fifteen minutes down the road. I felt a surge of… *warmth*… rush through me and knew that Annie was working late at the police station, as clearly as if she'd called to tell me. That *knowing* came from some connection through the petals of the Infernal Clock, the broken immortality that we both shared, and I got the feeling Annie often had glimpses of me, as well. We each knew where the other was, if we concentrated hard enough.

It had been a few weeks since I last saw my young detective. Safe to guess she was avoiding me, but that couldn't last, not with our newfound connection. Her desire for answers would eventually outweigh fear of those same answers.

I missed her. Funny, in a tragic kind of way, how quickly someone could come into my life and completely fill an unfathomable *need*. A need I had not really desired since the night I forfeited my shadow.

"So magic shotguns, is it?" Ethan clapped his hands together, pulling me from my thoughts, the sense of *knowing* where Annie was vanished for the moment. "Sure, why not? You got a spare?"

"You two stay here with Emily," I said calmly and lifted the shotgun to rest on my shoulder. The wind still whipped the rain against my windows, and a feeling that may have been an anxious sort of dread gripped my heart. "I'll go see what all the ruckus is outside. Faces in the rain, huh…"

I moved across the shop, through the book-strewn labyrinth of shelves, and paused before the front door. Steeling my resolve—a wearied kind of indifference, really—I flipped over the ward sign, grasped the handle, and stepped out into the wild night, making sure to reset the wards behind me.

The downpour soaked me in the first half dozen steps I took away from the relative safety of my shop. My fine leather shoes submerged in a flow of water about a quarter foot deep that ran down the plaza toward Sugar Lane.

I held the shotgun at the ready, barrel pointed just below the horizon, finger to the side of the trigger, and meandered over to the wide-rimmed marble fountain in the heart of Riverwood Plaza, putting myself at ease on the rim of the fountain and on display for anything that wanted to try its luck and take a bite.

The night was cold—colder than cold, heading toward freezing. In a few hours, dawn would break. Something told me I was going to be worlds away before then—call it intuition, but I'd played the game before. I shivered and watched my breath shimmer on the air, dance in the rain.

And all at once, the streetlamps went out, plunging Riverwood Plaza into darkness.

Well, that's an easy trick…

I snapped my fingers, and a burst of sunlight exploded from my palm, coalescing into a sphere of pure, white energy. *Bait for the hook.* I cast the sphere into the air, high above the fountain, and caught sight of a thousand tormented faces, screeching like bats on the wind, before something slick and black—tentacles of dark, seething oil—swallowed my light whole.

In that last instant before the light went out, I stood and fired, pleased that the creature had taken the bait. The shotgun roared, another flash of blinding fire like the crack of an immense lightning bolt burst from the barrel, and a flaming bombardment of enhanced buckshot tore through the air and into the mess of screeching tentacles slithering just above the plaza.

Something shrieked, sounding like talons scraped down a chalkboard, and howled in anger.

I pumped the gun and fired again and again across the sky, taking wild shots through the rain in a rough circle just above my head. Fiery trails of magnesium dug deep furrows in the creature—creatures?—and oily pieces fell like ignited ash. Most of the ash dissolved into the flow of water running down the street. One piece landed on my forearm and burnt like antifreeze before dissolving with the rest.

I quickly reloaded from the store of shells in my waistcoat pockets. *This is something new—or, as always, something rather old.* Of the Void, most definitely, and of a kind I'd never encountered before. More oil than solid substance, more fractured than real. Still, anything loosed from the Void, that impermeable space between universes, was cause for concern. At best my shotgun would only wound the beast, perhaps rile it up—as if it needed riling—and to use Will would be akin to pouring gasoline on a fire, which was why the beast had devoured my sphere of light.

But I had a unique protection against Voidlings, afforded to me by the sale of my shadow in Atlantis:

They hated me.

Even, I believed, *feared* me.

The rain lessened… But no, that was the Voidlings.

More had appeared, blocking the sky, and the rainwater sizzled as it struck their oily skin. I wasn't fighting one massive, seething creature but a flock of flying serpents that screeched like bats. The creatures drew closer, encasing me within a swirling mass of darkness—a darkness that radiated a subtle illumination, a *not*-light, just bright enough to see how royally fucked I was about to be.

Yet none of them dared touch me. *Trapped under a Void-umbrella…*

A vague, blurred form stepped out of the darkness, a twisted silhouette that seemed to bleed from the maelstrom of Voidlings under our umbrella. The form quickly took on a rough, humanoid shape.

The not-light of the Void shone all the brighter, an impressive array of greys and gloominess that, against all reason, offered illumination. The oily darkness faded and became a pale, white face—a face I recognized all too well.

"Huh," I said. "Hello, handsome."

The glittering, smoky creatures poured themselves into the abomination standing before me, and drops of rain from the real world slipped through the darkness, leaving ragged holes in our umbrella. Thunder clapped far overhead, but I kept my eyes on a face I'd last seen in the Black Mirror—a pathway into the Void itself, locked away in my upstairs bathroom like the dark, dirty secret it was.

"Declan," the abomination rasped. His voice, although strained, was as familiar as his form. He offered me a half-empty bottle of something amber and aged. Scotch. "Care for a drink?"

I was looking at what had become of my shadow.

CHAPTER THREE

Mirrors

I eyed the bottle of scotch and licked my lips. "No, thank you. I'm on the wagon, Shadowman."

The abomination's eyes were entirely devoid of warmth, and his hollow cheeks were as pale as a corpse dead three days or more. The eyes that had bled into his face from the serpent-like Voidlings had turned pale blue, as if coated in a cataract film, and his hair hung dark brown and lank. He wore a rough imitation of my standard collared shirt and waistcoat, but on him the clothing looked *old*—worn and ragged, as if he'd been buried in it a long time ago.

That was the general sense I got from the demon in human guise—something dead and buried.

"Shadowman..." He grinned, lips the color of bruised skin. "I like that. Yes. I am Shadowman."

"How did you escape the Void? And what, may I ask, are these creatures you brought with you?"

Shadowman smiled and ran his hand through the myriad squirming serpents just above him. "Void essence, Declan. Raw, malleable clay of the abstract—clay, which, in the right hands, can be molded to great effect." He gave himself a brief round of applause. "And I escaped because of you, because your… soul, for lack of a better word, has seen the world with a new perspective these last few months."

"What do you mean?"

"You are no longer exiled, and therefore, neither am I." He tapped his forehead and winked at me. "Perception, how we perceive our absolute reality, is the only real truth. And truth, buddy—truth is like looking in a mirror: quite often *familiar*."

I guess that made a twisted kind of sense. Whatever this *man* had become, he was a piece of me, and by more than a little bit. My shadow was something abstract made tangible by the Everlasting Oblivion in the ruins of Atlantis those long, short years ago, and the Void existed only in the abstract. That was why thinking too long and too hard on the Void—particularly if one was Willful—could attract the attention of creatures from beyond time and space. The danger grew several orders of magnitude for those scant few who had faced down Voidlings and survived—or, worse, traversed the Void itself and managed to escape with life and some small measure of sanity intact.

I had done all those things, more than once. So I did my best to not think of the Void at all. Not always easy, when the Void was often thinking of me.

"Lord Oblivion created me." Shadowman thrust a finger against my chest. "He tore me from you and cast me into the Void. The price for ending the Tome Wars, yes? Everything that I am, everything that I *do*, is your responsibility. You willingly allowed me to be birthed."

I maneuvered the shotgun into the comfortable nook

against my shoulder and curled my finger around the trigger. "Perhaps I absolve myself of such responsibility right now."

Shadowman grasped the barrel and pressed it against his forehead. His dark brown bangs brushed the sight, and he grinned. "You think a concoction of star iron and archaic runes can stop me? I'm far too *new* for such old tricks."

I tilted my head and smirked. Damn it all, but I believed him. Still, I kept the business end of the gun trained on his heart. "So what is it you want, Shadowman? Did you just come on by tonight to say hello? Give me a heads up that you're out and about on the winds of the rising storm? And tell me, did you damage sweet Emily Grace?"

"The Immortal Queen…" Something dangerous, a snarl mired in rage that ran as dangerous as an ocean in storm, flittered across his pale face like a—well, like a shadow. "I did not touch her. I would not dare. As for my purpose, I am here to slay the Everlasting."

"Hallelujah and amen," I said. The Void essence—still incessantly flying around us, blocking most of the rain and the wind—was beginning to make me dizzy. "But we're all out of elder gods around here."

Shadowman grinned and gave me a quick salute with his scotch bottle. He swayed back and forth, as if drunk. "Aye, keep believing that a little while longer. Perhaps I just wanted to meet you, Declan—face to face, without that dark mirror between us."

"Am I going to have to kill you?" The shotgun was beginning to weigh on me. My finger twitched on the trigger. "You said this won't do the job, but I'd still like to give it a shot."

"Perhaps I came to tell you that I may have used this handsome face of ours to stir up a bit of trouble in Ascension City earlier today." He reached into his waistcoat, retrieved a folded newspaper, and held it out to me. "Or yesterday, depending on the time lost between here and there. The Void can be tricky like that."

I didn't take the pages from him.

Shadowman shrugged and held up the paper so I could read the headline.

HISTORIAN OF FUTURE PROSPECT KIDNAPPED BY DECLAN HALE

I read the headline then read it again, just to make sure I had the right of it. "You're kidding," I said. "No, no you are not kidding. Christ."

Shadowman grinned and tossed the paper aside. "She didn't see that one coming."

"She's just a kid," I whispered.

The Historian was far more than a kid, even if she were only sixteen. I'd last seen her half a year before, in the forests surrounding Ascension City. A pretty little thing, wise in the eyes. The Historian was a baby girl born with a rare gift—a curse, really. She could *See* the future. All possible futures. She could even—as was believed by more than a few—influence events to some degree.

The Knights Infernal revered the Historian. Ascension City was never much for religion, but if there was one thing the Knights and the people of that world held sacrosanct, it was their belief in the purity and sanctity of the Historian of Future Prospect.

To have kidnapped her… To have endangered her at all…

"Where is she?" I demanded. "Take me to her now."

Shadowman waggled his finger back and forth. "You

see what I am doing, yes? What must be done. Too long have the Knights ignored your—*our*—warnings about the Everlasting. Too long have they idled. I am forcing them to act. They will hunt me as the Historian leads me and my Voidlings against the Everlasting. They will have no choice but to fight."

"And be slaughtered," I said, shaking my head. His plan was good in theory, but reality wouldn't be so kind. "You don't fight the Everlasting and win."

"Says the man who outfoxed Scion, the Younger God, only a few short months ago." He tipped an invisible hat toward me. "Bravo, by the way. Fuck, but you make us look good."

I shook my head. "I bloodied his nose, at best—"

"You plucked his eye from its socket with a weapon of celestial illusion. You did more than bloody the Everlasting. You made them *fear*. Can you conceive the breadth of time that has passed since the Elder Gods last feared anything?"

I tapped the eye patch covering my eye. "That was revenge, pure and simple. His machinations cost me an eye."

Shadowman sighed and took a heavy swig from his scotch bottle. "They'll be coming for you—sooner rather than later. And they'll come in force. Hell, they may just turn this entire corner of the world into a blackened crater to ensure your destruction." He snapped his fingers twice and pointed at me. "Oblivion didn't understand what he created when he tore me from your soul. Blinded himself from the start, yes? So you can't afford to sit on the sidelines any longer. Get your head back in the game, sunshine."

"They value this world. Scion wanted True Earth. Are you saying Oblivion is making a similar play?" I followed my shadow's twisted thoughts down paths as dark as the Void itself, but I only had pieces of the puzzle and no way to know what move I should make next. "Why *this* world? I mean, besides—"

"True Earth is the cradle of civilization," Shadowman said, spreading his arms wide. "It is, was, and will be the beginning of… everything. The entire Story Thread, the millions of worlds dangling from the blasted spider web—Forget itself—began here. True Earth is the strongest link in the chain, the linchpin at the heart of the whole immense machine." He laughed and precious scotch sloshed from his bottle. "Whoever controls True Earth controls all creation."

"If you've harmed the Historian in any way, I will end you."

"I believe you. Unlike the rest of creation, I'm not stupid enough to underestimate the fearsome Shadowless Arbiter." Then Shadowman laughed and slapped his knees, as if underestimating me were the funniest thing he'd ever heard. "Oh, buddy, she'll be fine. We're going god-huntin' on the morrow!"

"I feel as if I should end you anyway. You know, on principle."

Shadowman bowed. "It is going to come to that, of course. You and I were stained with the blood of the innocent long before we were torn apart. Heh, broken quill, we don't know how to do anything else."

I grunted and lowered the shotgun. "But not tonight. I'll be coming for you, though. For the Historian. So will the Knights. You may look like me, but don't for one second think that means you can play the game in my league."

Shadowman took another swig of liquid gold scotch, and my mouth watered. I wanted a drink more than anything in the world right then. He knew it, too. "No need to insult me," he muttered. "To your health!" He raised the bottle and hurled it into the cobblestones, where it shattered into a thousand shards.

The Void essence and Shadowman vanished in a clap of vicious thunder, and the rain poured down and swept the glass and scotch away.

I *hated* that disappearing trick. All the biggest assholes I'd faced over the years had been capable of it, something to do with stepping *sideways* into the Void and skipping across universes like a river-smooth stone on a pond.

The rain beat down harder than ever, plastering my fringe to my forehead again. I stood in the dark for a moment, accompanied by the deluge and the spent shotgun shells, and sighed.

Shadows and Void light… Just what in all Forget had I unleashed upon the worlds now?

CHAPTER FOUR

Reunited Petals

Back inside my shop, I filled Ethan and Sophie in on all that had happened, out in the cold and the wet and the... abstract. Rainwater pooled at my feet on the wooden floors as I cast a few quick heating enchantments to dry my soaked clothes.

"So," I said, once I'd relayed Shadowman's tale and Sophie had healed the burn on my arm. "Shit meets fan again, I guess."

"I don't get it," Ethan said. "He looked like you?"

"He *is* me, in a way." I rubbed at the back of my neck. "The part of me torn away in Atlantis, to end the Tome Wars. My shadow."

"Shadows are dark…" Sophie muttered. "He's you without a filter, isn't he? Like, he's Declan Hale unleashed." She shivered and crossed her arms over her chest. "You without five years of exile to calm you down after what happened in Atlantis. Broken quill, he's dangerous."

That was a fine way of putting it. 'Declan Hale unleashed'… as if I were naught but a weapon or a disease.

I threw up my hands, sighed, and sat down on the edge of the coffee table, opposite slumbering Emily. "You know, for the longest time I thought I was clear of all this… bullshit." I smiled grimly. "Most people can hide their darker urges. Mine broke away, drank a fifth of scotch, and just declared war on the fucking multiverse. The Knights… will be pissed."

Ethan took a deep breath. "You're going back to Forget again, aren't you?"

"I made Shadowman. He is me. I'll stop him or die trying."

"What about her?" Sophie nodded at Emily. "What's she doing here, you think? Bit too coincidental them both showing up, and she in such bad condition."

I nodded and stroked the rough stubble coating my chin. "Coincidence, no, but I believed that… shadow, out there, when he said he didn't do this to Em."

"So who or what did?" Ethan asked.

"Something competent," I said. "Something or someone who thinks they're beyond reprisal."

Out in the plaza, flashing blue and red lights played with the shadows and the rainfall, bathing my dreary shop in alternating splashes of color. Someone knocked on the door, and I had a good idea who it was. I stepped through the labyrinth of books, veered through endless shelves of fiction and horror, and opened the front door.

"Good evening, Detective Brie." I strained to keep the smile from my face. Annie Brie had been far too absent over the last few weeks, and I enjoyed her company.

It wasn't easy, stepping back into the real world, after

going through something like what she'd gone through. I feared she had been avoiding me, trying to make sense of things and no doubt questioning the strange connection we now shared.

"Declan." She stepped forward as if to hug me. She caught herself, blinked twice, and offered her hand.

We shook firmly. Behind Annie, out in the night, a patrol car idled alongside the road that ran around the plaza. Two uniformed officers stood in the rain, flashlights in hand, scouring the ground through the surge of water sweeping toward the Indian Ocean.

"To what do I owe the pleasure?" I asked.

Annie fixed me with a stare that suggested she knew that *I* knew just why she was brightening up my door in the early hours of the morning—a morning that was creeping up on a dawn I was probably going to miss. "Call came through on the scanner that someone was firing off shotgun rounds in the middle of the night. I caught the address and thought I may be able to crack this case in about five seconds flat. What happened?"

"Ah, it was meant to be a surprise."

Annie blinked. "What?"

"The shotgun—I was modifying the darn thing for you, give you a bit of an edge in case you came up against something like Emissary again." I stepped aside so she could cross the threshold and get out of the rain, which was dwindling. "Well, no, not like Emissary, but creatures of Forget that need a stronger wallop than that service pistol of yours can deliver."

Annie shook the water from her brown leather jacket and ran her hands back through her dark, wet hair. In the dull light afforded from my fleeting chandeliers, her face looked drawn, tired, and her jade-green eyes seemed a touch sunken. She was still pretty—beautiful, even—but the toll of our adventures those few months ago seemed to still be exacting a cost.

"So you were using an unlicensed firearm in the middle of the night?" She glanced over her shoulder at the uniformed officers sweeping the ground across the plaza. "Are those two going to find evidence of that?"

Had all the spent shells washed away? Doubtful, even in this rain. "Very likely," I said.

Annie sighed. "Do I want to know just what you were shooting at?"

I shrugged. "Essence of the Void, creatures spawned in the space between universes, and… well, my shadow. I was shooting at shadows."

"You don't have a shadow," she said wearily. "You sold it to save the world or something, didn't you?"

"Maybe you should come in and sit down. This…" I chuckled and closed the door behind her. "This may take a touch of explaining. Ethan and Sophie are here and…" I trailed away, thinking of Emily on the couch. She and Annie had met once, at Paddy's Pub, just before Emissary had blown up the damn place. Annie knew *who* she was, the Immortal Queen of the Renegades, but I doubted she grasped just what that meant. "And someone you've met once before. She's sleeping, and I only ask that you be kind."

Annie gave me a funny look as I led her to the windowed alcove near the register. "Who is it?"

I offered her a wry grin as we emerged from the stacks and beheld my companions in the half-light. "The woman who killed me."

Annie gazed at Emily, and her lips pursed together in a grim line.

CHAPTER FIVE

Hunted

"Hello, Miss Brie," Sophie said.

"Sophie, Ethan," Annie replied, inclining her head. "Could you not have stopped Declan from discharging that shotgun I see resting so incriminatingly on the counter?"

"You know what he's like," Sophie said softly.

"More and more I do." Annie rolled her eyes at me and leaned against the counter, inspecting the sleek silver shotgun. "And what's with the woman on the couch? She… Emily… doesn't look well."

"She looks a lot better than when she fell through my door," I said. "Someone tortured her rather badly. We've healed most of the damage, and the baby is okay, as far as 'Phie could tell. It's been a busy night, Annie."

Annie nodded. She seemed resigned, withdrawn. "The start of something? Like last time?"

I shook my head, considered, and then shrugged.

"Hard to tell—too early in the game. I don't see any direct threat to Perth yet. But there's nonsense afoot in Ascension City and across Forget—nonsense with my name written all over it."

Emily stirred, and I sat down next to her on the edge of the couch, near her knees. She was muttering again, so I leaned in close to try to tell what she was saying.

Her eyelids fluttered open, and her gaze found me first, since I was leaning down over her. She smiled softly, bemused for a moment, then a ripple of something awful dashed across her face. She *remembered*, and her hands flew to her stomach, cradling her baby bump.

"It's okay," I said. "You're okay."

Emily's gaze darted around the room, flying from Sophie to Ethan, and lingering on Annie for a long moment. She then grasped my head and pulled my lips down to meet hers, kissing me once and then resting her forehead on my nose.

"Thank you," she whispered. Tears rolled down her cheeks—warm and sure. "You're always there for me. Always kind."

"What happened, Em?" Despite the welcoming kiss, I was thinking of the dagger that Emily had slipped between my ribs not too long ago—and the stormy night in Atlantis when she had kicked me from the tower in the heart of the city to a certain death.

For some reason, I'd already forgiven her. That was odd. I usually nurtured a grudge with the best of 'em.

Emily gave a sad smile. "Just the past coming back to haunt me. Oceans of time washing away the sand and revealing secrets buried far too long ago."

"So we're going the enigmatic route, huh?" I asked. "Riddles wrapped in murky words? My patience for that has long since worn down to the bone. Tell me, and tell it true, Em. Who did this to you?"

"I'm sorry, Declan. I was trying to be kind…" Emily sighed, and I had the strangest sense that we'd had the conversation before, a long time ago. Déjà vu or something. "She had eyes of blood, Declan."

My heart clenched, as if Emily had plunged her hand into my chest and *squeezed*. Behind me, Sophie made a soft sound somewhere between a whimper and a gasp.

"We don't know it's her," I said quickly, staring at Emily but speaking to Sophie.

Sophie said nothing, which said enough.

"Of course it's her…" I muttered. "Him, I should say, in her body. Lord Oblivion."

"He's no longer bound to Atlantis," Emily said. "When you severed the Infernal Clock, you severed the chains binding that beast to the Lost City. The cruelest of the Nine. He's free and… vengeful."

Sophie wrapped her arms around herself, and her mouth wobbled, as if she were about to burst into tears.

Ethan frowned and pulled her close. "What's going on?" he asked.

"I'd like to know the same," Annie said.

I took a deep breath and waited for Sophie to give me a tiny nod before exhaling. "You've all heard pieces of this particular tragedy before. Annie, you probably least of all. Pieces of—broken quill—of what *had* to be done. Six… damn, nearly six years ago now, I stormed Atlantis and forced an end to the Tome Wars. I gambled and lost, lost hard, against one of the Everlasting."

"Lord Oblivion?" Ethan asked.

I shrugged. "Sophie's sister, Tal, was with me. We were… We loved each other very much. She taught me what love was, why it mattered…" *A broken kind of happiness.* "I'd just annihilated the Renegade legions at the Reach with the Roseblade. Things were spiraling out of control. It was madness, *madness*. I killed… I killed a lot of people, most of them far too close to innocent." I paused, reached for a bottle that wasn't there, and grimaced. Sobriety was fast becoming a crippled crutch. "Some of the backlash spilled over into Ascension City, burning great swaths of it. The largest, most catastrophic battles in the hundred years of the Tome Wars were fought that night. Broken quill, but it was raw nightmare I unleashed with that damned sword. I've been dogged by white roses ever since."

"You ended the war," Emily said softly, as if reminding me of the one good thing I'd done with my life. "I was *there*, Declan—one hundred years ago, when it all started. You were so young to do what you did, but you ended it. And it needed ending. Just like the Infernal Clock needed severing. It was the right time."

"At a cost, my dear," I said. "I did it all at sheer cost to your armies and your old husband Morpheus. I… I'm sorry I killed him, by the way. For whatever sorry is worth to you." I scratched at the band of my eye patch and grunted, more than a little frustrated. "No, I'm not sorry for killing him. He took something special from me, and if given the chance, I'd kill him again, a lot more slowly. I'm sorry for the hurt it must have caused you, though."

Emily sat up carefully, swinging her legs under the coffee table, a hand resting on her unborn child. "Morpheus and I were a marriage of long circumstance. I never loved him nor he me. I do not mourn his passing, Declan. His means to an end were far too cruel."

Something we may have had in common, I thought.

"Sorry," Annie said, "but did you say you were there at the start of the Tome Wars?"

Emily cast an unreadable gaze at Annie—something, perhaps, hostile and cold. "I am the Immortal Queen," she said simply, as if that explained her timeless grace.

In the somewhat awkward silence that followed, Ethan cleared his throat. "So, ugh, you mentioned something about unleashing raw nightmare, boss? Sounds spooky."

I blinked, lost for a moment before I remembered what I'd been telling them. "Ah, right. Anyway, using the Roseblade that night in the Reach tore openings in the Void. Pure nothingness began to bleed into reality from a few key wounds. My grandfather, Aloysius, summoned me to the Forgetful Library to seal one of the tears. I didn't know it at the time, but I prevented the largest incursion of Voidlings ever seen from pouring into Ascension City."

My companions listened in dead silence. For Ethan and Annie, a lot of the story was new, but all of them had been touched by the Void, Annie far more than she knew—far more than I'd told her, at least.

"With the Knights and Renegades still reeling from the Reach, I saw no other choice. It was my first real act of madness, even after the destruction of the Reach. The chaos was preferable to the Void. So Tal and I gambled on Atlantis, on what we knew was hiding there."

"Imprisoned there," Emily said.

"Aye, say it true, my dear. What was *rotting* in that cursed city."

Leaning against the counter, Annie tapped her hip. "The Everlasting, yes? Like that Scion son of a bitch from a few months ago."

"Scion's older brother, I suppose." Although his host body—what remained of Tal—was female. It was still a *he*, if any sort of gender could've been ascribed to something as ancient and alien as the Everlasting. "Bit of a nut job. It took my shadow and… Sophie, I'm sorry…"

"I've heard this before," she said, giving me a hard

look I knew well—a look that suggested it should have been *me*, that night, and not her sister.

I couldn't have agreed more. "My shadow and Tal's essence. It scattered pieces of us across the Void. I was granted a boon, in a way. Voidlings can't really touch me or work their awful magics to wound me. Shadowless, I am poison to them. And Tal… Tal was destroyed."

"And for your shadow and my sister's soul," Sophie whispered, "you got the Degradation, and Morpheus Renegade surrendered. The Tome Wars were over, and you didn't have to use the Roseblade again, which would've made the cracks in the Void, sprouting up all across Forget and the Story Thread, worse. Almost worse enough to pierce reality here on True Earth."

"Victory at a cost so high, it may as well have been defeat," I said. "The only clever thing I did that night was surrender the Roseblade to an old friend in Ascension City. Last I saw of it, though—you had the blade, Emily."

She offered me a small smile and patted my knee.

Ethan sighed. "So Oblivion is out and about in Forget. No longer in Atlantis. And it was Oblivion that hurt Emily, but it—he—looked like Tal?"

The Immortal Queen of the Renegades nodded.

"I get the feeling we're heading full circle toward something dangerous." I clenched my fists. "Why did Oblivion attack you, Emily?"

"No," she said.

"No?"

"That's the wrong question, Declan." Emily put a soft hand on the back of my neck. "What's the right question?"

Her hand felt warm, almost comforting. "I'm not sure what you're getting at—"

"Why does Oblivion choose to still look like Tal Levy?"

That… was actually a good question. Thinking on Tal hurt, and always would, but that question…

I feared the answer—not for my own sanity, but for what it could mean, after all these years, in which I'd loved and lost without Tal. I swallowed and hesitated for a moment, considering the answer from all angles, and then took the plunge. "Tell me then. Why does Oblivion still look like her?"

"To wound you." The Immortal Queen cupped my cheek in her palm. Out of the corner of my eye, I saw Annie tense, a hand hovering over her service weapon. "Oblivion is seeking revenge for Scion's defeat. You were a novelty to the Everlasting, all those years ago. A useful toy to their ends, to severing the Infernal Clock and the locks on the Eternal Prison. An unwitting pawn on the grandest stage in all the universes." Emily sighed. "Oh, Declan, better you had stayed that way. Because now the Elder Gods are coming for you."

Whoop-de-fucking-do. "And they hurt you to… what, get my attention?" I asked, a touch confused. Emily and I were friends, despite the occasional stabbing and murder, but there were faster avenues to draw my gaze. Better avenues.

"You're surprised." She laughed softly. "Forgive me, but I often forget how young you are. It's your eyes, you know, the eyes of an old man that watched civilizations burn. That *burned* them. You'll understand soon, I promise, why hurting me was the surest strike they could have made against you."

We fell into silence for a moment, and I scratched my stubbly chin. The red and blue lights from the police cruiser still splashed against the walls.

"I'm going to go see how those two are getting on outside," Annie said. "Declan, can I have a word, please?"

I stood and followed Annie back through the

labyrinth of high shelves once more, stacked with books and buried in the cool scent of old leather and vanilla.

When we reached the door, she put her hand on the knob, turned, and gave me a piercing stare. "That woman killed you, Declan."

"Yes."

"I don't trust her."

"No."

Annie opened the door and stepped out into the dreary night. The rain had almost entirely given over. Thunder still rumbled, but distantly. "Every instinct in me is screaming that something is amiss with her, Declan."

And, having said her piece, Annie trudged across the drowned cobblestones toward her colleagues, leaving me with that to think on.

I closed the door and left it unlocked, the wards down, and headed back through my shop. Sophie blocked my path halfway through the maze, somewhere between Crime and Sci-Fi. Her eyes glinted dangerously in the half-light.

"'Phie, I think I know what you're going to say and—"

"Do you think she's still in there?" Sophie asked, grasping my forearm hard enough to hurt. "Declan, Dec… *Could my sister still be alive?*" she whispered fiercely.

And then I was back on that tower in Atlantis, where I'd fallen through time and death. Where, all things said and done, I should have died half a decade ago instead of Tal. But that night of the fall, earlier in the year… The creature that looked like Tal staring down at me—hating and, perhaps, *fearing* me—as a storm of cherry blossom petals raged and burned like ash under a tormented, purple sky, something had changed that night.

"Did you see a future for us, Tal?" I asked, but she only stared. "Did you see us waking up together? Smiling in the morning? Did you see us laughing and growing old? Did you see me loving you even more, for every morning as the years flew past?" I took a deep breath and exhaled slowly. "Boy, I sure did."

I sighed, and it turned into a wince that brought me close to tears.

"Please, say something."

An arc of wicked purple lightning tore the heavens apart behind Tal.

"Oh, well. Songbird, I love—"

Tal pressed an ethereal finger against my lips. Her eyes, the eyes of a Knight, blurred from harsh crimson to soft pepper brown. For a heartbeat—or the moment between—she was mine again in mind, body, and soul.

"I know," she whispered, and she vanished like smoke on the wind.

I stared into Sophie's eyes and lied, "She's dead, 'Phie. We lost her a long time ago."

CHAPTER SIX

Renegade Ideas

Annie returned, a net of water droplets coating her dark hair, and stared out of the window alcove overlooking Riverwood Plaza. Her two fellow lawmen were still out and about in the rain, dusting for prints and looking for clues and what have you. The rain had hindered them somewhat, which was useful, but the storm was passing, and I was still trying to decide what my next move should be.

Indecision was usually the gamble of these games in the night—too many ways to move and far too easy to see all the mistakes I was about to make.

Should I go after Shadowman, my unholy twin, and mount a rescue for the Historian? What of Emily being attacked by the Everlasting Oblivion—attacked by what was left of Tal Levy, a girl I had loved and lost and spent the last six years trying to find again in the bottom of too many—*not enough*—scotch bottles? Hell, should I seek out the Knights in Ascension City, try to explain the latest round of chaos?

Safe to assume that King Faraday's patience with me may have worn a touch thin, despite my rescinded exile status. I could see them shackling me in star iron first and asking questions later. Or just lopping off my head and have done with it. Arbiter Drax and a few others would be chewing at the bit for that particular honor.

Annie said something that pulled me from my thoughts. "Sorry?" I asked. "I missed that."

"I'm stalling them," she said. "The officers outside. Against my better judgment. They'll want to chat soon. What's the move, Declan?"

Emily sat poised on the edge of the couch, amidst the stacked crinkled pages of my unfinished novel, watching me with a calm grace that belied the condition she had been in only a short while ago. Arms linked, Sophie and Ethan leaned against a creaky case of books, also watching me.

"Okay." I took a deep breath to steel myself. "Okay. Here's the thing. Twice in the last six months, I've been pulled back into Forget, once to my death, and second to the destruction of the Atlas Lexicon and Scion's incursion on Diablo Beach. Both times the Everlasting were playing me for a fool. Not again. Time to get back in the game properly."

Ethan gave me a quick salute. "With ya, boss."

I opened my mouth to shoot him down, thought on it a moment, and then nodded. Ethan had proven himself resilient this past year, and his Will training had progressed in leaps and bounds after he'd seen the kids at the Infernal Academy outperforming him. He wasn't afraid of a fight, either—or, more importantly, of taking a hit.

Sophie frowned but nodded. "I won't sit this one out, a prisoner of the Academy, or be left behind like on the Plains of Perdition. I'm with you, as well."

Annie wrapped her arms around herself and shook her head. "I don't know if I want to get pulled into another whirlwind adventure with you, Declan. Or, you know, another pub crawl. The last time…" She rubbed at the spot where Scion had shattered her skull and killed her. Her eyes filled with tears. "Why can I always *feel* you in my head? Like there's a compass pointing right at you in my mind!"

"Annie…" I didn't know what to say. Now wasn't the time. *Is there ever going to be a good time to tell her she died and you brought her back?* Ethan and Sophie stared at me strangely, confused, and Emily avoided my gaze. Em knew the truth—hell, she'd slipped the immortality petal into Annie's pocket in the ruins of the Atlas Lexicon. "I'm not sure."

"Could it have something to do with that, that dagger? Myth?" she asked wearily.

I glanced quickly at Emily again, an unspoken warning for Annie to keep her silence about Myth.

The Immortal Queen only offered me a small smile and a quiet laugh. "Oh, Declan, I know you found yourself another trinket of celestial illusion. I know you've hidden it somewhere nearby. The Creation Knife. You used it to blind Scion."

"Eye for an eye," I muttered, tapping the patch covering my left socket. The eye was whole but useless. I'd plucked Scion's clean out. The roughshod immortality afforded to me from the petal of the Infernal Clock in my heart made me something dangerous to the Everlasting, as the loss of my shadow made me dangerous to the Void.

"Yes. Well, you can use the knife to take us to Voraskel," Emily said.

I blinked, sure I'd misheard. Sophie chuckled uncertainly, as if responding to a rather tasteless and poor joke. Ethan chewed on the word, likely trying to remember where he'd heard it before. Annie just sighed, as lost as ever.

"I'm sorry," I said, pressing my thumb and forefinger against my brow, warding away the inevitable headache, "but did you say 'Voraskel'?"

Emily simply stared at me.

"New Voraskel?" I asked. "The bloody Renegade homeworld."

Emily *tsk*ed. "No, no. New Voraskel is far too, well, *new*. A certain lack of history there. Hidden on Old Voraskel, I have considerable resources and weapon caches. Among other things. You remember that world, don't you, Declan?"

All too well.

Sweet, bloody, broken quill. The Fall of Voraskel.

A battle in the final months of the Tome Wars that had spanned two worlds—Avalon and Voraskel. The Void had *split* between them through the sheer weight of the Will being channeled across the battlefield. King Morrow, the leader of the Knights Infernal at the time, had perished in that battle. My old friend Tia Moreau, as well—or so I'd thought at the time. Entire command vessels and legions of sworn men and women had simply ceased to be. I should have claimed the throne after Morrow, but then came the Reach, Atlantis, and the loss of Tal…

The rest was history. My half-brother, Faraday, stepped in, and I was exiled.

Broken quill, but half the Cascade Fleet, the elite of the elite, had fallen into the Void at the Fall of Voraskel and Avalon. The two worlds collided, and I'd played a literal part in destroying the Renegade homeworld. Another reason they didn't like me so much. The world—what was left of it—was still there, had merged with the ruins of Avalon. A slow death.

"Voidflood…" I muttered, and I instantly regretted

saying the word aloud. The creatures that swam through the murky nothing of the Void existed in the abstract. They could sometimes *know* when they were named, and voicing that particular word seemed like tempting fate to add another misery to the night's events.

Growing up and living the life I'd lived, not a lot in this or any other world could shake me. I was, for all that mattered, hardened and embittered against monsters, enemies, demons, spooks, and the general hatred across hundreds of Forgetful realms. But Voidfloods terrified me, right down to my core.

I still had nightmares about the Fall of Voraskel. To see the canvas of reality tear away so easily and pure, dark *nothingness* seep over the thin—*oh so thin*—paintwork of the world, unmaking the laws of physics and sanity in one fell swoop. Indeed, worse, rewriting those laws into something twisted and cruel in the ruins of Voraskel and Avalon.

The Void had *offended* me that day. Loss and death were part of the natural order. What had fallen through the shattered sky above those worlds had burned the natural order and pissed on the ashes.

"Why oh why, dear Emily, would you ever want to visit Voraskel?" My hands were shaking—I shoved them into my pockets. "And what could possibly make you think I'd want to go there?"

"Simple, really," she said. "Voraskel is where you'll recover the Roseblade."

CHAPTER SEVEN

Shining Armor

I let Emily's words hang in the air for a long moment, getting a taste of them as they aged, and found them sour.

Annie broke the silence. "The Roseblade. So it's a sword, yeah? Made from the same stuff as Myth?"

I nodded. "Of celestial illusion, which is kind of a super rare and entirely unpredictable alloy. Looks like crystal. Legend has it the weapons were forged in Atlantis, and the color of the rose petals in the blade is important. White petals were said to be… purest."

"Purest?" Ethan asked.

"Reactors to generate and amplify raw Will," Emily said.

"Unfettered and uncorrupted—pure power in a raw form." I forced a rough chuckle. "Our Will power—or maybe what the Everlasting call Origin, seeing as how the weapons were created a very long time ago. Even shards of celestial illusion could topple empires…"

The history of the blades was murky and sordid. For the longest time, celestial illusion was thought to be the stuff of fairytales. But in my experience, fairytales could be very real—with exceptions. Most worlds and thoughts, written into existence by Willful authors, could become a jewel of the Story Thread, a new universe to be charted, but the limits on such seemingly infinite power of creation were complex, and the consequences for a misstep were catastrophic.

The Tome Wars were a fine example of Willful men and women abusing the power at their fingertips. The war had begun over a splinter group of the Knights Infernal, my people. The splinter group evolved to become the Renegades—in name and belief. *Perhaps Emily was one of them, all those years ago…* The Renegade agenda was to write worlds into existence that could be… plundered, for want of a better word. I might have been the one with an eye patch and a thirst for some dark grog, but the Renegades were the real pirates. It had taken a century to stop them, and in that time, a lot of the Story Thread's light was overwhelmed by the Void. The Forgetful Realms were almost torn asunder.

Then I came along, not only living in fairytales but living *off* them, and bargained for peace.

Well, not so much *peace* as Renegade destruction.

Anyway, there were rules to the game, and certain materials could not be written into existence. Veins of celestial illusion to be mined—or whole weapons forged from the alien substance—were pretty high up on the list of things that simply couldn't be created by the Willful. I didn't know why, and Willful Mechanics had been the subject of study at the Infernal Academy for centuries. Call it divine providence or just simple human ignorance—either it was forbidden by some unknown law or edict of all creation, or we just weren't clever enough to figure out how. I was a fan of the former explanation—but then, my ego would demand nothing less.

"So how is it you keep running into these weapons, Declan?" Annie asked. "If they're so rare."

I could only shrug. A few months before, Annie and I had spent some time in the Dream Worlds—worlds sealed away by the Knights for the danger they represented to Forget and the Story Thread. Our visit itself should have been impossible, let alone what we found in a ruined old temple and *what* led us to it.

Scion, in the guise of a child, had outplayed me that day. He'd needed me to retrieve the dagger—Myth, the Creation Knife. Because the bloody thing had been placed in a pedestal of dusty stone for me, by people—*perhaps* people—from ages long since buried under the weight of time.

On that plateau, in a garden reminiscent of Eden or Shangri-La, had been an inscription in archaic glyphs:

Here rests Myth, the Creation Knife,
Forged in Atlantia for the Nine to slay,
Forged to light the Shadowless way.
Paths unbroken, unsung, unfound
Await the Immortal King to be crowned.

A tool of immense power, Myth could cut the fabric of reality, allowing me to slip between worlds as quietly as a thief in the night. Certainly there existed a number of other ways to cross the Void and travel to other worlds. The Atlas Lexicon, once it was repaired, was the surest and the cheapest for those lacking Will. For the Knights, pages of a good book could be used to open pathways through the Void. But the latter method kept the traveler linked to the point of departure—sometimes a positive, often a hamstring. The Willful could only move once, in one direction; one Knight needed another to cross more than one world at a time, and even then the link could be severed, the traveler left stranded. Myth cut paths through all that bullshit.

"Trust me," I answered Annie and sighed. "If I knew how to avoid them, I would. Celestial illusion has brought me nothing but pain."

"And yet—" Emily rose to her feet, swayed, and then steadied herself. "And yet if you do not aid me in retrieving the Roseblade, Declan, then all that pure and unfettered power will fall to Oblivion. An unfavorable outcome, yes?"

That sword, in the hands of one of the Everlasting, would be akin to a nuclear arsenal the size of a galaxy in the hands of a madman—with someone daring him to push the button.

Broken quill, when having the blade in *my* hands was the kinder option… "Bloody hell. Okay, Voraskel it is."

"Shit," Sophie said.

"Indeed. You two want to back out now—or head to sunnier shores and inform the Knights of all we've discussed tonight? That could be helpful." I would be hunted for what Shadowman had done to the Historian. Perhaps sending a messenger to my vengeful brother, King Faraday, could prevent some misery down the line. "What d'you say? Ascension City?"

Ethan looked to Sophie.

After a moment, she nodded slowly. "But they'll have to throw me in Starhold before I let them tie me to the Academy again."

"As a reinstated Knight Infernal"—I inclined an invisible hat—"you two can claim my protection. I'll sign a runeletter deputizing you as my official emissaries. You'll be free to move about the palace, for the most part. Not even Faraday, Fenton, or Drax would violate an Infernal seal."

Emily stood tall. "Very good. But we must hurry. Oblivion knows where to find the Roseblade. We do not have much time."

"How did you escape?" I asked, perplexed. "Seriously, that doesn't add up. Oblivion had you, *tortured* you, so how did you come to find yourself on my doorstep?"

Emily shivered. "He let me go, of course. So I could tell you all of this—so you'd go running across worlds after the Roseblade. So he could kill you, sweet Declan."

"Well, the math on that reads a bit better." Christ, but the world-ending catastrophes on my to-do list kept changing in priority. *Recover the Roseblade, stop Oblivion, rescue the Historian, destroy Shadowman*… "I need a drink."

"You and me both," Ethan said. "This is getting intense."

"Declan…" Annie took a deep breath. "I'm stepping out again—walk me to the door?"

We went once more through the labyrinth of haphazardly stacked books until we reached to door, which she opened. The rain was nothing but drizzle now, but the wind still had a bite to it.

"Are you coming back?" I asked, standing in the doorway and looking out at Riverwood Plaza. "Annie, there's work to be done."

"My shift was over an hour ago, Declan. I'm going home to my fiancé, and tomorrow I'm going back to work." She gazed at me, not with defiance, but with a knowing kind of regret. I liked her, and she knew it, that way women always do. "I'm not a Knight Infernal or a Renegade or one of the Unfound like Ethan… You go take care of the universe. I'll just take care of Perth."

"Well, if you're not coming with me, then I'm taking the cool new shotgun," I said, hating that I felt slighted.

Annie stepped forward and caught me in a quick hug. The infernal compass in my head spun as if magnetized, making me dizzy. We were far from done with one another, Annie Brie and I. Of that much I could be sure.

"Stay safe, Hale," she whispered into my ear. "We need to talk when you get back."

~~*~*

"Okay, 'Phie and Ethan—you're on supplies. Go fill a backpack with some perishables and water in the kitchen." I clapped my hands together, trying to convey an air of confidence about the upcoming venture across the Story Thread. *Fuckin' Voraskel…* "Emily Grace, is there anything you need? Baby-wise? Should you—"

"If you're about to ask me if I should be accompanying you to Voraskel, I would rethink such a foolish question." The glimmer in her eye promised another knife to the heart if I pushed my luck.

"Right. Of course." She *was* the Immortal Queen, after all, and although she didn't look much older than thirty, she was at *least* a hundred and ten years old if she had seen the start of the Tome Wars. Something told me Emily was far more timeless than even that—something, perhaps, to be discussed on our journey to the Roseblade. "Still, is there anything you require?"

"Just my knight in shining armor." She smiled. "And his dagger of celestial illusion."

I stroked the buttons on my waistcoat. Part of my armor, this old waistcoat. The fabric was imbued with layers of Willful protection and painted with unseen Infernal runes. The weight of such incantation and enchantment was burdensome, adding actual pounds to the thin fabric, but the benefits far outweighed the cost. The waistcoat could and had stopped a high-caliber round from a sniper rifle. Emily would have a hard time slipping a dagger between my ribs while I was wearing my armor. I'd enchanted similar protections into my trousers and shoes.

Although I didn't look it, I *was* Emily's knight in shining armor. "Let's be getting this over with, then."

I followed Sophie and Ethan into the kitchen and retrieved Myth, the Creation Knife and a weapon of pure celestial illusion, from the cutlery drawer.

CHAPTER EIGHT

Old Voraskel

I stood next to Emily, wondering on our time together and why she kept spinning back into my life, as Ethan shouldered the backpack and Sophie filled the side pockets with shells from the cash register. I carried the sleek shotgun itself over my shoulder, and I held Myth in my left hand, poised to cut between worlds.

For the first time in a long time, I actually felt prepared for whatever madness lay ahead.

"That's everything, I guess," Ethan said.

"Pen and paper," I said. "Make sure there's some in the pack. Once we get to Voraskel, get the lay of the land, you'll need a formal letter of introduction to move about the Fae Palace on Ascension as my emissaries."

Ethan snorted. "Instead of just showing up out of the blue like the last few times?"

"Don't think they've forgotten you and Clare Valentine hijacked my shuttle to Starhold earlier this year, mate," I said. "Or that with your potential skill, you'd make a fine recruit—albeit a shade old—at the Academy."

Sophie zipped up the pockets on the pack, fit to burst with shotgun shells, with some effort and ran a hand through her boyfriend's mop of dark hair. "They can have him—few years at the Academy would do him good."

He smirked. "You mean I could grow up to be just like Declan?"

"Declan Hale is unique in the universe," Emily said softly.

I glanced at her with my good eye and chuckled. "Yeah, sure, I'm a unique little snowflake. Please, Emily. Let's just be about this dark business, shall we?"

I stepped into the clear space before the counter, between my writing alcove and the first of the dusty old shelves straining under the weight of forgotten libraries, and gripped Myth's hilt. The trick to using the dagger was to open unfound and unseen paths through the Void—which meant avoiding known waypoints or written gateways, as the knife refused to allow passage along those thoroughfares. The Creation Knife *created* new paths, so long as I held the way clear in my mind, and it closed them just as quickly if I broke that clarity.

As if cutting through warm butter, the tip of the dagger disappeared into the air, like a pin through cloth, and I sliced the fabric of reality down toward the floor. Reality split and peeled back, curtains undrawn, and formed a gateway in the air about seven feet tall and three feet across.

Sunlight, warm and bright, poured in from another world. Used to the dull light of my shop, I squinted to let my good eye acclimate to the sudden change of scenery. The scent of spring flowers and the sound of trickling water filtered through the gateway—as did another scent, something old and indescribable that permeated all the realms of Forget along the Story Thread. A world scent. Once my eye adjusted, I could see gently sloping grassy hills through the gateway, overlooking the mosaic marble ruins of what had once been the capital city of the Renegades on Voraskel.

The sky blended from pure azure to violent purple and was strewn with the debris of Avalon—of an *entire world*. The burning planet, cracked and bleeding, eclipsed the sky. Small moons of jagged rock peppered the heavens and Avalon's ring system, similar to the rings that banded Saturn, had slowly dispersed along Voraskel's upper atmosphere and into space, as if emerald-green and ruby-red ribbons were caught on a slow, interstellar breeze.

"Look at what happened here…" I whispered. My companions, my friends and whatever Emily was, stood at my back, gazing in awestruck silence through the gateway from our small corner of True Earth to Voraskel. "When they write the history books, if I have a say—a chance to explain *why* I ended the Tome Wars the way I did—I'll point them here. It was Voraskel, more than anywhere else, when I decided that there could be no more of this. When I decided that if my elders and the supposed wiser men and women of the Knights Infernal wouldn't take action, then I would."

"Beautiful horrors." Emily stroked the back of my neck and scratched softly at my hairline with her nails.

"This is insane," Ethan rasped, barely above a whisper.

"Why did you hide the Roseblade here, Emily?" Sophie asked.

Emily removed her hand from my neck and stepped through the portal. Her sandals clicked on hardwood floors in one step, and sunk into yielding grass in the next. She turned to face us, standing an entire world away in just a few feet. "Who, save the creation's most mad, would dare come looking in these ruins?"

"It needed hiding," I said. "Although Voraskel… Broken quill, anywhere but here. How far do we have to travel?"

"Through the old forests on the other side of the city." Emily gestured over her shoulder at the crooked splendor of two dying worlds on the very edge of crashing together. "An enchanted forest, naturally. One of the oldest in all existence. I hid the Roseblade in the Tomb of the Sleeping Goddess."

CHAPTER NINE

'Ware the Everlasting

The Sleeping Goddess. Fair Astoria. One of the Everlasting. Another of the blasted Nine.

I was never one to put much faith in fate or destiny, but if Emily was telling the truth—and, indeed, she had never lied to me—I could almost feel another gigantic piece of some predestined puzzle locking into place. It weighed around my neck like shackles of heavy rusted cast iron.

If the game was already decided, the moves already determined, then nothing I could do would prevent the inevitable Everlasting war.

Which, if you're being honest, Hale—can we be that, you and I, just this once?—you want to fight such a war, to throw your immense skill and sheer dumb luck against the might of the Elder Gods. The voice in my head sounded a lot like my half-brother and king of the Knights Infernal, Jon Faraday.

"Be quiet, you bastard…" I muttered.

Sophie gave me a strange look, a single pale eyebrow raised in question. We had passed through the portal back in the bookshop just a minute ago and we now strolled along a path of broken cobblestone down the hill toward the ruins of the Renegade city. Next to her, Ethan carried the hefty pack, playing with the silver shotgun I'd offloaded on him as soon as we'd cleared the portal. The sun overhead felt warm with the breeze, but overshadowed by the cracked sphere of Avalon dominating half the damned sky. Night would fall early, once the sun disappeared behind that… beautiful horror.

Emily strolled just ahead of our little group, cleaning the blood from her white dress through Willful means. The blue shawl around her shoulders trailed in the breeze. Long curls of her red hair fell in gentle waves down her back and I thought, not for the first time, that she was beautiful—regal. An Immortal Queen.

As if reading my thoughts, Emily turned and pierced me with her sapphire eyes. *Curse all women and their knowing stares...* The persistent memory danced through my mind of Emily dressed in sheer red, face hidden behind a white porcelain mask in the grand entrance hall of the Fae Palace, her lips pressed against mine as she slipped a dagger between my ribs, harvesting my blood to travel the path to Atlantis.

That had been one hell of a kiss.

"Penny for your thoughts, Declan," she said.

I cleared my throat. "The Sleeping Goddess. Fair Astoria… she's dead, and her tomb is here on Voraskel?"

Emily sighed and gazed out at the vista we commanded from the hill leading down toward the city. From the white ruins of the fallen city, to the blight of Avalon in the sky, across acres of what would have been farmland years ago before the Fall of Voraskel, and finally into the distance beyond the city—under the vast shadow of the planet-sky. A large swath of forest disappeared over the horizon, spreading north to south and creeping up the sides of distant, snow-capped mountains.

"This world holds a great many secrets," she said. "She's one of the oldest in the Story Thread, you know. Her true age is lost to time, in eras and empires that do not even exist as half-remembered scraps or myth… A great many of those secrets will burn when the fall of Avalon tears this world apart."

"One of the Everlasting is dead," Ethan said, panting under the weight of the pack. "That's a good thing, isn't it?"

Emily ignored him and strolled on ahead. Sophie shrugged and glanced at me, perhaps wanting an answer. I was, when all was said and done, the Knightly expert on the Everlasting—having met two and blinded one—and I was inclined to agree with Ethan.

"We'll have a chat about the Everlasting over something to eat," I said. "Before you and 'Phie disappear to Ascension."

Journeying across other worlds could be somewhat disorientating with the time difference. On Voraskel, it was early afternoon, as best I could tell, which meant we'd skipped breakfast. Just ahead, alongside the meandering cobblestone path down the hill toward the city, were some fallen stone pillars that would make fine picnic tables for lunch. Also a fine spot to have a chat and send Sophie and Ethan on their mission. In unspoken agreement, we trekked off path to those stones.

The slabs of fallen stone were warm to the touch. Emily leaned casually against one, hands around her unborn baby, as Ethan unshouldered the pack with a grunt and set about raiding the provisions within it for a spot of lunch. A small stream of crystal-clear water, just a few feet across, bubbled on the far side of the fallen pillars away from the path and trickled down the hill in little waterfalls. Sophie kicked off her shoes and dipped her toes into the water, humming softly to herself, before pulling herself up onto one of the pillars and basking in the sun, as Ethan prepared a plate of food.

Lunch was a near-silent affair and comprised of red apples, almonds, some ham that needed to be eaten before the heat spoiled it, and jellybeans. The last I had taken a particular liking to, back on True Earth. The butternut and watermelon beans were like a drug. My larder was stocked with enough of the tiny sweets to wait out the next two or three end-of-the-world adventures. *Damn, but it's good to be back on the road…*

I was always and ever at my best when I was working against a clock. During my exile, I'd felt a lethargy and a sense of becoming obsolete. The feelings had been a cancer on my soul, making me miserable and, slowly but surely, had sent me seeking happiness at the bottom of a bottle.

Five long years of searching bottles, and I hadn't found a scrap of happy, only a numb sort of indifference that had gotten me killed.

"So we've been hearing about those Everlasting a lot," Ethan said to me, drinking stream water from a plastic cup he'd retrieved from the pack, "but in only bits and pieces, mate. There are nine of them, yeah?"

"Always nine," Emily said, stroking her baby bump. "Never fewer, and never more."

"Scion," Ethan said. "That's one."

Sophie, resting on her side on top of one of the smooth warm pillars, said, "Oblivion, with eyes of blood—that's two. There are seven more. We're taught all about them at the Infernal Academy, growing up, but no one ever thought they were real. Or at least, if they ever had been, they were believed long dead."

"Not dead. Imprisoned by the Willful of Atlantis ten thousand bloody years ago," I said. "I broke the lock on that prison, apparently, when Oblivion tricked me into severing the Infernal Clock in Atlantis earlier this year. My bad, I know, but it was the only way to end the Degradation and restore life to the Story Thread… You all know that part."

"Severing the Clock allowed Scion to reach across the Dream Worlds and force you to retrieve Myth," Emily said. "But there are layers to the prison of the Everlasting, Declan. Severing the Clock, while vital, did not release them all—at least, not all at once. Imagine they've been released from their cells to find that the Knights of old, of Atlantis, are no longer guarding the prison. They still need to navigate through barbed fences, among other layers, to escape."

"And make a play for True Earth," I surmised, given Scion's intentions a few months ago. "How do you know that, Em?"

She flashed me a secretive smile I knew all too well, a smile that suggested I should have figured her out long ago. "I have lived a very long life."

"So Oblivion was hiding in the ruins of Atlantis, yeah?" Ethan asked with a frown. He joined Sophie on her pillar as she sat up and took his hand. "Scion was in the Dream Worlds—which I'm going to need to know more about at some point, boss—and the other seven?"

"Locked away in corners of Forget that were, well, *forgotten*," Emily said. "The Knights all those millennia ago made sure of that. Scion was sent to the Dream Worlds because they were inaccessible—but no longer, with the loss of the Infernal Clock, as Declan and Annie Brie can confirm all too well. Oblivion was shackled to Atlantis, to the Clock itself, and the city was cast back into a pocket of faux time until Declan discovered it in his youth. Always trouble, weren't you?" She gave a small chuckle. "And set this ancient game in motion once again. War is coming, perhaps the last war of this age, and this time there are no Knights worthy of the title to stand against the Everlasting."

"There are thousands of Knights Infernal…" I muttered, but my mind was troubled—and my heart felt sick. Too many jellybeans.

Emily rolled her eyes, not unkindly. "In Atlantis, where the Order of the Knights Infernal was born, they could work legends and miracles with Origin—with what you now call Will. They created the Infernal Clock, the Roseblades, and other weapons of celestial illusion. Today's Knights are less than a pale shadow of their former glory. A bonfire diminished to embers. None of the Order could wield Origin with enough conviction to even blemish the Everlasting." She grinned and gave me a wink. "Well, save perhaps one shadowless fool."

I crossed my arms over my chest, feeling a chill despite the warmth of the day.

Ethan pulled Sophie close. They both looked troubled—no, more than troubled. Afraid. "What are the rest of their names?" he asked.

Sophie sighed and sat up straight. "They each have two names… or titles, I suppose. I've never thought on it much, but their names and titles sort of reflect who and what they are, you ken? There's a rhyme…" She cleared her throat and recited a poem most children in Ascension City and all across Forget knew before they were three.

'Ware the Nine Forgetful Tomes
Storied names carved of old bone.
For the Nine see you as clear rose-light

Etched to stand against their blight.

Bitter Child craves his father's throne,
Yet Younger Scion sits all alone.

Dark travesty surrounds the Age Flood,
Lord Oblivion drowned in fire and blood.

The Sleeping Goddess can never forget
Fair Astoria, lost in time's tangled net.

Mind the snare of the Nightmare Sea—
Madness, the realm of Iced Banshee.

Distant threads tie the Ancient Bane
Pained Hail and his forever game.

Hear the wrath of the Marked Fear—
Harbinger Chronos is drawn near.

Starless paths through the Lost Sight
Dread Ash turns cold day to night.

Watch Fated Legion be destroyed
Scarred Axis fears the rampant Void.

The World-Eater, last in shadow's husk
The Never-Was King—Lord Hallowed Dusk.

So 'ware the Nine Forgetful Tomes
'Ware the Elder Gods from your home
Ageless, hateful, dull blight-flame—
The Everlasting know your name.

Sophie's voice faded away, and the world felt a whole lot darker. Even Emily's face had lost some of its timeless grace. Her eyes were far away.

"Well, they're certainly not a cheery bunch, are they?" Ethan said, trying to sound upbeat and failing. "Blimey, and they're all loose now?"

"Well on their way." Emily sighed. "As you two should be, so Declan and I can hurry and retrieve the Roseblade before Oblivion does—which he will undoubtedly use to free his siblings."

"Right," I said and then blinked a few times. I had to force myself into action. *Scion… Oblivion… Astoria… Banshee… Hail… Chronos… Ash… Axis… Dusk…* And Myth, forged in Atlantia for the Nine to slay. Forged for *me*, damn it all. "Get me the pen and paper from the pack, and I'll write the both of you up for Ascension City."

The letter only took five minutes and afforded Sophie and Ethan my protection as a Guardian of the Knights Infernal. Once I had held the rank of Arbiter—the highest honor of the Order—but that had been stripped from me in exile. Honestly, I still thought of myself as an Arbiter, and I was sure most of the Knights—and my brother the king—also thought that way. Hard to take something like that, well earned in fighting during the Tome Wars. Still, Guardianship was enough to bestow the rite of passage and protection upon Sophie and Ethan from—and against—the Knights Infernal.

I signed my name and ignited just the tip of my index finger with a point of thin light, no wider than a pinhead. Will-light flowed through the door in my mind that tapped the raw power in the heart of creation. With that finger, I inscribed three glowing Infernal runes onto the page, making the document somewhat official.

"Now doesn't that look pretty?" I folded the page in half.

Sophie took the letter from me and glanced at Myth, tucked under my belt and resting alongside my leg.

"Any particular place you want to step out on the other side?" I asked, as she and Ethan stood and moved behind me. He left the pack and the shotgun on the fallen pillar for me and Emily.

"Maybe Aaron's shop?" Sophie asked. "Or his villa? I don't know what time it is in Ascension, but if we could have a chat to him first, see what's going on with the Historian before we storm the palace, I'd feel a lot better about all this."

I nodded. "Good call. The villa, then? I think I can picture it clearly enough to cut a path." I bit my tongue and frowned, concentrating as I unsheathed Myth—careful not to cut my belt in half—and found a point in the air to tear asunder.

Myth caught, as the dagger always did, and I drew the curtains back on Lake Delgado at sunset. Small, speedy craft darted along the lake from our view on the balcony of Aaron's villa. In the distance, I could see the forest city of Farvale, nestled into the mountains. Ascension City was a smooth half hour's journey from the villa by shuttle.

"End of the day," I said. "If Aaron's not home yet, he will be soon. We got lucky."

Sophie wrapped her arms around me, giving me a quick but firm hug and a kiss on the cheek. "Take care, you hear?" She stepped in front of the gateway to Lake Delgado, and the smooth, glowing edges of the portal framed her auburn hair like a halo. "And if you see… Oblivion. Well, if you…"

"I'll be kind," I whispered.

Sophie nodded and stepped back through the gateway. Her feet left the soft, grassy earth and clipped the wooden decking of Aaron's villa yet another world away.

"Stay out of trouble, boss." Ethan shook my hand. He offered Emily a quick smile and then followed Sophie across worlds—just doing what I've always done, really, by chasing the pretty girl.

CHAPTER TEN

Warming Up

A few Willful enchantments somewhat lessened the weight of the pack as Emily and I continued our trek down toward the city. I'd have to teach Ethan that trick, eventually. He was a good kid—powerful, even talented—but often lazy. Time would tell if he would ever push himself to learn a touch of finesse when it came to Will, as I could only carry him so far.

Emily and I soon stood on the outskirts of the city, amidst the ruins of cracked stone buildings and fallen aqueducts. Closer to the heart of the city, the buildings I could see from our vantage point became progressively more modern—even a few skyscrapers graced the inner blocks. Vines and weed grass had broken through the cobblestoned streets. Only six years—just over six years—had passed since the Fall of Voraskel, but nature had well and truly reclaimed the city.

Voraskel was a pretty world, lush and green. A shame that the entire planet was destined to be torn apart in the near future.

For an abandoned, doomed world, I felt an awful lot of unseen eyes watching from the shadows.

I held the silver shotgun, barrel pointed away from Emily toward the road, and double-checked that it was loaded with some of the special shells. Call it a sixth sense, a kind of intuition honed and sharpened over the long years of my short life, but a stirring in my gut spelled trouble ahead. I couldn't shake the feeling that we were walking into a trap—perhaps not meant for us, but a trap just the same.

"There's no one living here, is there?" I asked. Even the sound of our footfalls seemed to echo for miles through the forsaken ruin. "The planet was evacuated. The Renegades abandoned it."

"None would dare stay," Emily said. "The Void presses too close against this world, since the flood."

I nodded slowly. "Still, let's be quick about our business. What's the best way to the Tomb from here?"

"The fastest road to the forest is through the city's eastern quarter." Emily pointed at two dilapidated skyscrapers—one half-slumped against another and supporting a wrecked Eternity-class starship, fallen during the final battle. Faint light still shone from the crystal cores in the massive engines of the ship. It would take decades for the energy to bleed from the core, and even then, the damn thing was still liable to explode at any minute.

"If we can find a path through the chaos, that is," Emily added. "Perhaps over the Narrow Bridge, if it's still in one piece."

It was definitely too quiet, here in the ruins of Voraskel and under a planet-devastated sky. The sun would soon disappear behind Avalon, leaving us maybe an hour or two of daylight at most. My palm was sweating on the stock of the shotgun. "What say we backtrack and walk around? Avoid the city altogether? If I knew what this Tomb of the Sleeping Goddess looked like, I could see about using Myth to make us a shortcut."

Emily gestured to the far side of the city, beyond the skyscrapers and the crashed starship. "Could you cut a path over there? Would the Creation Knife work like that? Cut a path from one point to another on the same world?"

"I… don't know." Strange that I hadn't thought of such a move earlier. Too many things on my mind—Shadowman, Tal, Oblivion… "Only one way to find—"

A man stood in the road just ahead.

I took a step to the side—in front of Emily.

The man rocked back and forth on his heels in a fine Armani suit, smoking a thick cigar. Emily saw him and sighed, as if she'd been expecting him all along. I got a good look at his face and cursed. "Emissary," I greeted the monster in human guise. "Didn't I kill you already?"

"Declan Hale," Emissary said, his voice a deep *thrum* like colliding boulders caught in a deep current. "I was told you'd be coming this way, partner. Totin' a six-shooter and that can-do attitude that gets you into such miserable strife." He threw his head back and laughed at the sky. "You cannot kill *me*—for I am *legion*."

"The Emissary are servants of the Everlasting," Emily said calmly. "There are more than just the one you destroyed. Hundreds of the winged beasts, even."

"Dragons," I muttered.

"Yes, dragons," Emissary said.

He snapped his fingers, the sound echoing through empty streets, and from the ruined buildings emerged flocks of ragged creatures—monsters I had met before, on a hundred different battlefields. Forget-full hell-spawn, foot soldiers pieced together from the dregs of a thousand poorly written stories. The Knights suffered their existence only because they bred faster than we could stamp them out. The Renegades—as well as Willful pirates and crime syndicates—often used them as cannon fodder.

"Behold the Orc Mare," Emissary snarled. "Another race loyal once again to the true masters of Forget: the Everlasting."

From behind Emissary, dozens of Orc Mare unfurled semi-translucent wings. They were skeletal creatures, with wasted leathery skin that stretched taut over their elongated and misshapen bones. Burning, insane eyes of black coal glared at me, and fanged maws dripped yellow pus, which sizzled against the road. Even from fifty feet away, they stank of sulfur and death.

Not overly worried just yet, I gripped the barrel of the shotgun and frowned. "Em, you seemed to have some control over these beasts earlier in the year, when you stabbed me—"

"They owed me a tentative allegiance then," she said, hands protecting her baby. "King Morpheus held some command over them in the outer territories of Voraskel. They do not owe me allegiance now… and Morpheus is quite dead."

"Ah, right." I shrugged out of the pack, keeping a firm grip on the shotgun. When—not if—the attack came, I wanted to be able to move quickly, unencumbered.

"Now I'll take the dagger, if you please," Emissary said. "And the woman."

"You would dare…" Emily said softly but loudly enough to carry the distance between the monsters and us.

"My lady," Emissary said, his smile all charm and eyes alight as he stomped out his cigar. "Your race is run, your game is over. Lord Oblivion was quite clear. I'm to slice you open and feed that abomination in your belly to the Orc Mare."

Well, that settled who would die first and, if I could swing it, slowest.

Emily pursed her lips into a thin, dangerous line. "Declan, I would very much like you to destroy that creature."

"Well, Hale?" Emissary snapped. "Have you nothing to say?"

"Oh, aye. Just one thing, you ken?" I leveled the shotgun at his head. "Knight's bite repels the blight, *motherfucker!*"

"Bah! Mortal weapons are—"

I fired—the shotgun *roared.*

The scatter from the shells of Infernal-runic star iron tore a hole the size of a grapefruit in Emissary and ripped his right arm from its socket. Emissary wailed, spun on the spot, and struck the ground in a bloody, writhing mess. Purple ichor spurted from its wound, and if I knew anything about the creature, it wouldn't stay down for long. They needed to be beheaded good and proper with a piece of star iron—preferably a sharp piece—to finish the job.

I didn't have a sharp piece of star iron, but I had my grandfather to thank for teaching me their weakness. As Chief Librarian of the Forgetful Library—at least, before my downfall—old Aloysius Hale had held and read books most Knights didn't even know existed. He had picked up an old scrap of law: Knight's bite, star iron, repelled the blight—repelled the Everlasting and their servants.

The Orc Mare charged me en masse, howling, raving, slathering at the mouth and coal-black eyes burning.

Now, that was a challenge I was more than capable of meeting. I stayed in front of Emily, tossed the shotgun aside, and pooled smoky, luminescent light into my palms.

It had been a good long while since I'd fought foes that could fall under simple Willfire. I'd been one of the Academy's best students when it came to combat enchantment. That skill had served me well in the Tome Wars, ensured my rise through the Knights and access to battle enchantments better left alone.

I cracked my fingers, fell into an old stance, and began to *carve* through the Orc Mare. "Come on, then, you sons of bitches!"

I summoned needle-thin beams of pure energy, borrowed from the world of Coyle's *Reborn*—a story where the characters could manipulate light and string together weaves of crippling power. The barrage of white fire cut through the first wave of Orc Mare, slicing them in twain and twain again. The ragged flesh burst like swollen sacks against a hot stove. The battle howls turned to shrieks of dismay, of agony.

Still the horde attacked. Some took to the air, while others stumbled and clawed over the squirming mess I'd made of their brethren.

I stood my ground and gave Emily a quick glance over my shoulder. Picking idly at threads on her blue shawl, she seemed content to just watch me work. This ugly work was what I'd been born for, twenty-five years ago, and bred for through all my time at the Infernal Academy and in the Tome Wars. I kept one hand firing pellets of crackling energy into the snarling crowd and used the other to create a whip of bright red flame. I cracked the whip through the air and struck the beasts that had taken to the sky, slicing limbs from torsos and heads from necks. It started to rain monster blood and sizzling chunks of charred, rotten meat.

A wave of heat, backlash from the whip, washed over me, carrying the scent of burning flesh. I took a step back.

The Orc Mare ranks broke and turned to flee, but I didn't let them get far. I clapped my hands together and sent a crippling explosion of wind and fire after them. The chipped cobblestones broke further under the force of my power and downed the last of the Orc Mare, their bones liquefied.

Quiet fell.

Slow trails of luminescent smoke spiraled up from around my hands.

"It is truly something to see you… unleashed, Declan." Eyes alight and wild, Emily was breathing hard, flushed with adrenaline.

I hadn't even broken a sweat.

Emissary, amidst the carnage, started to laugh. That particular asshole had been slowly pulling himself back together during the festivities and was almost whole again.

From within the ruined buildings, howls of anger began to rise.

More Orc Mare. By the sound of it, a *helluva* lot more. In the dead years since the Fall of Voraskel, it seemed that the city had become infested with the worst kind of scum.

"Time for us to depart, I reckon." I quickly strapped the shotgun to the pack, shouldered it, and pulled the straps tight against my chest. I reached into the pool of Will once more, palms aglow, and offered Emily my hand. "I'm barely warmed up, Your Majesty. May I?"

Emily grinned—her timeless smile that always hinted at secrets I was too stupid to see. "I thought you'd never ask…"

One arm under her knees and the other under her shoulders, I picked her up, baby and all.

The Orc Mare were regrouping and pouring from the ruins of the city like shit from a burst pipe, howling for my head. The creature I knew as Emissary had nearly succeeded in pulling itself back together, but it was having some trouble with the star iron shells fused into its flesh.

"*Hale*!" Emissary roared.

"Overstayed our welcome," I muttered and concentrated on the ground at my feet. Passages of Raymond Germaine's *Gravity Boots* swam through my mind. Cords of liquid light fell from my hands, and a warm breeze swept Emily's hair into my face as a bubble of invisible energy began to form around us. Cracked stones and pebbles began to float up toward me, the pressure building. "Hold on tight, my dear!"

The bubble of Will burst, and I was *flung* up into the sky, high above the city. A hundred feet, two hundred, three hundred—higher! Wind rushed past my ears, and Emily laughed, delighted, as we arched over the ruined skyscrapers and crashed starship. We gracefully fell on a platform of glowing smoke beneath my feet, the remnants of the bubble.

I wasn't flying—that wasn't quite possible, as far as the Knights knew. Well, it was possible, but required such an understanding of aerodynamics and air pressure as to be a wholly ineffective means of getting about. But I could leap several hundred feet into the air in a single bound, and fall with a bit of style and grace. We were taught the technique from a very young age at the Academy, from books written expressly for the purpose of teaching young Knights how to survive. Or, as the case may be, how to make a swift exit from a dangerous situation.

I landed outside the other side of the city, as gently as if stepping off a curb, and placed Emily on her feet.

The air behind us was rife with the frenzied screams of the Orc Mare. They'd soon be hot on our tail.

In front of us were trees, leafy and green and a good hundred feet tall. Thick bands of roots, as thick as I was wide, had grown together in a tangle that seemed impenetrable.

"Well," Emily said. "Right where we need to be. The Forest of Astoria, the Sleeping Goddess."

"Best we hurry," I prodded. The fight with the Orc Mare had sapped my strength a bit. I wasn't keen for a rematch any time soon. "Which way?"

"This way, sweet Declan." Emily headed along the edge of the trees. "If we—oh, oh my." Her hands flew to her stomach, and her face clenched in pain.

I was at her side in a heartbeat. "What's the matter?"

"Hmm… nothing, I'm fine. I don't think the bairn enjoyed your leap through the sky as much as I did." Emily Grace smiled and wiped beads of sweat from her forehead. "Come along, then. A few miles farther to travel yet."

CHAPTER ELEVEN

The Enchanted Forest of Astoria

Emily led the way under mighty boughs and over tangled roots, seeming to know where she was going. She moved with that timeless grace of hers, each step certain, and I sensed that Emily Grace had spent distant years wandering the paths of this forest. *Too much I don't know about you, Em…* After all that had happened between us—my *death*—the last thing in the worlds I should've been doing was helping her. But she was lovely and pregnant, and I cared for her deeply.

"Take me for a fool…" I muttered and swatted at some tiny fireflies dancing around my face. The air was warm under the tall, leafy trees, and charged with scents of earthy grass and something that might have been lavender. We'd left behind the sounds of the Orc Mare and the ruined city howling for my head.

Only an hour after the fight in the city, and Willful energy still jolted through my veins, making me eager for more, to drink as deeply from the fires of creation as

I could, to bask in the light as I burned. Only my discipline and my years of training kept me from doing just that.

New recruits at the Academy had horror stories drilled into them on their first day. The power of Will itself was infinite—forever and eternal—but human capacity to use and abuse the fuel was limited, sometimes severely. That was why I'd taken Ethan under my wing earlier that year—if someone didn't guide him, he'd trip up one day and burn himself or others to ash… if he even left that much. He had that potential in him, buried under years of pretending magic wasn't real, but channeling vast amounts of Will came with one *helluva* high. Thankfully, only the strongest practitioners, the elite, ever became Knights—and therefore those able to channel vast amounts of Will were taught the skills to manage it.

Ascension City was full of people who could use Will, but the vast majority—ninety-nine percent, even—could never reach the apocalyptic amounts the Knights were capable of wielding. Those people could use small enchantments all day, every day, and feel nothing more than a caffeine buzz from their efforts.

The Knights were orders of magnitude above the vast majority. That was why we ruled the world.

I wondered if Emissary had managed to pluck the star iron buckshot from his chest—were we hunted yet?

Emily did not seem concerned, for she stopped to smell a copse of colorful wildflowers.

"How far to go?" I asked, glancing up at the sky I could only glimpse through the canopy. Avalon hung over most of the heavens, but the sun had fallen behind the planet. A dusky sort of twilight, blurred by the planet's broken rings, dominated the sky.

"Not far now, Declan," Emily said, holding her stomach again. "Little lad is kicking up a storm in here."

"Lad?" I raised an eyebrow, somewhat startled to learn the baby's gender. "You know, back at the Academy, the recruits used to tell stories. One—well, more than one—was about prophecy. I've never been much of a fan of prophecy. Still, the story goes that the son of the Immortal Queen would both save and destroy the world… Or destroy it *to* save it, or something. I forget the details. And it never said which world."

Emily laughed, high and true. "Well, if he's anything like his father, then I imagine he'll get up to all sorts of mischief."

"Who is his father, if I may be so bold?" I'd assumed it had been Morpheus Renegade, a few months before I'd driven the Roseblade through his heart.

"A man I met some years ago." Emily's face grew wistful. "All charm and kindness, but underneath a layer of unbreakable iron. He was handsome, too—inside and out. And a few years older than you, Declan."

I pondered Emily's description for a moment, stroking my chin. Nothing in there that gave away much. "Sure, but I bet he didn't have rugged good looks and a kickass eye patch like me, did he?"

Emily smiled. "No, he certainly did not."

From the copse of flowers, Emily led the way along a rough path through the forest. The path took a turn down into what I could see was a deep valley between a range of distant peaks, collaring the valley almost like a horseshoe. Nearby I heard gushing water. Great boulders the size of minivans lined the path, caught between the trees as if dropped by ambling giants. Thick, green moss clung to the rock and the air took on a cooler bite, less humid, more charged with negative ions.

I felt more alert and energetic—ready for anything.

"If I recall, we're close to the outer ring surrounding the Tomb," Emily said. "There's a hidden glen, a sort of secret grove, where we can rest and plan for the assault on the Tomb."

A rest, something to eat, and maybe an hour or two of sleep sounded ideal. Long shadows and the onset of night drew close. "An assault? What are you expecting to find there? This far out in an empty forest on a relatively empty world?" I sighed and answered my own question. "Lord Oblivion—you think he's here already." *Inside what's left of Tal…*

"Yes, I imagine he is close by. The Emissary and the Orc Mare were, I believe, an alarm to alert Oblivion of our arrival. Now, we'll soon pass over an outer ring of star iron," Emily said. "When we do, you may find yourself cut off from Origin, Declan. The Tomb is surrounded by deep layers of runic star iron, buried hundreds of feet down into the earth."

I hesitated, just for a moment, one hand leaning against a heavy old oak tree for support. Star iron had a plethora of wonderful uses beyond beheading demigods. The Knights forged blades that couldn't be manipulated by enemy Will-casters from star iron. They also—and I knew this firsthand—made shackles that dammed the Willful's ability to access their power.

Emily had just informed me that I was about to be hamstringed and, likely, trapped with one of the Everlasting.

"Great. Anything else you want to tell me? Perhaps that I'll need to be blindfolded for the next round? One arm tied behind my back, maybe?"

"Oh I'm sure a resilient young man like you will find a way to save the day." Emily grinned, showing perfect white teeth and soft dimples. "If we hurry, we'll be hidden in the grove before true nightfall."

~~*~*

The grove was secluded—secretive, even—and for the first time that day, I felt almost safe. The feeling was an illusion, perhaps—given where we were, what was on our tail, and what lay ahead—but for the time being, we could rest under the shattered sky.

We had crossed the star iron bindings surrounding the Tomb of the Sleeping Goddess a half-mile back. Doing so had dealt me a sore blow, as if all the air had been pushed from my lungs. Crossing the wide, deep ring had felt like wading through waist-deep treacle, slow going and sticky. Entering the binding's ancient power had left me a touch groggy and Will-less, while the pack and the shotgun became a whole lot heavier.

I'd grumbled and moaned the whole half a mile to this little slice of enchanted paradise.

Emily's secret grove was nestled up against a wide pool of near-still dark water reflecting the ruins of Avalon high above. A small, trickling waterfall fed the pool from a series of cracked boulders that had fallen into the valley like misshapen stairs—a natural windbreak against the weather rolling in over the mountains. On the north and south banks of the pool, small smoother rocks—natural seating—were scattered on the dry green grass, and to the right, a border of impenetrable ancient trees covered in velvety moss hid us from prying eyes.

In the air hung sparks of ethereal white light, as if a light snowfall had been set on fire. I reached out to touch one of the sparks, but it darted away. *Huh. They're alive, whatever they are…*

"Oh, it is good to be back here." Emily removed her sandals, took a seat on one of the rocks, and dipped her toes in the pool. "Nowhere else in all the worlds I'd rather be…"

"Paddy's?" I offered, slipping out of the pack and unclipping the shotgun for ease of access. I took a moment to reload the darn thing from the stock of shells in the pack. "I hear it's rebuilt and better than ever, after Emissary's attack earlier in the year. I don't think I ever thanked you, by the way, for warning me about that."

Emily rolled her eyes and grinned. "For a man known during the Tome Wars for his strategic mind and cleverness in plotting and planning the downfall of empires, gods, and the almighty rulers of Forget, Declan,"—she gave a wry chuckle—"you can be hopelessly predictable."

"But never boring, eh?"

"You are many things, but never boring. A little maudlin, at times—not without reason, I know. But if you wore a little more happiness every now and again as well as you wear that waistcoat..."

I snorted laughter and set about preparing a small meal in the last of the light. The snowflake creatures provided a subtle ambience, as did the bands of torn planetary rings in the night sky, creeping in between the canopy and reflected in the pool.

Dinner was a small, intimate affair. Emily and I sat, tired but warm, on boulders near the water and feasted on warm apples, squashed bread rolls, handfuls of salted almonds, and a small helping of comfortable silence. I kept an ear perked back toward the city, listening for the snapping of branches or disturbed underbrush. Emissary and the Orc Mare would not have given up.

"Do you ever give any thought," Emily asked after dinner, "to what you want from life, Declan?"

"Honestly?"

"Honesty is all that binds us, my dear."

"Then honestly I didn't expect to live this long," I said, with a short chuckle that was one part wry humor to two parts bitter terror. "And I technically didn't, thanks to you and Morpheus."

"Would you still blame me if I knew Aloysius Jade would return you to life with that stolen petal?"

I regarded Emily, resting my elbow on my knee and my stubbly chin on my palm, and saw a great deal of kindness in her eyes. "I've never blamed you, not really, and I don't know why."

"Honesty, again? Perhaps some measure of trust from the legendary Knight Infernal Declan Hale? The Shadowless Arbiter… So many silly titles we collect, hmm?"

"Yeah tell me about it." I ran a hand back through my hair and shrugged. "I don't know what I want from life. Who does? Do you?"

"Peace in our time?" Emily asked, seemingly to herself. "Peace for our children. An end to a conflict spanning countless universes and endless ages of creation? A normal life, away from angels and demons? Freedom, Declan, is what I want from life."

In the warmth and the gentle light of the grove, I found my eyes were growing heavy. It had been a long day. "I used to think that my exile meant I could live a normal life—find a girl, nine to five, and so on. Even thought I could go out to a pub, Paddy's, and meet a girl—just a normal girl, whose biggest problem was finding a job, finishing her degree, or calling her mother. Simple, you know? But every time I'd sit at that bar… every time a girl would smile at me or catch me looking… I'd wonder if she was really normal or just sent to play normal. If she were real or a Renegade assassin or a monster in human guise. I know now that, even if half a century had passed in exile, I would still be sitting at that bar, wondering.

"The life I've lived, the wars I've fought… it's too late to have 'normal.' Best I could have would be a lie, a lie spent looking over my shoulder and wondering if the normal girl I met at the bar would stab me in the back—or, worse, step in front of me at the wrong time and catch a stray bullet."

Emily patted my knee. "You need to rest. Sleep for a spell, my dear. I'll wake you."

Having been awake for nearly thirty hours, that sounded like the finest damned idea in all Forget. Let the Story Thread plummet into the Void for an hour of blissful, uninterrupted sleep. I used the pack as a pillow, propped against one of the small rocks, and lay down on the grass next to the pool.

The soft trickling from the waterfall was cathartic, sleep-inducing. Emily remained seated and silhouetted against the ruined sky, humming a soft, somewhat familiar tune, as I drifted away.

CHAPTER TWELVE

A Tomfool of Cherry Blossoms

Emily woke me in what felt like thirty seconds later. I sat up, groggy but better for the sleep, and cleared my throat. "Morning already, eh?"

"You slept just under two hours," she said. "And now it's time for you to storm the Tomb and recover the Roseblade."

"Don't you mean, 'time for *us*' to do that?"

Emily shook her head. "No, I did not. I will remain here, Declan, and risk no further harm to my unborn child."

Quite right, too.

"Here then." I unsheathed Myth from my belt. The celestial crystal was cold under my fingers. "I won't leave you unprotected. If things get dicey, I want you to cut your losses and run. Don't wait for me." Things would probably get dicey.

Emily hesitated, searched my face for something, and then took the Creation Knife. Her eyes glistened with tears, and she chuckled softly. "Oh, Declan Hale. Just when I think I know you so well… you surprise me. Do you know how valuable this blade is?"

I sniffed and stood up. "You're worth more."

"You're young and kind," she said. "Too young and too kind. But I believe there will be peace by the time you're done. I pray I'm there to see it…"

I did a few stretches to wake my sleeping limbs and popped my neck to work out a kink left from using the pack as a pillow. "Really glad I brought that shotgun," I said, now without Myth as well as my Willful power. "I'd hate to get into a fight with Emissary or Oblivion with just my considerable charm at my disposable."

"You're more liable to cut yourself than an enemy with that," Emily commented, stroking her baby bump. "I will be here when you return. I promise."

"First sign of trouble—you get out," I said. "No arguments."

Emily's lips quirked. "Very well. You'll find the Tomb about a quarter mile through the trees. Head out the way we came into this grove and turn left behind the copse of oak sentinels. You'll… you will know when you've arrived."

I nodded, committing the directions to memory. "Right then. So where did you hide it? The Roseblade?"

"I… cannot say."

I shouldered the shotgun and nodded again, relaxed and confident. "Sure. I guess this was already too easy. Need a bit of a challenge to keep things interesting."

"I cannot say because in the Tomb of the Sleeping Goddess… memory pervades. The corridors twist toward your memories, Declan." Emily's expression fell. "And I am sorry for that. I know your memories are not happy."

Ah, bugger. I'd encountered something like pervasive memory before, in an old, broken temple hidden on one of the Dream Worlds—Scion's prison, if I had my head wrapped around all that nonsense right. Annie Brie and I had stepped through a memory of my time as commander of a bombardment inter-dimensional cruiser and part of the Cascade Fleet. Good times, back in the day.

"Not really, no." I could only agree, for the most part. "But now and again, something happy. I wear it better, remember? Maybe I'll get lucky and the Tomb will show me nights at Paddy's or my old friends from the Infernal Academy. Or that time you and I kissed in the Fae Palace, eh?"

"I stabbed you and left you bleeding on the marble floors…"

"Still one of my happier memories," I quipped. "You made that red dress look stunning, Emily Grace."

A faint blush rose in Emily's cheeks as she stood there in the grove, heavily pregnant and clutching a dagger of celestial illusion. "Thank you. Best you be on your way now."

~~*~*

Although true night had fallen on Voraskel, enough ethereal radiance from the snowflake creatures and the planet in the sky lit the overgrown path through the enchanted forest to guide my way. I was, of course, on guard for any sign of the enemy. Orc Mare didn't seem to possess much in the way of stealth ability—I'd hear them coming miles away—but the Emissaries could be a tricky bunch. I kept my shotgun at the ready.

About five minutes' walking from the secret grove, the trees started to thin, and more of the sky broke through the canopy. I stumbled onto a road, ancient and cracked, unkempt and tangled with twisted tree roots. The forest was silent—perhaps *too* silent—and I clutched the shotgun tight. The eight remaining shells of packed star iron and magnesium were all the defense I had against… well, anything.

Up ahead I glimpsed the tomb, and I didn't have to wonder anymore just how one buried a god.

A large pyramid structure, lush with old vines, stood at the heart of a vast courtyard at least two hundred meters across and as long as it was wide. Stone pieces of what had once been walls, mosaics, gargoyles, and statues from the land before the Knights Infernal littered the roadside. At the end of the road, where the trees ended and the courtyard began, the remains of a pillar that must have risen a good twenty meters in its prime had collapsed and cracked.

Next to that pillar was a statue of a woman, covered in white roses and thorny vines. I glanced at the statue and then stumbled. The statue's cruel face struck me as familiar—so much so that my heart leapt into my throat—but I couldn't match the worn stone to anyone I knew.

I stared at the features for a good minute, and the longer I concentrated, the more it slipped away. Whatever my mind had intuitively recognized escaped my grasp like water in a sieve.

I shook my head—it was gone. But the answer would come to me, I was sure.

"All of this feels far too familiar…" I muttered, and breaking the silence felt like committing a sin, like drunken laughter at a funeral.

As I entered the courtyard of wild grass and cracked stone, a cool breeze blew a smattering of fresh dew-soaked cherry blossoms toward me. The petals swirled up and around me, as if I were wearing a cape caught in the wind, with a scent so familiar that it made my knees wobble.

Funny how smell could be the strongest of the senses. The aroma in the cherry blossom petals took me back years, to the final weeks of the Tome Wars…

Someone wrapped her arms around me from behind—tiny, olive-skinned arms with crimson fingernails—and pressed some of the swirling petals between our bodies.

"You came," she said. "I knew you would. Even though it's going to hurt."

Gently, I broke the embrace and turned on the spot, careful to keep the barrel of the shotgun at the ready but not quite pointing at the woman before me. "How much of you is *you* and how much the Dread-Lord Oblivion?"

Tal Levy's eyes were honey brown, but she had been host and vessel to the Everlasting Oblivion for over half a decade. Oblivion had eyes of pure blood—no whites, no pupils, just orbs of blood-red menace.

Those brown eyes in the woman before me were Tal's eyes. Her dark hair and soft skin were Tal's hair and skin. Her face was Tal's face of oh-so-familiar soft angles, although looking a shade older than when we'd last met in Atlantis. She wore a simple garment, a sort of inky black pantsuit with a deep V-neck.

I reached out, slowly, and cupped her cheek. She felt real and warm and, worst of all, alive.

Tal sighed against my palm and gripped my hand. "I am me," she said. "But Oblivion is watching."

If I hadn't been standing so near, I might have missed it, but a crimson sheen flashed across her eyes. *Well to remember you're not face to face with Tal, but with the creature behind the myths of the Beast, of the Devil—the very personification of evil and enemy of humankind. Well to remember, Declan.*

I took a deep breath and exhaled slowly. "And here I was hoping we had this forest all to ourselves."

"Lord Oblivion will let me stay in control," Tal said. "So long as you recover the Roseblade for him we can have some time together."

I wanted to laugh, to dismiss Oblivion's offer for so much bullshit, but… but here was Tal, my Tal, who had spent six years as host to fucking Beelzebub. Any moment she got to be herself instead of the beast had to be rare. Indeed, that may have only been the second time since we bargained with Oblivion those long years ago. The first being a brief second atop the tower in Atlantis, after I severed the Infernal Clock and just before I died. Why did the cost of such a moment have to come at so high of a price? Or, worse, a price so easy to pay? The Knights would hang me for it, but I would trade the Roseblade for even just this brief moment with Tal.

"I told Sophie you were dead," I said. "Broken quill, for the longest time I thought you were. But you've been in there this whole time, haven't you? Tal, I'm so sorry."

Tal sniffed, and her gentle smile faltered. "You know you can't give Oblivion the Roseblade."

"Why not?" I rasped. "If it gets me you."

Her smile returned, a lot sadder. "And that's what the Everlasting is counting on, Declan. Your weakness for me."

"Songbird, we used to call that weakness love."

Tal's expression hardened into something as cold and as distant as one of the fallen statues littering the courtyard. "He needs you. And he thinks he knows you, knows you to your very core—so much so that he doesn't *care* that I'm telling you this. He could stop me in a heartbeat. Smother my mind and take my body. He could stop *your* heart in less time. He believes you'll do what he wants… for me."

"He's right," I said simply, not even having to think about the situation. "So that's the deal, is it, Oblivion? I get her back, if only briefly, while we recover the Roseblade?"

"As much as it irks him, Oblivion needs a human, one with strong memory, to navigate the corridors of the Tomb. This place was built so many thousands of years ago by Fair Astoria herself, before she fell from grace." Tal's brow furrowed, as if she were listening to something only she could hear. "Her presence and power still encircle her tomb. It was designed with purpose—and to keep her brothers and sisters, the Everlasting, from ever reaching its heart."

Fair Astoria fell from grace? Is that the same as dying? So little was truly known about the Everlasting, beyond their names and crimes. I half-expected to find Astoria alive and well inside this damned tomb.

"I accept," I said, because I already had, but my mind was racing. To have Tal back at all meant… so many possibilities. A chance to save her, to bring her back, and perhaps learn more about the nature of the Everlasting than any Knight in history, And I was willing to gamble handing over the Roseblade, the most powerful weapon in existence, to Oblivion for a chance at such possibilities.

Hell, I'd done worse.

Tal nodded, resigned, and her eyes changed again, from honey brown to tainted crimson. "Try anything," Oblivion growled, his voice like flat river stones colliding and smashing in a flood, "and I'll make Tal Levy eat you alive, piece by piece, until all that is left of you is your abandoned shadow. I will be watching, Arbiter."

Tal shuddered, and the blood drained from her eyes. She took a hold of herself again, met my gaze, and tried for a smile. "I've missed you."

"Let's be about our work," I replied and offered her my hand.

Tal entwined her fingers in mine, and together we started for the Tomb of the Sleeping Goddess, one soft step at a time, as if we were old lovers merely strolling through the park.

CHAPTER THIRTEEN

The Tomb of the Sleeping Goddess

"What does he want the Roseblade for?" I asked, resting the barrel of the shotgun in the nook below my shoulder. "Besides the obvious, of course."

Tal shook her head. "I'm… not permitted to say."

I looked at her sidelong and nodded slowly. "He binds you, is that how this works? He's behind the scenes right now, keeping you on a short leash. I thought you dead, Tal—in Atlantis, when we made the deal for the Degradation and the war's end."

"In every way that that matters, I *am* dead, Declan, and have been for six years." She shivered and wrapped her arms over her chest. "I forfeited my essence to Oblivion, so you… so you didn't have to. I belong to him: mind, body, and soul."

To that I had nothing to say, save something that could not be articulated by mere words. Perhaps a gut-wrenching scream would've come close, but only in the sense of expressing just how inexpressible some thoughts and feelings were and had to be. A *yûgen* of misery once again. I'd been thinking on that word—*yûgen*—a lot lately. It was a Japanese aesthetic, a set of ancient ideals, and *yûgen* could refer to a glimpse of the profound, mysterious beauty of the universe… or the sad beauty of human suffering.

Not a bad way to view the world, I thought.

"Shall we head inside, then?" Tal asked.

A series of wide steps, in ruins much like the rest of the world, led up to what I assumed was the entrance of Fair Astoria's tomb. I wondered if her remains were actually buried there or if—as had been the case of Oblivion in Atlantis—Astoria were imprisoned there. That didn't seem likely, but perhaps I should have asked Emily, given that she had secreted the Roseblade somewhere within the structure.

The great door of faded marble hung open on rusted hinges, just beyond a circle of what I assumed was star iron, given the Infernal runes etched into the metal. I chanced a glance at Tal, unsure who I'd see there, but she didn't seem bothered by the symbols. Scion, the last Everlasting I had met, had not been able to approach a place protected like this. The old runes afforded some protection against the Elder Gods.

"Another reason he's giving me control," Tal said. "Oblivion exists as… an idea, Declan. Which is not to say he isn't real. I think we're long since past doubting the existence of Elder Gods, hmm? He is abstract, like a Voidling. You saw in Atlantis, when he took me—he was naught but mist and malice surrounding the Infernal Clock, shackled to it. But now, nestled away at the back of my mind, festering on my soul, he can pass these old wards, so long as I'm in control. The only Everlasting with that abil—" She gasped and doubled over, as if struck in the gut.

"What's wrong?"

Tal stood and offered me a grimacing smile. "He didn't want me telling you that."

I made a mental note to think on just what had been said later, if I survived the next hour or however long it took to find the Roseblade. *He's the only Everlasting who can bypass wards? Why's that important?*

And once we did recover the Roseblade, what came next? Oblivion was raw power, even if he were as stunted by the star iron in this place as I was—same shit in different ways—but, given the Roseblade…

Not even star iron could overcome the power in that sword. Of that, I was quite sure.

"Let's head inside," Tal said. Her olive skin had paled and she sounded as weary as… well, as someone who had been possessed and abused for six lonely years…

~~*~*

The first few feet of the tomb were dirty and dusty, the air musty, and the light rusty. Old torches in cast iron brackets long past their use-by date flared to life with oily orange flame as we drew near, as was usually the way of such forgotten places. Emily might have been there recently, but I doubted the Tomb of the Sleeping Goddess was a tourism hotspot on Voraskel, even before the Voidflood. Save Emily, Tal and I may have been the first two people to set foot there in a long, long time. The torches offered just enough flickering light to mark a path ahead.

The wavering firelight was disorienting to my one good eye, after the ethereal light outside. I blinked a few times and got my bearings. The corridor ahead, all spider webs and dust, seemed to head underground.

I sighed and rubbed my arms. The way forward felt cold and lonely, but turning back was not an option.

Off we trotted, our footsteps echoing in the hollow space, and I couldn't help but keep glancing at Tal, making sure she was still there. To see her again was like a dream come true—a dream wrapped in an Everlasting nightmare, to be sure, but now and again I was allowed to live in the present and not worry on the future.

The corridor widened and revealed a dimly lit chamber, held up by crumbling pillars that seemed to lean like loose fence posts. Still doing their job of holding the roof in place, but one good gust of wind away from unemployment. More torches lined the walls, illuminating a colorful mosaic. Although covered in centuries of dust, the tiles on the wall were clear and told quite the story—one I'd heard before, as a fairytale told with slight smiles, as if it couldn't possibly be true.

"Holy hell," I said, lowering the shotgun. "This is the story of how the Knights were founded in Atlantis, ten millennia ago…" I circled the room, avoiding the curious white platform in its heart for now, and read the story as best I could from the ancient hieroglyphs interspersed between the vast pictures. "An order of men, to fight the blight…"

Tal followed silently in my wake. I was more aware of her presence, like a hot flame on my back, than anything else in the chamber.

"Something… It's old Infernal, I can't quite make it out… Something about a Knight lost to the ages. The Everlasting waged war against True Earth and ravaged the planet until only Atlantis was left, the last bastion against the blight."

"Yes," Oblivion snarled in Tal's voice. I didn't turn, not wanting to see his eyes marring her pretty face. "Eternally vexing, that city. We had the planet, True Earth—we *had* it! All save one small corner that somehow managed to forge the prisons and banish us for ten thousand years. Curse that wretched hive and all who called it home!"

"How did Atlantis end up on the Plains of Perdition, then?" I asked. "If it was originally on Earth?"

Oblivion was silent for a long moment, perhaps deciding whether or not to tear out my spine. "The Atlanteans forfeited their city to a Voidflood in order to ensure my imprisonment. They purposely opened the Void above the planet. What remained of Atlantis, and all its wonders and treasures, washed up further down the Story Thread and far from True Earth. Lost to time, my prison—until you came along, Hale."

Atlantis had fought the Everlasting Oblivion by *hurling* the bastard and their city into a Voidflood?

"Wow." Now *that* was certainly a piece of forgotten history. The Atlanteans were lucky the flood hadn't overwhelmed the entire planet. "I guess they thought it crazy enough to work."

"Yes," Tal said, and it was Tal again. "Don't get any ideas. True Earth used to have two moons, before this... debacle."

I turned and grunted. We'd reached the end of the story told on the mosaic. It ended just as Oblivion had said, with the city washed away in a great flood. *I guess that's where the myth on Earth comes from… The flood that drowned Atlantis did happen. A Voidflood.*

I hadn't seen any corridors or doorways in the chamber leading elsewhere through the pyramid. A dead end, for all that I could tell.

But there was that platform of pure white stone in the center of the chamber, seemingly untouched by time or dust. The platform, rising just a foot off the floor, looked simultaneously inviting and ominous. I could almost smell unseen enchantment breathing through the smooth marble.

"That looks like it may descend, doesn't it?" I asked, speaking mostly to myself. "Down in to depths unknown. Goblin town, eh? You want to go first?"

Tal smirked as we walked over to the heart of the room and stood just before the platform. "Ever the gentleman, aren't you?"

"Got you fooled." I took a deep breath, a touch apprehensive at how *well* this venture seemed to be going so far. "I'll go first then, but tell me, what's your favorite story, Tal?"

"I haven't read it yet," she replied.

"Oh, good answer." I stepped onto the platform, and the old stone shivered and began to sink into the floor. The grinding sound of stone on stone echoed through the chamber. From above, a thin beam of white light shone down on me, as if I were on stage under a spotlight.

I squinted against the brightness, and when it dimmed, I was no longer in the Tomb of the Sleeping Goddess. I no longer had only one good eye to my name and a possessed girlfriend escorting me down to goblin town with one helluva malevolent monkey on her back.

I hadn't felt a thing—no step between worlds, no teleport, no impending sense of the Void pressing close. In less than a heartbeat, I'd simply appeared somewhere else, without my awesome demigod-slaying shotgun.

*Some*when *else*, I realized, as I got a hold on my new surroundings and found them familiar.

I was young. I was a *kid*.

In a single step I'd not only crossed worlds but time.

Bugger.

SALVO II – PUT YOUR LIPS ON ME FOR NO GOOD REASON

Hello, babies. Welcome to Earth. It's hot in the summer and cold in the winter. It's round and wet and crowded. At the outside, babies, you've got about a hundred years here. There's only one rule that I know of, babies — "God damn it, you've got to be kind."

—Kurt Vonnegut, *God Bless You, Mr. Rosewater*

CHAPTER FOURTEEN

Old and New

I was seated in a comfortable green leather armchair in front of a drooping old table stacked with about a hundred books. Disoriented after having lost sight of the tomb and Tal, I whipped my head around to get a good look at just where I'd ended up.

Funnily enough, it was somewhere awfully familiar. I'd been getting a lot of that lately—a sense of familiarity. It was worrying, in an I've-got-bigger-problems kind of way.

I wasn't alone.

Tia Moreau, my old mentor when I was in school, waved her hand in front of my face. "Hale?" She snapped her fingers. "You're zoning out, kid."

I tried to focus on her, but my gaze was drawn to the room around us. We sat in one of the small study nooks built in the outer wings of the library at the Infernal Academy, surrounding the perimeter of a wide quadrangle of garden and just up the road from Edgar's, the oldest and greatest pub in Forget.

I'm in a memory. Come on, get it together—you knew this would happen. You're still in the tomb with Tal. Some enchantment is just dicking around in your head…

It wasn't quite like the memory-journey experience in Scion's temple on the Dream Worlds with Annie. Similar, yes, but not the same. Here I was a part of the memory, as if it were happening again at that very moment—or as it had happened on that day in the past. Last time, I'd just been an observer, unseen and confused.

Now I have to participate? Is that how we journey on?

Tia was looking at me, a severe frown of disapproval on her stern, lovely, *teenage* face. This had to be at least ten years ago, probably a few more.

Well, there were worse memories that the enchantments could have recreated.

"Sorry," I mumbled. Of Tal, of Oblivion, there was no sign. Which made sense, I supposed. I hadn't known Tal when that memory had taken place. "So what's the plan?"

"You have to retrieve four elements, using your wits and the books in this room," Tia said. "You've got an hour to construct a reality beacon that harmonizes between the Academy and our bases on Avalon. Easy, for the most part, but I bet the worlds in between will hold a few surprises."

We were definitely in the Infernal Academy—which existed on a world hidden from all tomes and accessible only through the Fae Palace in Ascension City. Night had fallen outside, and I glimpsed my reflection in one of the long windows.

I was a kid. Thirteen, at the most, when this had happened. And so much more had happened since that I only vaguely recalled this memory at all.

"Huh," I said, admiring my old trainee uniform in the window—a charcoal suit of enchanted cloth, trimmed in braided yellow around the shoulders and down the button line. I wore an empty sheath for what would, in a year or two, hold my Infernal blade—something they had taken from me a few years later, just after the Degradation and just before my exile. "Time flies."

"Where are you tonight?" Tia asked, exasperated. She was pretty and tiny, just about five feet even. I think she looked so young to me because she didn't yet carry the worry lines or the scar that cut her face in two. Her lightly freckled nose was unblemished, her eyes were full of yet-to-be-corrupted life and her raven-black hair was pulled back in an easy ponytail. "Concentrate, or we'll fail."

"Sure. Right. You're still as sweet as lilies in May, Tia." I cleared my throat and tapped on the old wooden table with my knuckles. "Reality beacons. Cool. I know all about those."

Blimey, it had been a while since I'd had need to create a beacon. Truth be told, once I'd graduated, I'd had a slew of less powerful Willful at my disposal to do what was, if I were being cruel, grunt work—and if I were being less cruel, basic programming for charting paths through the Void. Reality beacons were installed on starships and cruisers, or the trains at the Atlas Lexicon. They could be used to navigate universes like lighthouses in mist, to avoid treacherous shores.

"So the assignment is pretty straightforward and your mentor," Tia grinned and winked, "can only intervene if you're going astray." She fixed me with a fierce glare. "Do not go astray. This may only be a few theory points toward your grade, but it's worth fifteen percent of my final in Leadership."

I struggled to keep a wry smile from my face and gave Tia a quick, sure nod. Broken quill, but it was absurd to think there had ever been a time when we worried about grades and results. A time when we cared what the Knights above thought of us and our progress. A time when we *wanted* to fight a war.

Young and stupid, the pair of us.

As for the assignment, the memory may have been a touch buried in my head, but I'd remembered. Tia and I would find the raw elements for the beacon easy enough, but at each off-world site was an ambush of lesser Forgetful spawn. It was my first real test without an instructor, just a fellow student. Tia was my senior by three years, at that point in our training, and she was more than capable of dealing with the parameters of the assignment.

"So what do we need to make this work?" Tia asked.

I looked around again, searching for a glimpse of the tomb or of Tal through the walls of this illusion, but the memory was complete. Outside the room, the Academy hustled and bustled, and inside it, I could hear the creak of the joints in our chairs, smell the old books, and taste the library dust in the air. It seemed the only way ahead—indeed, the only option I had to get out of the memory—was to play the game.

I took a breath and blew the air out between my lips in a huff. "Okay. Reality beacons. The four elements we need are earth and stone from the Academy and from Avalon, a codex pod, and some sundrops. Also Byrd's *Elemental Pathway Inscriptions…* Volume Two… to transcribe the enchantments."

"Volume Four," Tia corrected. "Not so much of a hotshot when it comes to the theory, are you?"

Well it's been over a decade, through a war or two, and once into the jaws of death since I had need to check my math, sweetheart… "More of a hands-on son of a gun, Miss Moreau."

Tia frowned, bemused, and I had to remember I was only just thirteen. *Am I really here?* It was mere illusion, pulled from my mind, wasn't it?

I was more than a touch concerned that I found it hard to tell reality from the fiction. *Story of my life, for the most part.* I kept trying to see some flaw in the memory, some small glitch in the illusion, but it was seamless. In all the ways that mattered, I was there.

"So what do we know about codex pods?" Tia asked.

"They're grown from channels of Will funneled through an irrigation system in East Ascension markets. About five gems apiece, yeah?"

"Pretend for a moment you don't have access to the markets. Where would you look?" She gestured to the stacks of books on the table. Hundreds of worlds in hundreds of pocket universes, all within arm's reach.

"The natural glades on Mandeelos," I said.

Tia raised an eyebrow and smirked. She picked up a book from the top of a stack. Blythe's *Fall of Heaven*, a sci-fi adventure that spanned a whole galaxy of bright and sparkling worlds—one of which held codex pods. "Mandeelos. You know it's not settled, right? Could be anything there."

I grinned. "Then what are we still doing here? Mandeelos also orbits a blue supergiant. We can get our sundrops at the same time."

Tia blinked, and I realized she was impressed. She hadn't thought of combining the worlds. Two birds, one interdimensional portal through the Void.

"Well," she said, "do you have your earth and stone from the Academy? Probably best to get that first before we dive across to Mandeelos. That way we can head straight to Avalon. How long do you have before the pod turns sour?"

I slapped my forehead and nodded. "Yeah, of course." Codex pods, once plucked from the vine, had a limited shelf life. They needed to be refrigerated or used, or they withered and died. Again, I was a long, violent decade away from having to know all the theory. "Stone and dirt first. I'll be right back."

I left Tia twiddling her thumbs and stepped outside into a warm night.

The small study room on the ground floor of the Academy's library bordered a nice patch of green grass in the quadrangle garden. I heard revelry and merriment from Edgar's on the air and thought about testing the bounds of the illusion. Could I get a drink?

No, even though for the moment I was a kid again, I still had memories of the years to come and, in the future, was still working on being sober. I'd spent the best part of the last five years in a drunken stupor. My liver was scotch-proof but highly flammable. So far I'd lasted a good few months off the booze. Not a day or even an hour went by that I didn't *want* a drink, but one could never make the argument I was short of willpower.

Still, something amber and aged would have taken the edge off my nerves.

I didn't have time to saunter down memory lane. I had Tal to worry about—and Emily all alone in a forest soon to be overrun by Emissary and Orc Mare.

Time or not, I guessed I could enjoy the glimpse of the past while it lasted. *But no sense in dragging it out.*

I headed into the garden and grabbed a fistful of soil and tiny pebbles, plenty of source material for the reality beacon, to tether the Academy to a faraway land through the Void.

Avalon, the assignment called for, which was a link to the mess I was in at that very moment—that is, in the future, from the perspective of this memory. Before

Avalon had been swept away in the Voidflood, it had been an outpost of the Knights Infernal. And from the timeline of this memory, it was set to become the site of one of the hardest fought battles in the hundred-year history of the Tome Wars.

I turned back to the study room, and the memory changed.

Again, there was no sense of stepping between worlds, but reality simply reeled forward a slide, and I was somewhere new and familiar. The fistful of pebbles and dirt also disappeared.

"Guess we're not making reality beacons today…" I muttered.

In this memory I was older, but not by much. A year, at most, maybe a shade under. Fit, healthy, and full of ambition that would one day—one day soon—tear worlds apart.

The sun shone bright and warm overhead, and I was wading through knee-deep mud with three dozen of my classmates. We were running the physical obstacle course on the far fields of the Academy's training wing as fast as we could. Course record, set by me, was eleven minutes, twelve seconds—if memory served, and why wouldn't it here?

I wondered briefly if that record had been broken yet in the present.

Tia was with me again, a grim, determined smile on her face. She, my mentor, yanked me forward, and we surged through the sludge, firing beams of concentrated Will at targets that popped up from the sidelines or fell from above. The funny little wooden targets had snarling, monstrous faces painted on them—at the time, I hadn't been clever enough to see it, but the Academy had trained us well to be soldiers and killers. Life at the Academy had made us *want* to be soldiers and killers.

And I'd been the best recruit those bastards had ever seen, rivaled only by a scant few such as Tal, Marcus, Tia… and Clare Valentine.

The whole memory shuddered as my thoughts settled on Clare, and I went from being near-submerged in cold muck to stumbling on a hardwood dance floor. *Why am I being shown these memories? Why Tia? And what do I have to do to break the enchantment?* Oh, and the latest memory was pleasantly unfair. One of my favorites, remembered only with a fondness for something I once had but could never have again.

I was dancing with a pretty girl—Clare, who ended up dying for me. We were amongst friends, and fast music played through the air in the dim light of the bar. Everything was as I remembered it, of course. Every face, every corner of the bar—

Everything except the menacing and otherworldly stone arch resting on the stage near the far wall. A crooked arch of obsidian stone, polished to a fine glassy sheen. For no reason, I hated and feared that arch the moment I saw it. The arch framed a rippling portal of neon-blue energy.

"What's wrong?" Clare Valentine asked, moving against me with a little more pressure. Her breath was warm and carried the pleasing scent of some strawberry-flavored vodka.

I met her eyes and found them sultry. That night had been the very first we spent together. Tal was still a year away, and we'd been graduated Knights for only weeks. Already we were known for our skill and prowess in the minor skirmishes we'd had with the Renegades. That night was Clare's birthday, and we'd all gotten together and rented a bar in Farvale on Lake Delgado, just over the mountains from Ascension City.

"Nothing," I said. No one else seemed to give the dark arch or the pulsating light any mind. Indeed, the wraiths of my past stepped right through the arch as if it wasn't there. They blended with the stone and emerged unscathed and unbothered.

"Come on, Dec." Clare laughed and spun me around by the waist. "Dance with me!"

I laughed and fell into the moment. Clare had always been tiny, petite—and her ever-changing eyes, as I remembered them, had been wild and bright. Her blue and indigo orbs certainly were shining that night. With a wicked grin, I swept my arms under the back of her legs and picked her up, pressing our bodies together and lifting her just a head above me. She looked down, placed her hands on either side of my face, and kissed me.

The bar erupted in cheers and catcalls, wolf whistles and applause.

Clare withdrew her tongue from my mouth and pulled back, still a foot above me in my arms, and blushed beet-red in the dizzying lights and the loud music. She swatted my shoulder, and I let her down.

"It's about time you two got it on," Tia Moreau said, holding a fresh drink for Clare and wearing a devastating, sheer blue dress of her own. Never mind the warships, the battlefields, or the endless skirmishes—Tia could cut through the Renegades in that dress alone. "We all thought it'd happen weeks ago when we were stationed out at the Reach."

"No fraternizing while on duty," I said, and both girls rolled their eyes.

"How was it?" Tia asked Clare, a devious glimmer in her eye.

Clare smirked and gave me a wink. "Sloppy… but effective."

Tia burst into laughter. "Declan's never been anything else."

I chuckled and looked across the dance floor again, keeping an eye on that arch of rippling light. I wasn't sure, but I thought that maybe the light had grown a touch dimmer. A sense of distant urgency and unease settled in my gut. Wasn't I supposed to be doing something else tonight? Wasn't I—

On Voraskel.

—looking for something or someone?

"He's not even listening," Tia said. "Declan, we're going to the ladies'. Watch our drinks, would you?"

"Sure," I said, distracted. I'd forgotten something important. "Watch your drinks."

Clare and Tia linked arms and wandered off in the direction of the washrooms. I watched Clare leave in her tight green dress, pale shoulders bare, and she made sure it was worth watching. I ran my hand down the buttons of my waistcoat and—

This isn't real.

—couldn't shake that feeling, like a maddening piece of gristle caught between my teeth, that I had somewhere else to be tonight.

"You can't stay here…" I muttered to myself. "This was long ago, and most of the people here are dead or insane."

And that's the perversion of this particularly brand of enchantment, isn't it? It makes you want to stay. The defenses protecting the Roseblade in the Tomb of the Sleeping Goddess were designed to be unfairly kind, I saw now. Memory could be pervasive. The enchanted defenses wanted me to stay, to get lost in the past—so much so that I was beginning to believe the illusion was real.

And therein lay the insidious danger of the tomb's enchantments. I'd live in this dream world, flittering from memory to memory as my body in the tomb dehydrated and succumbed to an agonizing death that I would never feel.

The arch called to me.

Time slipped by, and Clare had returned from the washroom. No sign of Tia.

"Let's get out of here," Clare whispered, her warm tongue darting across my earlobe. "It's your lucky night, Declan Hale."

"It sure was." I took a step back, grasped Clare's hands in my own, and raised them to my mouth. I kissed the backs of her fingers, trying hard not to picture them as they were now—naught but rot and bones in the World Cemetery. Better to remember Clare this way, wasn't it? I let her go and took a step back.

"What's wrong?" she asked.

"Everything," I said. "And nothing, I suppose. Happy birthday, Clare Valentine."

A few more steps backward, and I felt the heat of the arch at my back. I took a snapshot in my head of Clare in her dress, young and beautiful and—for a short while, ten years ago—mine. Then I stepped through the archway, giving up relatively *Matrix*-style happiness, and the whole shambles disappeared in a flash of hot white light.

My head spun, and the ground shifted beneath my feet.

Noiseless air rushed past my ears, but I was falling through a void of nothing. Not *the* Void, but *a* void—of pure white nothing. That nothing marked every direction, and I only knew down from up because I was falling.

Long minutes passed that way.

I thought on my memories of Clare and of Tia before her. Of Tal yet to come, and the heartache we had wrought in each other. Of all my friends and the best people I'd ever known.

After what could have been hours or minutes, I started to think on something else.

Somewhere else.

Someone else.

Let me out, I thought, speaking to the enchantment messing with my head. *I didn't yield. You couldn't make me stay. My present may be dull and devoid of these people you keep flinging at me, but it's real. These dreams are pale shadows of what really happened, how we really felt, and how much we mattered to one another while it lasted.*

I sensed I was heard by whatever intelligence was in the enchantments, guiding me through my memories. Not so much alive but aware, and capable of vast and terrible understanding.

You could have all these lives, whispered a soft voice that sounded male and female and neither. *You could live a dozen different lives here, and only seconds would pass in true reality. Declan,* the voice said, kind and soothing. *You could be happy.*

This isn't real. This does not matter. I wanted to slam my fist into a wall to drive that point home, but I could only fall. *And what I have—what I lost—defined me. I can't play pretend with all the ghosts of my past, you hear me? I could never live in these 'perfect' worlds. I need loss. I need cruelty and a hard slap in the face every now and again. It's how I know I'm still alive. Now release me!*

Like everything I touched, the void of nothing shattered in a blaze of reality, and the enchantment was broken.

CHAPTER FIFTEEN

Each Breath She Takes

The platform in the Tomb of the Sleeping Goddess, which had held me prisoner to my memories in a beam of light, shuddered and descended below the level of the floor as true reality reasserted itself. I took Tal's hand, and she took a small step onto the platform as it fell toward the bowels of the tomb.

"How long was I caught?" I asked. My mouth felt dry and my throat sore, as if I'd run a marathon without water.

"You were only a few minutes," Tal said. "I tried to rouse you, at first, but then I sensed the enchantment."

"You didn't see any of it?" I asked as the platform slowly spiraled down, grating against the stonework. A cylinder of dark stone encircled us now, and the chamber above had become a circle of white light.

Tal shook her head. "Your eyes grew distant and your face went slack, and you had your fists clenched as if you were fighting it."

"I didn't even feel it coming on," I admitted. "I took a step here and then I was thirteen years ago… in the Academy."

"What happened?" Tal asked, her jaw set hard and grim. I had a feeling she was being forced to ask that question.

"Nothing exciting. Honestly, I'm not sure what the point of that was. We were just… working on an assignment. Constructing a reality beacon, you know, and then I was running an obstacle course, after that at a bar in Farvale. I think the enchantment wanted me to get lost in the memories, you know. Blissfully live in the past as I died out here."

Tal seemed to relax. "Is that all?"

"I don't know what you want me to say."

She rolled her eyes. "An apology for what's happened to me would be a fine start—but then, you've got nothing to apologize for, do you? Save perhaps acting when no one else would dare. Let's keep going and see this done."

~~*~*

The platform lowered us under the temple and came to a stop in about an inch of clear water, speckled with blue sparks of energy. Thick beams of light, coming from some unseen source, filtered in through yellow stained glass windows that reached up toward the ceiling in the cathedral-like space, which, I realized was actually the top step of a large spiral staircase. I could smell fresh rainfall and hear the trickling of distant streams from within the walls.

"Oh, this place is beautiful…" Tal said, a hand over her heart. "Like an old church in Rome or somewhere."

"Flooded, somewhat, but yes, I have to agree." The Tomb of the Sleeping Goddess was a work of art.

"We're fortunate to see this." I looked at her sidelong and found half a smile. "Circumstances being what they are, and all."

Water trickled down the spiral staircase, which was at least twenty meters wide and made of old marble and descended before us in a wide curve in dozens of little waterfalls. The staircase was lit well every ten feet or so by a narrow, tall window. I couldn't glimpse just what the light behind the windows was—it certainly wasn't sunlight, so far beneath the surface of Voraskel—but it provided more than enough illumination to guide our way.

On the sill of each window was a white rose—*always white*—and I leaned in close to get a look at one. The roses were real, but they had been dipped in some sort of resin to preserve the blossom. The stems were plated in gold, as were the thorns and leaves.

These flowers are likely older than the Egyptian pyramids, I thought idly.

The steps led us further underground, and I was expecting the air to grow foul from centuries of stagnation, but a warm breeze wafted up from below, carrying hints of wildflowers and spring rain.

"This is a peaceful place," Tal said. "A shame it'll be lost when Avalon finally pulls Voraskel apart."

"Do you think she's really buried down here?" I asked. "Fair Astoria? The Sleeping Goddess? What does…" I didn't want to have to address the Everlasting again. "What does Oblivion have to say on the matter?"

Tal shook her head, uncertain. "If he knows anything, he's not talking."

I squeezed the grip on my shotgun all the more, feeling a touch of trepidation bleeding toward fear. An Everlasting snarling in my face I could deal with. One who was subtle and silent put me on edge.

The steps ended in a shallow pool of softly glowing water, just a few inches deep. White petals floated on the water, and in the center of the small chamber was a raised dais and a gray stone sarcophagus. Atop the tomb was a small, narrow pedestal, and sheathed in that stone was the Roseblade.

Tal and I stepped forward at the same time. I was shocked and a little surprised to actually have stumbled upon the sword without having to give up a limb or a piece of my soul to the enchantments in this place.

I felt the pull of something buried in the floor, unseen but just beneath our feet in the water, and grasped the significance of it a split second after Tal did. The pedestal was protected by yet another ring of star iron—hidden to trick any wayward Everlasting.

Tal's words at the entrance to the tomb rushed back to me. *But now, nestled away at the back of my mind, festering on my soul, he can retreat and pass these old wards so long as I'm in control. The only Everlasting with that abil—*

So long as she was in control… Oblivion had to retreat deeper into her mind, relinquish a few inches of his leash, in order to pass star iron wards.

"Declan," Tal whispered, far quicker than me to realize what was happening. "Run and get it—*now!* He'll kill us both before he lets—"

Tal was flung into the wall, as if some unseen force had hooked her on a line, away from the star iron trap. She screamed—a sound of such hopeless, ageless agony that I stifled a gasp and ran toward the pedestal, even as she fell to her knees, clutching her head and clawing at her face.

I crossed the band of star iron a heartbeat before crimson devoured Tal's eyes and Lord Oblivion stood, using her small feet.

Terror shot through me like a jolt of electricity. I didn't hesitate to pull the Roseblade from the pedestal, pulling the sword up and over my head with a ring of crystal on stone.

Power surged through me, a torrent of water bursting over the dam of star iron, and I drank in the creation light pouring through my mind like water to a man who hadn't known he was dying of thirst. I'd been right—not even star iron could eclipse the power in the sword.

I leveled the tip of the blade toward Oblivion. My other hand still gripped the shotgun, loosely and off to the side.

Had Emily known the cards would fall this way? Had she hidden the Roseblade here on purpose, to lure Oblivion in close and give me a chance—a split second of a chance—to cross the star iron band before the Elder God could reclaim his control of Tal?

I sensed the hand of some greater mind than mine at work in this game. It had been a simple trick to fool a being so old and sure of itself, a being that was probably expecting something a touch more clever.

"That sword," Oblivion growled, "does not belong to you."

"Deal with it, shithead," I snapped, at the end of my very short fuse. "Now let's have a talk about what you can do for me—"

Oblivion roared and threw Tal's body through the air toward me, arms outstretched and fingers elongated into razor-sharp claws. Madness spun in the red orbs of her eyes and I—*forgive me, songbird*—didn't hesitate to swing the shotgun up and open fire.

The Everlasting Oblivion took two shots of star iron-infused buckshot to the face, and his roar of outrage turned into a shriek of pain. Tal's body spun back through the air and struck one of the stained glass windows, shattering the glass, and slumped down the wall. A trail of blood and ichor smeared the marble stonework.

"Broken quill…" I whispered harshly.

Tal lay slumped as if dead, her head lolling on her shoulder, as if two rounds from a high-powered pump-action shotgun point-blank to the face could kill a god. I took a step down off the pedestal, Roseblade in hand, and Oblivion snapped Tal's head up.

He glared at me through a face torn apart. Tal's lower jaw hung from her face. Her nose was gone, and one of her eyes had been obliterated. The other eye, as red as blood, seemed to dance with laughter and raw, insane anger.

Oblivion laughed. "You think you've won," he hissed somehow, his voice more of a loud echo in my mind than actually emanating from Tal. Even as I watched, her jaw snapped into place and the ragged flesh of her cheek sealed over seamlessly. "You think I didn't *intend* for this? I had ten thousand years of imprisonment to plan my resurrection, Declan Hale. You think this a victory?"

I shrugged. "It's a point on the scorecard in my favor, at the very least."

"Surrender the Roseblade!"

"How about I scatter you across the Void instead?"

Oblivion grinned with half a mouth of splintered teeth. "Follow me, if you dare." He crossed Tal's arms over her chest.

I took a quick step back as her entire form dissolved into thick, oily black smoke. Red lightning rippled through the cloud. One lashed out like a whip, and I caught it on the Roseblade. The tip lashed the back of my hand, drawing blood. I'd seen the cloud of mad smoke and terror before—it was Oblivion in his true form.

With a shriek loud enough to bring the whole tomb crashing down on my head, Oblivion fled back up the spiral staircase—shattering windows and cracking stone in his wake.

CHAPTER SIXTEEN

Birth and Death

My shoes barely touched the floor as I hauled ass back up the spiraling steps, crushing shattered glass underfoot. I found that I couldn't manage a steady pace with both the shotgun and the Roseblade, so I tossed the silver-barreled mosquito aside—it had served me well, but I had a god to outrun and outfox before Oblivion made me pay for swiping his prize out from under him.

And how will he do that? I wondered, with a dread conviction gripping my heart. *He'll hurt someone close to you, of course. They always do.*

Right now, both in terms of distance and friendship, that was Emily Grace—alone in her secret grove, pregnant, and armed only with Myth to defend herself against the blight.

I ran. I ran hard and fast. When I reached the stone platform that had brought Tal and me below the tomb, I used the Roseblade to cast a quick invocation and flew up through the dark cylinder, back into the mosaic chamber. The oppressive weight of the star iron ring, which had restricted my Will, was now just an annoying, buzzing bee in the back of my head, silenced swiftly by the Roseblade.

Having a clear line of sight up the corridor, I worked some speed enhancement enchantments on my legs—at a cost that would leave me shaking and fatigued if I maintained the speed for more than a few minutes—and *shot* up the corridor, as if I were an arrow loosed from a bow. The walls and torchlight *blurred* in my wake and I leapt out of the Tomb of the Sleeping Goddess and landed in a defensive crouch next to that fallen statue with the familiar face.

"Ma'am," I said, panting hard, and began the run back through the forest to Emily's secret grove, already fearing that I was too slow, too late, too much of a fool to think more than five minutes ahead. I had to go slower, lest I slam into a tree or low-hanging branch at speed and snap my enchanted neck.

I scattered dozens of the floating snowflake spark creatures as I darted through the forest, mindful of tree roots and loose rocks. My arm grew heavy from hefting the Roseblade a few miles in under ten minutes, and I rounded the copse of old oak sentinels that shielded Emily's glade from prying eyes.

With my heart pounding in my ears and my lungs on fire, I returned, victorious and terrified.

Emily rested serenely against one of the boulders, her head held high. Just above her crouched Oblivion, eyes blood-red and bristling. Tal's body was healed and unblemished from my shotgun blast.

And Oblivion was grinning wickedly and holding Myth to Emily's throat.

"Fuck me," I cursed. Too slow.

"One step," Oblivion said simply, his voice an arrogant mix of Tal's and a steel edge on grindstone, "and I'll slit her throat."

Emily's white dress was stained with blood between her legs and over her stomach. Her pregnant belly looked as if it had *shrunk*.

If I'd been afraid for her before, that fear just strapped on a jetpack and burst through the atmosphere.

"Hello, Declan," she said.

"Hello, Emily. Are you okay?" Her shoulders, which she had kept wrapped in her blue shawl since we left the bookshop, were bare.

"All is well in the world," she quipped, and smiled as if a blade of celestial illusion to her throat was nothing more than a fancy necklace.

I'd caught my breath, but my legs still shook from the exertion of my mad run. I met Oblivion's gaze and leveled the sword at him. "You kill her and there's nothing to stop me ending you with this sword," I said—and at least a part of me meant it—but what of Tal?

"She's old, this one," Oblivion spat. "But there is power enough in this dagger to end her life and repay her *betrayal*, once and forevermore!"

Her betrayal? "What's he talking about, Em?"

"Oh, I'm sure nothing important." Emily gave me a slow smile.

"I tire of our posturing, Arbiter. Perhaps I move this game along a few moves, yes?"

And then Oblivion did the unthinkable. He drove Myth into Emily's chest, between her breasts, and into her heart. The knife slipped into her flesh as easily as if she were as solid as warm butter.

"*No!*" Without any rational thought, I raised the Roseblade and tore the Creation Knife from Emily's heart and Oblivion's hand with a quick, fierce invocation of intent. The knife flew through the air, and I caught it in my free hand. Armed now with two weapons of celestial illusion, I gritted my teeth and advanced.

"Stop please, Declan," Emily said softly. Blood flowed from the stab wound in her chest, thick and steady, down her white dress and onto the forest floor. For her part, Emily seemed mildly inconvenienced by the blade to the heart. Her hands still cradled what I was sure had been a larger bump when I'd left her there a few hours before.

"How… are you still alive?" I managed. "Emily, how…?"

Oblivion chuckled, tone low and cruel. "How, indeed? You never did like revealing yourself to your pets, did you? What little of your *self* remains…"

"I've grace enough left for what must be done." Emily's voice, although faint, held a cord of unshakeable command. "Declan, Lord Oblivion has overstayed his welcome. If you could show him the door, my dear."

Oblivion clenched Tal's fists and glared, daring me to attack. Given the power I held in my hands, the combined strength of two blades of celestial illusion, I might very well have been able to unmake the Elder God—but by doing so I would also destroy Tal, once and for all.

And that I could never do.

Oblivion knew that truth. He probably considered my feelings for Tal a weakness, but those feelings were the only real strength I've ever had. I couldn't destroy that strength, not even if the fate of the whole Story Thread hung in the balance—as it so often seemed to be.

Show him the door… A bulb lit up in my head, a way to survive, but it would mean sacrificing the Roseblade. No other option—at least, none I was willing to take.

I looked to Myth and was sickened by the sight of Emily's blood dripping from the blade.

And something else was happening to the knife. The petals in the crystal were changing color. They withered, shriveled, and turned a deep, dark, midnight black.

I had no idea what had happened, but I sensed a corruption in the blade. From Oblivion… or from Emily? It didn't matter, so long as the knife could still do its job. *Quickly now.*

With a thought, I carved a portal between worlds just on my right, six feet tall and three wide. The portal opened up on a world from the novel *Auron's Folly*, atop a cliff overlooking a cold deep sea scattered with icebergs made of diamond. Clare Valentine and I had visited that place, more than once. It was a world about as far along the Story Thread as you could go, way beyond the Outer Territories. Before I could lose my nerve, I tossed the Roseblade through the portal and over the cliff's edge.

The sword tumbled through the air and disappeared below the sea.

Nausea washed over me, and blood trickled from my nose. I didn't pause to ask why, and I quickly turned to my left and cut another portal with Myth. That portal came harder, and I had to split my concentration—not entirely sure it would work—to carve a second gateway somewhere new while maintaining the first. Myth bucked in my hand, and tearing open the air felt like wrenching two pieces of Velcro apart—but I managed it.

"What are you doing?" Oblivion snarled.

Sparing him a glance of contempt and regret, I tossed my other hard-won weapon of celestial illusion through the gap in reality. I let that portal close as soon as the knife was through, but I maintained the first.

"There," I said, dizzy from the strain. Why had the petals blackened? And what had using the knife afterward done to me? "Now you've got five seconds to step through that portal after the Roseblade before I close it, after which I'm all out of ways of opening it again."

Show him the door…

Oblivion looked as if he were about to hurl himself through the air as he had done in the tomb, when I'd fed him two rounds of buckshot. I didn't have the shotgun now, and I'd just tossed away my only real defense—gambling on Oblivion's greed and machinations winning over his desire to lop my head from my shoulders.

"You kill me and the gateway closes—and you'll spend the next ten thousand years searching the Story Thread for the sword," I pointed out. "Leave us alive, Oblivion, and you'll have your prize."

I could see the creature behind Tal's eyes evaluating the situation and swiftly coming to the same conclusion I had: We were going to have to settle our accounts at a later date.

With a snarl of suppressed rage and an unspoken promise of horrors to come, Oblivion stepped away from Emily and toward me. He came close enough to shake my hand, his expression on Tal's face alien and cruel, and then took a step sideways through the gateway and after the Roseblade. I didn't hesitate to close the path the instant he was gone.

Broken quill, but I had just done the unthinkable and armed the Everlasting with a weapon of celestial illusion.

Also rather stupid of me, I'd tossed Myth away to save our lives. Using its path-cutter enchantment had caused me a pounding headache and a bloody nose.

At least I knew where to recover the dagger, even if something had happened to corrupt the petals set in the crystal blade.

I rushed over to Emily and fell to my knees before her, placing a hand just below her breasts and trying to stem the flow of heart's blood. I was no Healer and, indeed, I had no idea how Emily was still alive. Her poor heart must have been shredded. *If Sophie were here…*

"Across the stream," she said softly, "in that tangle of old tree roots—you see where the sparks gather?—I left something important. Declan, my dearest, while there's time, could you please fetch it for me?"

I nodded. We needed to move… It wouldn't take Oblivion long to recover the Roseblade from beneath the waves.

I left Emily, waded across the stream, and approached the knot of thick brown tree roots. The roots belonged to the oak sentinels guarding the secret grove and were twice as thick as a man if they were an inch. I ducked beneath the overhanging roots, weaseled between the thinner strands, and found what I'd half-expected to find:

A newborn baby wrapped in Emily's blue shawl, blinking up at me curiously with tired, half-lidded eyes.

"Damn it all…" I muttered, and retrieved the little bugger from his soft nest of foliage within the maze of roots. "I should never have left her here alone."

I returned to Emily, taking careful steps back across the stream, and placed her son in her arms. Emily had paled, but the blood seemed to have stopped flowing from her chest. For a long moment I watched them, mother and child, and then knelt down on my knees before her.

"How is your heart?" I asked.

She smiled. "It has taken worse strikes than this in the past…"

"We have to go, Em, but please tell me who you are?" I whispered. *What you are?*

"Oh, Declan, you sweet man," she said, holding her son in bloodied arms. He was so quiet, aware, fragile—and he couldn't have been born more than an hour before. "I will always be Emily Grace to you. Please remember that. But I have had other names across the ages. The Immortal Queen, least of all. Once upon a time I was even known as… Fair Astoria."

My heart leapt into my throat, and I forgot to breathe, to blink, for about half a minute. A startled deer in headlights had better reaction time than me in those thirty seconds. The look on my face likely would've made quite a good passport photo. But my thoughts and resolve were crushed under the weight of Emily's revelation. *Fair Astoria… The Sleeping Goddess.*

Emily, my timeless Emily Grace, was one of the Everlasting.

"Oh…" I sighed softly. A million tiny pieces of a puzzle I hadn't even realized needed putting together, tumbled into place. I was rocked by Emily's confession, but I *believed* it. Wholly. She wouldn't lie—she had never lied—and it made far too much terrible sense. "Oh, Emily."

No wonder she had been able to survive a knife to the heart. Emily was… a god.

"Now kiss me," she commanded. "Declan, you will kiss me once more before I rest."

And I did just that, as the baby stirred between us, gurgling softly and perhaps the only other person on this entire planet save Emily who knew what he was doing.

Emily's lips were hot and tasted of copper.

I saw things in that kiss—images of people I had never known and places I had never been. I saw Atlantis, alive and new, a city of True Earth before it was lost to imprison Oblivion. I saw war—the Great Everlasting War, and how one after another the Everlasting had been imprisoned, with Astoria's help. *Her betrayal…*

And then I saw Emily and me alone in a garden, a place I didn't know and had never been. Wildflowers were abundant under an azure, cloudless sky. I looked older, but not by much. I wasn't wearing an eye patch, but the skin around the eye was scarred from the wound, and in that glimpse of a moment that hadn't happened yet I felt a truth echo through my mind.

"He's yours…" Emily whispered against my lips. "This child belongs to us both, Declan Hale."

I broke the kiss and reared away from the Everlasting Astoria, falling onto my ass and panting as if ten thousand years of past, present and, indeed, *future* history had just been French-kissed into my mind by a goddess. Emily—Astoria—paler than ever, regarded me with that infuriatingly soft smile.

"We never…" I shook my head. "Emily… Astoria, we've never slept—"

"Not yet, we haven't. At least, not yet for you."

And I knew that to be true. The memories Emily had *kissed* into me, through some unseen and unknown enchantment—a part of her magic and, perhaps, the essence of who and what she was—had shown me glimpses of the future. My future and her past—which should have been impossible, for all save the Historian—but we had tired of impossible a long time ago.

A creature like the Everlasting—a woman like Emily—was not bound wholly to the laws of star iron or even to the known laws of Will and Origin. She had never been imprisoned with the rest of the Everlasting. She was timeless, ageless, yet older than entire universes. Fair Astoria, the Sleeping Goddess, *lost in time's tangled net*, as the old schoolyard rhyme went.

And what of the woman I knew as Emily? Emily Grace was… as real, or as close to human, as an Elder God could have any right to be.

"I forfeited a significant amount of my power in Atlantis to see my brothers and sisters imprisoned by the founding members of the Order of the Knights Infernal," Emily said, as if reading my thoughts on my face. "Oh, you would have liked them, Declan. I retained my immortality, some measure of grace, my power—which I just gave to you, to show you the truth—and command over Origin. For that, Declan, and for so much to come, I am sorry."

"You've nothing to be sorry for," I said, almost on autopilot, but I did mean it. Emily was dying, and I would not have regret or apology left unresolved between us. Whether that meant Astoria, the goddess she had once been, would die as well or continue to exist in some fashion… That didn't matter. "Broken quill, but this is a lot to take in."

"I have a lot to be sorry for," Emily said. "Regrets enough to fill ten thousand years and ten thousand lifetimes. And this, my last. Leaving our child without a mother and with a father who must fight, and fight hard, at the forefront of the coming war. The final war against the Everlasting. Oh, sweet mercy, let it be over this time. Let us all die and return to the Void…"

I stared at the baby in her arms with growing near-nauseating trepidation. He was *my* son. Mine. The memories she had shown me, of events that had happened for her but not for me—yet—revealed the truth. I *felt* the truth, as if I'd known it all my life. *Blimey, I can't even take care of myself.* A weary drunk with a million powerful enemies and the ire of millions more… What in the seven levels of hell was I going to do with a child?

"You… you're going to die," I said, surprised she was still alive at all, given her state.

"I'm weak. I am old and tired, and the Everlasting were never meant to mother children." Emily was crying quietly, tears that followed the curve of her face and fell onto the baby's blue shawl. "What we've done, Declan, and what you will do to bring this child about… Well, let's just say that laws and decrees as old as creation have been violated. And there will be consequences."

"Aren't there always?"

"Would you hold him?" Emily asked. "My arms grow numb."

On my knees as I was in front of Emily, I reached out, and she put the delicate bundle into my arms. He was lighter than I expected, something I hadn't noticed retrieving him from amongst the tree roots, but given the life in his tiny eyes and what I knew of his parentage now, perhaps that wasn't so surprising.

The blue shawl was warm from the bundle and the fire of his short life. *If you live, what will you make of all this? Of your father?*

"I waited a very long time for him, Declan," Emily said, her voice the failing whisper of autumn leaves chasing the wind. "He's someone that should not exist. Someone that the Edicts of Creation demand does not exist."

"Do you have a name for him?"

Emily shook her head. "You will stumble upon a name for him, I'm sure."

"Declan Jr.," I quipped, but my voice was distant, distracted by the shiny new eyes blinking up at me. *If your mother was a god and your father a shadowless mess, just what are you going to grow up to be?* Something set to destroy the world, if whispered prophecy was to be believed.

Emily smiled at me and, with the last of her strength, cupped my cheek with a bloody hand. "I hope you find your girl at the bar. And peace or something like it, Declan Hale."

Her hand fell away, and her gaze lingered on mine for just a moment before dropping to the bundle in my arms.

Emily sighed contently, and then she died.

I expected the ground to crack, the sky to fall, but then I remembered that had already happened here. Ribbons of burning light from the rings of Avalon were strewn across the sky, like paint splashed against a canvas. It seemed that Lovecraft had the right of it—even gods of death could die, after strange eons, and their dying was no different from any of the hundreds of other deaths I'd seen in my life. Some died screaming, some died so quick they were gone before realization gripped them—most died quiet, alone even if surrounded by friends.

Fair Astoria, my Emily Grace, had died human.

"What now?" I muttered.

I was alone and deep behind enemy lines, a thousand worlds away from anything even close to safe haven.

Worse, the Orc Mare and Emissary could not be far away. And Oblivion could return with the Roseblade, looking to settle old scores once and for all. I looked down at the newborn in my arms.

His curious eyes, sharper than rose thorns, seemed to look right back at me and *through* me. He gurgled, as if uncomfortable.

The dark, fierce wail of an Orc Mare echoed through the forest somewhere off in the dark—far too close. We were to be hunted, it seemed.

"Okay, little fella," I said. "It's cold, we're hungry, and we've got no magical shotgun and only one very slim chance of getting off this world unscathed. Welcome to the party, son."

CHAPTER SEVENTEEN

Dragon's Fire

I needed to move, but it didn't seem right leaving Emily bloodied and on display. I took a moment to fix her clothes, to place her hands on her stomach, and close her eyes. She looked almost peaceful, alone in the grove, and if not for the blood on her clothes, she could have almost been mistaken for someone resting her eyes.

A Sleeping Goddess.

I realized with a grim smile why that statue back in the courtyard of Astoria's—of Emily's—tomb had struck me as familiar. Centuries of wear had weathered the pale face, but it had undoubtedly been Emily. *I'm a blind fool.* If I'd made the connection earlier… I never would have left her alone in the grove, but done was done.

And dead was dead.

Only… "I died," I whispered, speaking half to myself and half to the kid. "So did Annie, but the petals of the

Infernal Clock revived us… And Emily had those petals." I felt a surge of hope, almost relief, quickly squashed by a harsh realization. "Even if she hadn't used them, they're not here… Damn it all."

An angry shriek echoed through the forest—the cry of the Orc Mare after me. And what of Emissary? I couldn't stay there any longer. I would have to leave Emily alone and to the elements.

Still, I hesitated another minute, kneeling in front of her, and gave her forehead a quick kiss.

She already felt cold.

"I'll come back and bury you," I promised. The baby's tiny arm fell loose of the shawl, and—quite accidentally I was sure—his tiny fist brushed against my stubbly chin. I laughed to keep from sobbing. "Broken quill, kid, already throwing punches far outside of your weight class. You're definitely a Hale."

Two shrieks cut through the quiet air of the enchanted forest, from the east and south, answered by a third somewhere away to the north. That last shriek was close enough to raise the hairs on the back of my neck. I was out of time for grief and sentiment.

I washed my face in the stream, took a few swigs of river water, and decided to abandon the supply pack—the weight would only slow me down. Before I left the pack, I retrieved a small leather purse with a handful of gems, the Forgetful currency, worth about a hundred bucks. If we made it through the forest, I'd need money on the next world.

"Okay," I said, mentally preparing as best I could for the chase to come. One stray step, one misjudged moment, and I could snuff out the life in my arms before he'd even lived a day.

In the past I'd shouldered some significant responsibility, but none seemed as heavy as my current need to ensure the little one's survival. "We've got one way off this world, back in the ruined city. You've been good so far, so do me a favor and be as quiet as you can, okay? Okay."

~~*~*

A low mist coated the ground as I jogged as quickly as I dared back through the enchanted forest and toward the ruins of the Renegade city. After a few minutes at a steady jog, I crossed back over the star iron ring surrounding the tomb and felt my Will come back to me. The return of my power was encouraging, but the forest was no longer a pleasant place, alight with snowflake sparks and inviting spring scents.

The twisted trees seemed menacing, a dark and infested wood. Monstrous creatures, so far unseen, circled closer as they hunted me and my son. The air tasted stagnant, alive yet dangerous, and it stank of musk. I was painfully aware that if I left the path, we could wander lost for days and no doubt stumble upon a whole plethora of unimaginable horrors.

At least the planet in the night sky provided enough light through the canopy to keep my one good eye on the vague, fogged path back to the city.

"You're going to have to take my word on a lot of this," I muttered. My son's small eyes blinked up at me and out at the strange world. How well could newborns see? Fatherhood and baby care were not subjects taught at the Infernal Academy. *Am I holding him too close? Can he breathe?* "The sky usually doesn't look like that, you know. More stars and less strewn with planetary debris."

My innate sense of impending danger kicked in a split second before we rounded a curve in the old path that led back to the city. Sure enough, two Orc Mare armed with wicked, curved blades of black steel barred the way. Their black eyes widened when they saw me, and the one on the right opened his mouth to shriek—

"Bang, bang," I said between heavy breaths. A bolt of white-hot energy about the size of a marble ran under my skin and burst from the tip of my index finger.

The Willful bullet took that Orc Mare on the right between its eyes. The other advanced on me, sword raised, and I shot that one dead, too.

"Nothing to it—"

A third monstrosity came flying out of the darkness to the right. It didn't have a sword, but I raised my arm in a block and caught the tip of its sharp, fetid claws. Hot lines of pain tore through my arm but I shoved the creature back. I punched the Orc Mare in the jaw with my bloody arm and was rewarded with a sickening crack. The creature stumbled back, howling in pain, and I had sense enough to shoot it dead before it recovered.

"Bugger," I cursed, inspecting my arm. The cut didn't look deep, but I was worried about infection. Something to worry about further if I survived the next hour's run back to the city. "And are you okay?"

The kid made a curious gurgling sound and closed his eyes, off to sleep. *He'll need feeding soon. I have to hurry.*

Ignoring the stinging in my arm, I continued down the winding, overgrown path.

The night had fallen quiet, which was somehow worse. At least if the Orc Mare were wailing, I knew where to expect them. Silence, on the other hand—well, damn near anything could hide in silence.

"We need a distraction, little fella," I said. "Something loud and noisy and confusing to draw them away… or to send them every which way."

I snorted a rough chuckle and decided to set off some Willful fireworks.

I'd never make it back to the city using stealth—not if the last encounter and the stinging claw wounds on my forearm were any measure—so a blazing display of confusion and fire seemed like a fine Plan B.

Those with enough ability to channel vast amounts of Will got recruited into the Academy and were taught how to manipulate the magicks and enchantments of a million different worlds, written down in novels. For the most part, we learned soldiering skills and survival enchantment.

Yet, more often than not, we did a bit of reading on the side and taught ourselves impressive yet relatively useless skills, like juggling or coin rolling.

Or, in my case, fireworks.

And while what I had in mind did have certain military applications, it was about as subtle as a brass band parade and certainly beneath the lauded and powerful image of the Knights Infernal. I set to work.

"It's going to get a bit noisy, kid," I whispered as white light flowed under the skin of my arm, illuminating the blood from the claw wounds, and entered my palm. Smoky, luminescent light fell from my fingers. Holding the enchantment in my mind like the answer to some simple math problem, I raised my palm to the sky and fired.

A streak of purple sparks and whistling fire spiraled above the trees and exploded in a dazzling display of cascading embers and thunder. I fired off more fireworks into the forest at random as well as overhead. Soon enough, the shrieks of the Orc Mare rose again.

I decided to set the whole affair on fire.

I wreathed an old oak tree in a coil of superhot flame, which ate into the bark and burnt into its heart. The tree ignited as if it were nothing but scraps of kindling, and soon a thick cloud of white smoke bellowed above the forest.

I shot off a few more fireworks, adding to the cacophony of noise and confusion. The forest fire at my back spread dangerously fast, sprinting along the network of tree roots and brush coating the ground to lick at my heels. I coughed on the smoke in the air and made sure to cover the kid's mouth and nose with the shawl.

The flapping of rotting wings joined the shrieks of the Orc Mare as they took flight, fleeing the flames and chasing the thunder of the fireworks, trying to track me down.

Finally, I cast a subtle perception enchantment over me and the kid, which would make us even harder to spot within the maelstrom.

~~*~*

A few hours later, after having lost the path once and thankfully finding it again—and without further molestation from the Orc Mare—I emerged from the forest just north of where Emily and me had entered the forest that afternoon, on a small grassy hill overlooking the heart of the ruined city. Of Emissary there had been no sign, which bothered me more than it should've. *No news is good news…*

Smoke clung to the air from the fire, which burned through the forest like—well, like wildfire, and made me dizzy. An orange glow emanated through the trees, and I could hear the distant crackling of wet trees burning. Muffled explosions echoed through the forest from trees splintering under the intense flames.

I looked to the city, just a few hundred feet below. The ruins seemed quiet, and I hoped most of the Orc Mare were still in the forest, hunting me and burning. The skyscrapers holding up that wreck of a starship between them, her fusion engines still glowing softly against the night, were a brisk ten-minute walk through the streets, assuming we didn't encounter any resistance or blocked avenues.

That starship was where I wanted to be.

"Close now, kid," I said, counting a thirty-second rest in my head and catching my breath. "Blimey, I need to run that old obstacle course back at the Academy a bit more often, eh?"

My infant son winked one eye and then the other, so I took that as endorsement and began the quick descent into the outskirts of the city, following the dirt path cut into the hillside.

Back down in the city, my shoes clicked on old cobblestone streets as I clambered over chunks of torn-up asphalt. I kept an eye on the shadows in the abandoned doorways, as well as up in the sky above. *Well to remember that those bastards can all fly…*

That part of the city had been laid out in a convenient grid pattern, much like Manhattan, which allowed me to keep the tall towers supporting the wrecked ship in view on my right. I cut down three blocks, feeling a rising trepidation and that everything was progressing far too easily.

Soon enough I stood on the corner about a half dozen streets over from the dilapidated skyscrapers. The prospect of climbing through the buildings only to have the foundations give way made me rethink my plan, but I was out of options—and sooner or later, my enemies would catch up with me.

The baby needed food. I needed bandages, rest, and a stiff drink.

Running on fumes, I jogged down a desolate avenue of fallen rubble, crushed cars, shattered glass, and at long last neared my goal. I could hear the mighty starship's engines thrumming overhead and the sound of the ship gave me my second wind—I was close.

"Just might get him out of here, Em," I said, mostly for the baby to hear. But then something up ahead pulled me up short and I cursed. "Damn it all, spoke too soon…"

Emissary stood in the street just before the entrance to the skyscraper I needed to climb, as if he'd been waiting for me all this time. Quite possibly he had been. At this point in the game and after all the years of impossible realizations, Emissary anticipating my next move was small potatoes.

His suit was repaired through some enchantment, after I'd scattered the few rounds of buckshot into him, as was most of his face. Ragged scars ran up his neck and under his hairline, where the star iron had burned his skin. "Ah, Declan," he said. "How nice to—"

In no mood to chat or match wits, I hugged my son against my chest with one hand, and with the other I sent an ugly unguided wave of brute concussive force, designed to simply knock the bastard dragon from my path.

The cannon of air struck Emissary like a freight train and hurled the creature across the street and into the dusty, unbroken glass of an abandoned storefront. The glass shattered, of course, and swallowed the beast whole. I used what little time I had to run.

"That was an assho—bad guy." I stepped over some rubble and inside the skyscraper holding up the starship. The air inside was dank, dirty. I cast a glowing orb about the size of a tennis ball with a click of my fingers and tethered it to hover in the air just a few feet above my head. "Generally best avoided, but I've found they're a lot like bad pennies—keep turning up."

I found the eastern staircase and, after shoving the emergency door aside, breathed a sigh of relief to see that the stairs seemed mostly intact, crisscrossing back and forth up through the skyscraper. *A bit of luck, finally*… Grim-faced and running on less than fumes, I took the first step of hundreds and headed up as fast as I could.

"Forgive me, but I'll have to concentrate on breathing for a while," I told the little fellow.

After about five minutes, my legs were on fire, wobbling from the strain, but I'd managed to climb most of the way up the building. I'd reached the floors where the impact from the ship had torn the structure open. Cool wind ruffled my hair, under that amazing and terrifying planet-ruined sky. The ship was only a few floors above me, and I thought I could see a way aboard, through the exhaust ports.

In the distance, smoke rose from the enchanted forest. I wondered idly just how much of the forest would burn. From the base of the skyscraper came a bellow, and a burst of green flame illuminated the side of the building, melting glass and scorching concrete. I felt as if I were standing near a bonfire. *Emissary's back on his feet and pissed.*

Two floors of rubble took a minute to navigate, but finally I stepped from the skyscraper and crawled into the ruined ship, searching for each step and making sure it could take my weight. I climbed in through one of the leeward-facing exhaust ports, almost level with a balcony and the stairwell on what felt like floor ten million to my abused legs.

Down below, a dragon unfurled its wings.

"And I'm going to make damn sure most of your days aren't like this," I said, panting from the strain. We emerged on one of the upper decks. I knew the layout of the ship—I'd learnt to fly on one just like it, ten years before—and we'd reach our destination in about thirty seconds, barring any surprises. The gravity elevator probably wouldn't work, but there should be a service ladder. "I mean, the forest was nice, wasn't it? But the demons, fire, and homicidal dragons? All that bullshit—ah, pretend you didn't hear that—all that… bothersome to-do won't be your life. I promise."

Old skeletons, grinning—mayhap screaming—skulls, lay slumped against the dull walls of the corridor. Six years' worth of dust and grime, long-dead soldiers in their uniforms, entombed in a dying ship.

I jogged up to the next floor, midway along the length of the cruiser, and headed toward the bow of the ship.

The kid sneezed, and I almost dropped him in surprise.

"Oh, you scared me," I said between heavy breaths. My shins had split and fallen off a few miles back, I was sure, along with my knees. Blisters the size of cannonballs had formed on my heels. "People do that to each other, though, when they're holding onto something precious. That's a nose, by the way, what you just sneezed out of. Two eyes, a nose, a mouth, ten fingers, and ten toes. You're off to a good start, kid—for the most part."

I slid open a long door on rusted hinge rails, wincing at the shriek of metal-on-metal that hadn't been oiled in half a decade, and stepped through the gap. "And this is the bridge and control column of a crashed inter-dimensional Eternity-class starship, Fourth Inked Battalion, Cascade Fleet, commissioned by the great and powerful Order of the Knights Infernal."

I cleared my throat and saw what I'd come all this way to see. "You know, your dad once commanded the entire Cascade Fleet. Oh yeah, legions of soldiers and hundreds of ships just like this one. They asked him to fight a war…"

I picked up Myth, the Creation Knife, from the torn and dusty leather command chair where I'd sent it from the forest and took a seat. I'd doubted the knife would be here, until I'd seen it with my own eye, but Emily had been right—as always. The knife could carve the distance between two points, even just a step away, on the same world.

Useful… but why are the petals black? Back in the grove, where Oblivion had killed Emily, using the knife had hurt. The blasted thing felt different, too. Holding the hilt before had produced a warm, almost inviting, vibration. Now the damn thing shook and jarred, as if it were snagging on the threads of a hundred unseen worlds.

Myth felt… *defiant.*

A dragon's roar pulled me from my thoughts. I gazed out the forward-facing windows, twice-shielded enchanted glass, and saw the city street far below. A sleek, oily black dragon about the length of half a football field furled its wings and shot a river of hot fire up toward the ship. One yellow eye pierced me from far below.

Emissary could see me, even up here in the ship.

"Time to go, little fella," I said.

The control column flickered with light from the dying fusion engines, but it was more than enough for my purposes. Working quickly, as Emissary flapped his wings and took flight, I tripped the engines and—given the state of the wreck—set them to ignite. A vibration shook the ship, and newly loosed dust rained from above.

Calmly, I took a deep breath and stepped behind the command chair, leaning on the faded leather with my back as the ship began to tilt entirely toward the city street below. She was about to fall, as Emissary raced up the side of the building, wreathed in fire and a wicked wingspan.

I hesitated only a moment, fearing the consequences, and then sliced open a way between the worlds with Myth.

A sharp pain just behind my eyes tried to blind me, and I almost let the portal slip, but I'd been trained long ago to deal with pain under stressful circumstances. Old warning bells and harsh red lights began to blink along the walls of the bridge and the control stations.

Pushing off the back of the command chair, I took a long step forward and ducked through the portal. The step was disorienting, as I went from leaning at a forty-five degree angle on a shaking ship to flat, grassy ground in a single step.

I'd moved on an axis with and—ever so briefly, on Voraskel—*against* gravity.

The baby frowned, and I'm sure he felt the same momentary disorientation.

"How was that?" I asked, in the clean air on the new world, somewhere I'd been once before. "First trip across universes." Through the portal at my back, the warning sirens on the ship were eclipsed by Emissary's frantic, ferocious roars. I turned back to see the dragon flood the shielded glass with green liquid flame. The creature slammed into the outside of the bridge, claws digging deep furrows in the broken metal of the hull.

"Here's the fun part," I told my son, smirking grimly.

The engines I'd set to cycle overloaded, the crystal cores ruptured, and the pressure forced a final burst of energy from the rear of the ship. The entire wreck flew forward—downward—with Emissary wrapped around her bow.

A lizard clinging to the nose of a makeshift crystal fusion missile. I wanted to think the son of a bitch knew what was about to happen.

Gazing through the portal at the wrecked starship was almost like watching events unfold on a television screen. The thousands upon thousands of tons of steel, crystal, bones, and dirt *drove* the Emissary into the city street.

I'm sure a colossal boom and explosion, perhaps mixed with the shrieks and roars of the creature, followed next. I didn't keep the gateway open to find out, certain that fire and shockwaves of energy could travel across worlds through the portal just as easily as my son and I had done.

Walk away from that, asshole.

"And that's why they asked me to fight a war," I whispered to the kid, enjoying the cool air and the scent of honeyberries on the wind. It made my eyes water, and I rubbed at my patch-less one with the back of my hand, still clutching blackened Myth.

Bright spots of pain exploded in my skull, and the liquid I wiped away from my eye wasn't tears, but blood. "Right… okay."

I stared at the dagger, at the sinister darkened petals, and thought the defiant vibrations felt a lot more like a low, dangerous growl.

CHAPTER EIGHTEEN

A Distant Star

In the memories Emily had shown me through her dying kiss, I had seen her change over the millenniums since Atlantis had fallen and the rest of her kin had been imprisoned in some of the darkest corners across Forget. Back then, she had not been Emily. She had been Fair Astoria—and entirely alien.

But for whatever reason, as I understood it, she had given up what was known as *grace*, her power as one of the Everlasting, and slowly but surely turned human. Not entirely human, of course—not even close to entirely human, given her immortal status—but enough so that she could conceive the life in my arms and, unlike her brothers and sisters, come and go on True Earth as she pleased.

That last distinction seemed like a significant slice of the pie.

A few months ago, Scion had needed Myth to leave the Story Thread and access the real world, and from what I'd gleaned through Oblivion and Tal, the Everlasting coveted True Earth but could not travel there through 'conventional' interdimensional means. But with the Roseblade, Oblivion would have more than enough strength and means to access True Earth. The war would start with an Everlasting beachhead on the most precious planet in existence, where the books that formed the Story Thread were written.

Trouble ahead and in my road… Yet none of that seemed very important when compared with the need to find some formula for my son.

From the wreck of the starship on Old Voraskel I had travelled to the familiar honeyberry fields of Meadow Gate, one of the accorded neutral territories of Forget, and home to Miss Tia Moreau—now an ex-Knight, trying to stay that way—but more importantly pharmacies and markets where I could get some sort of food for the little fellow in my arms. And some bandages and salve for me. The gems in my pocket would be enough to cover those slim expenses.

How much time had I spent dodging fire in the forest? Three hours? Four? Again, I didn't know much about parenting, but I knew newborns needed feeding. Hell, I could go for a good steak and chips—none of that salad nonsense—the plate stacked with garlic mashed potatoes, burst cherry tomatoes dipped in basil and olive oil, as well as a schooner of delicious golden beer. My stomach rumbled at the thought of such a feast. *Baby first, you second.*

I'd cut a path to Meadow Gate just along the farm roads that I knew led up and around to the main streets. The sun had disappeared behind the western ranges, spilling a tin of mauve paint across the sky. A few stars blinked overhead as dusk became true night. The town—more accurately a mini-city—had been built around a tall but gently sloping hill in the shadow of nearby snow-capped mountains. Cottages, buildings, roads, waterfalls, and all manner of stalls, cars, and hovercrafts used these hills as home.

Luckily, the farm road—the same Tia had arrested me on a few months ago, with Annie—seemed empty. No one had seen my abrupt arrival, but I had to get out of sight soon. Meadow Gate kept a check on the use of Will and Will-related magical items like Myth. My use of them had triggered the buried sensors dotted under the landscape and announced my arrival up in the sheriff's office. Deputies would be on their way to investigate, and while I might get lucky with the regular townsfolk, too many people knew my face—my infamous, exiled face.

I'd lost my eye here in Meadow Gate, to an unruly mob.

So I ducked into the honeyberry fields alongside the farm road, hiding behind the vines, and kept my remaining eye on and an ear to the road.

Sure enough, about five minutes later, a pair of revolver-wearing, sword-wielding toughs sauntered past my hiding spot within the honeyberry vines. One was telling a story, mumbled just too low for me to hear, and the other bellowed great guffaws of laughter. Clearly they didn't expect to find Declan Hale, the Shadowless Arbiter, exiled-but-not-anymore, architect of the Degradation and Hero-Villain of the Tome Wars, squatting in a field of ripe, juicy honeyberries.

Once they had scuttled down the way a bit, I emerged from the field and marched a quick step toward Meadow Gate. After the mad dash through the forest and up a thousand or so flights of stairs, my legs had settled into a numb sort of indifference. The baby was drifting in and out of sleep now but kept making soft mewling sounds—the closest he'd come so far to crying.

"That's right, kid," I said, as we rounded the hill and left the honeyberry fields behind. "Hales don't cry." *Well, not often.*

A walk of only a few minutes brought me to the well-traveled road that led up the hill and into Meadow Gate proper. Streetlamps slowly flickered on to greet the end of the day as I hobbled along, keeping my head down and avoiding staying too close to other folk. As I limped past a small tavern that reminded me of Paddy's, an idea occurred to me, and I ducked inside. Sure enough, just along the entrance corridor was a coat rack. The coats on the rack were varied—leather jackets, tweed blazers, and cloaks—both hooded and hoodless. I casually borrowed a long matte black cloak with a deep hood and stepped back out into the late evening air. I took a moment on the tavern's porch to swing the cloak around my neck, straining to do the clasp with one hand, and then slipped the hood up and over my head, concealing my face in its velvet shadows.

"There now," I said. Enchantments existed to alter one's face, but I'd never been good at the subtle stuff. A cloak was easier and less likely to fail. "We can walk with our heads held high, aye?" I bobbed the baby up and down a few times in my arms, and he yawned, which was catching, forcing one from me. "Let's see about getting you something for dinner."

The main street branched off near the top of the hill into dozens of winding cobblestoned lanes that rose and dove through uneven levels around the surrounding hills and down into long valleys between the mountain ranges.

Meadow Gate was a shining example of worlds settled by the Knights Infernal, comprised of scattered buildings both modern and medieval, as well as structures that wouldn't have looked out of place on an episode of *Star Trek*. The people were the same mix, pulling wagons that hovered about a foot above the ground and talking into displays wrapped around their wrists, or piloting small hovercraft in old suits of clothes in fashion roughly two centuries ago.

I followed the laneway Tia had shown me during my last visit, up a set of limestone steps curving around a hill dotted with white stone houses and warmly lit windows. The scent of sizzling meats, fried onions, fresh garlic, and dozens of other homely smells permeated the air.

At the top of the steps, the laneway opened on the heart of Meadow Gate, built just above the crest of the hill. A wide-open plaza, holding a series of mismatched buildings around its perimeter and a variety of stalls and food carts across its center. Roadside food vendors rubbed shoulders with silk merchants and bankers. Armorers forged Will-enhanced plate mail next to rare and exotic spice dealers. Mingled within all of that, a hundred other trades had set up shop.

I caught sight of a pharmacy on the other side of the plaza, lit with neon signs, and meandered through the crowds to the storefront. The building would not have looked out of place back in Perth, and stepping inside, I saw a lot of familiar products that had been imported from True Earth. Cadbury chocolate and cans of soda, alongside a variety of over-the-counter medicines, toiletries, and—most importantly—baby care products.

The air was cool inside the pharmacy and held that faintly clinical smell of a hospital. Identity concealed by my cloak, I scanned the shelves for a tin or box of infant formula, as well as a bottle. About a dozen different brands, all with smiling babies in their mothers' arms, faced me down like a line of Renegade soldiers.

Better for me if it had been a line of the enemy facing me down, as I knew what to do in that situation.

I grunted and spun the first tin on the shelf, having a read of the directions and the ingredients. "Powder and liquid concentrate… soy protein based… Blimey, kid, are you in the mood for a helping of partially hydrolyzed nucleotides? Between you and me, it's when you can start eating steak and chips that life really gets interesting."

I managed to find a bag of three small bottles, but as for the formula itself, I was flummoxed. I spent a few minutes perusing the products up and down the aisle. Some of the directions seemed to call for certain types of water; others seemed to emphasize the importance of folic acid, while one or two seemed to think niacin was of vital importance.

"Do you need any help here, dear?" asked a kind-voiced elderly woman.

I turned and glanced at her from within the folds of my hood. She was a few steps away—perhaps due to my reluctance to reveal my face—but when she saw the baby in his blue shawl, a genuine and warm smile spread across her face. She moved in close and cooed at the little fellow.

"I'm not entirely certain which formula he needs," I admitted.

She pushed her glasses up the bridge of her nose and blinked at me. "Well, young man, that entirely depends on a few things. How old is he? Does his mother breastfeed him? Any known allergies?"

"About half a dozen hours; no, I'm afraid she can't; and… allergies?" I shrugged. "He sneezed a few hours ago, but I think that was environmental. Lot of dust."

The lady peered at me, as if to see beneath my hood. "His mother can't feed him?"

I took a deep breath and exhaled slowly. "She died… not long after he was born."

"Oh, dear. I'm sorry for your loss. And you're his father, I take it?"

"That I am."

"You know, perhaps he needs to visit the hospital on the far side of Meadow Gate. I could call you a taxi… Or my son, Arl—he's out the back—would be happy to drive—"

The only thing that would keep my son alive in the year to come—the *only* thing that gave this tiny speck of life in my arms even a sliver of a chance of seeing his first birthday—was keeping secret just who his mother and father were.

Particularly his father. If word spread I had a son, entire worlds of my enemies would mark him for death. *Guilty by association…*

"I just need a bottle or two of formula," I said, trying to keep my tone light and even jovial. I held up the packet of bottles. "If I could use your kitchen to prepare…?"

The old woman stared at me in silence for a long moment, her expression blank and unreadable. Slowly she reached out and grasped the hem of my stolen hood and lowered the cowl to my shoulders. I blinked in the light with my one good eye, my face surely a mess of cuts and bruises from the events of the last day, and gave her a tired, sad smile.

The look of mingled fright and awe on her face was all I needed to know she recognized me. I was, after all, the infamous Declan Hale—hero and villain of the Tome Wars, Commander of the Cascade Fleet, and almost-king of the Knights Infernal.

Calmly, the old woman pulled the hood back up over my head and then grabbed one of the tins from the shelf, tucking the formula powder under her arm.

"Follow me," she said, and to her credit, her voice didn't shake. She led me through the pharmacy, around the counter, and into a small kitchen out the back.

Asking no questions, the old lady set a pan of water to boil and set about sterilizing the capped baby bottles, one at a time. "Biscuits on the table," she said over her shoulder as she worked.

I took a seat at a small round table and helped myself to a bit of shortbread, chewing softly and being mindful not to drop any crumbs on the baby. He fidgeted a little bit in my arms, yawned again, and made a tiny sound of discomfort. He was hungry, I was sure. I watched the old woman work with the ease of long practice, mixing the formula and sealing the sterilized bottles.

After about five minutes, she splashed a bit of formula on her arm, testing the temperature, and gave a satisfied nod. She handed me one of the bottles. "Now, you make sure he finishes all of this, young man."

"Yes, ma'am. Thank you. I will."

"Here's another. Give it to him in a few hours, and make sure you burp him gently." She stuffed another capped bottle of formula in the deep pockets of my stolen cloak. "Now best you be on your way. Somewhere s-safe."

"Thank you," I said again, ignoring the hitch on the word *safe*. I placed a handful of gems on the table for the formula and let myself out.

~~*~*

I hadn't just come to Meadow Gate looking to steal a cool new cloak or brew some baby formula. If all I'd needed was the formula, I could have cut back through to Perth where hiding my face wasn't a necessity.

No, as I wound through the streets of the town, working from my memories of a few months ago, I made my slow but steady way to a tiny little bar, tucked under the eaves of a two-story wooden cottage on a busy lane overlooking the valley—a bar that belonged to Tia Moreau. The baby had taken quickly to the bottle, during our brief walk from the pharmacy, drinking the warm formula slowly and surely.

The strong, caramel scent of honeyberries wafted up from the vast fields below, and above the bar, a sign swung gently in the breeze, secured to an awning on rusted iron hooks: *The Reminiscence.*

The reason I had come to Meadow Gate and sought out Tia was simple enough. The jaunt down memory lane in the Tomb of the Sleeping Goddess had shown me several memories, all of them containing Tia. Whether I knew it or not, my subconscious trusted her. Needed her, if my son was going to have any chance at all. Perhaps never more so now that I knew she was alive, even healthy and strong, after we'd all written her off as dead during the Fall of Voraskel and Avalon—but that was more for myself, than for the infant in my arms. If Tia could make it through the bad times, then perhaps I could, as well.

To be fair, her command ship, the *Reminiscence*, had been swallowed whole by the Void. She had named her bar in honor of the ship—and the two thousand lives lost under her command—when all she wanted to do was forget most of her life as a Knight. I could understand that want—*need*—as well as the next man.

She was out of the game, simply refusing to play—which was just what I needed. Tia did not have my enemies.

I let myself in through the sturdy wooden door, and a wave of merriment, drink, and mouth-watering aromas washed over me. Any properly cared-for pub, bar, or tavern in the world always felt like home.

Tia's bar was lit by a twin pair of crystal chandeliers, which sent a soft light cascading over the long mahogany bar and the lounge area. Oak tables and comfy leather couches took up most of the space near a large, roaring fireplace. In front of that flickering blaze was a small stage supporting a stool and a microphone, lacking only a musician.

None of the patrons in the bar spared me more than a second glance. Wearing a hood might have attracted a few concerned stares back on True Earth, but here in the outer territories, people didn't ask too many questions. I was just another face in the crowd, caught between the absurd mess of past, present, and future that held Forget and the Story Thread together.

It was nice to see that the bar hadn't burned entirely to the ground a few months before, though a lot of the fixtures looked new and shiny. I guessed Tia had cleared up the unpleasantness and rebuilt her bar. I hoped the mongrels that had thrown bouncing incendiary bombs through her windows had been strung up and left for the fucking crows. A bit of a morbid hope, perhaps—but then they had cost me an eye and nearly killed my friends.

I claimed a seat at the bar between a gorgeous woman in a pleated green skirt and white blouse, her lips as red as rose petals, and a scruffy blue-skinned kid wearing big round glasses and a pair of rainbow suspenders. Meadow Gate—home to all sorts.

The bartender, I recognized. The gargantuan man, Ace, had saved my life, carried me out of the burning inn while I was unconscious and blind, and he was Tia's partner on the city watch when they weren't tending bar. If he was there, odds were, so was Tia.

"You and the little one here for the music?" Ace asked, his voice gruff but kind. He'd barely acknowledged me last time I'd been here. Not without good reason, as all said and done I'd nearly gotten Tia and Annie killed not six feet from where I was now sitting.

"We sure are," I said, keeping the angle on the kid's bottle at a steady decline. He seemed happy enough sucking at the nipple and slurping up the formula.

"Something for yourself?"

"Could I just get a water?" I asked. "Waiting on some friends."

Ace nodded, clearly not too interested in who I was beneath my hood. I guessed the baby might have taken some of my mysterious, dangerous, devil-may-care aura away from me. He placed a tall glass of icy water on the mahogany bar. "Your friends best hurry. She's going on in two minutes."

"Thanks. I'm sure they'll be along soon."

"You enjoy your night." Ace moved off to tend to his other patrons.

The bar was busier than I'd ever seen it. In truth, I'd only seen it closed, but a steady stream of people—jovial, happy people—let themselves in and greeted one another like one big extended family. The atmosphere was warm, inviting, and not too loud. Just the right levels for conversation over a crackling fireplace. The smell of good food wafted in from the kitchen, too, adding a homely touch to the whole affair. I was of a mind that The Reminiscence was a bar I could quite comfortably grow old in.

And then I saw her emerge from the kitchen and knew for sure.

Tia Moreau, all five feet and a dime of her, stepped up onto the small stage in front of the fireplace to a round of raucous cheers and wild applause. She carried an acoustic guitar strung over her shoulder. Her bare shoulders, below raven-black hair, revealed soft curves and unblemished olive skin. A white dress, splashed with a pattern of blue roses like spilt ink and the risqué hemline just an inch short of proper, hugged her tiny form.

She was beaming from ear to ear. Her smile was infectious, and I caught myself mirroring it, hidden within the folds of my hood.

Tia's emerald-green eyes seemed too kind and full of life for someone who had traveled the Void and survived. She had commanded the Cascade Fleet before me, and it was only at the Fall of Voraskel—when we lost her and King Morrow—that I had been given command. Such command had ruined me inside of a year. Even now, over half a decade later, I was still shattered.

Then again, apart from a brief foray back to True Earth to stop Scion a few months ago, Tia had been happily presumed dead for that same half decade. I'd never let the Tome Wars go, and even exiled, I'd wallowed in scotch and misery, drinking to days that were and days that had never come.

"Oh, broken quill," I cursed. "She's *happy*..." And better off not knowing me anymore. Or my son. The damage our family name could do to a place as innocent as Meadow Gate...

The only mark on Tia that hinted at the travesties in her past was the long, thin line of scar tissue that slashed diagonally down from her eyebrow, along the bridge of her nose, and into her cheek. A souvenir from the Void. The vain and the selfish would say such a scar turned her pretty face into something less—something flawed that marred her beauty. To me and to all who mattered, such a 'flaw' made her one of the most beautiful women we'd ever had the pleasure to know.

"Do you like it here?" I whispered to the baby. He'd finished about half the bottle. *Make sure he finishes all of this, young man…* "Big open countryside. Friendly folk, for the most part. Clean air and healthy living."

"Good evening," Tia said into the microphone. Her voice echoed nicely through the bar, over the hum of conversation and the clink of glasses empty and full and all levels in between.

"Sing us a song, Tia!" someone called from the back.

Another round of cheers and applause seemed to agree with the sentiment. Tia blushed and inclined her head. She took a seat on the stool, one foot on the ledge and one on the hardwood stage. She swung the guitar up into her lap.

"She's going to sing…" I muttered, with a soft grunt of disbelief. The Tia I remembered from the Academy, the Tia I knew from the Tome Wars, had been fierce but kind, loyal but vicious. She had been a soldier—a Knight Infernal, like all of us. We didn't sing. We didn't… live this kind of life.

It might have been a mistake coming here.

"Here's a new one I've been working on," Tia said, her amplified voice warm and confident. "I hope you like it."

The bar fell into an appreciative silence as she strummed her instrument and started to hum, softly at first. The guitar was high pitched, like bell chimes tuned to match the upper range of a piano. I liked it—liked that the melody made me think of springtime on Lake Delgado, of late nights in Farvale with Tal, Clare, Sophie, and all my old friends, Aaron and even Marcus.

The amber bottle was far too open
The clear lens, long since broken
Maps that showed the way ahead
Were meant for those happier instead

And all I knew was a distant star…
Strung along the roads of gleaming hearts
We stood alone, but we stood for what was ours
Oh, quills did break, and night did fall…
Honey, we were better off apart

We surely were. But not just yet, not now. For now I sat at the bar, listening to Tia's music, a lump in my throat and a scar on my heart. *To keep the Everlasting apart…*

My son—and I was not at all surprised to find that I did think of him as *mine*, beyond a doubt—gurgled softly around the bottle of milk. His eyes fell heavy above puffy cheeks unblemished by time or the ravages of growing up Infernal.

If my son was to have any kind of life—indeed, if he was to have any chance of seeing his first birthday—then he could not be my son. I could not be his father.

And if Emily was to be believed, then I would see her again. At some point in her past, which added a whole new way of looking at the world, didn't it? I'd travelled back through time once before, after Atlantis, just in time to die. Was my ragged immortality bolstered by the knowledge that I wouldn't die and stay dead until the boy in my arms was conceived?

"Oh, Emily…" Elder God Fair Astoria or no, she would always be Emily Grace to me.

Perhaps kind but worse in the long run
They tell me I wear happier better today
And we're all fools just trying to have some fun
So I stand tall, I smile… but I'm a coward anyway

I'm sure this truth I've tried to deliver
Is not the pain, but all that I am
I could be honest, kinder, harder, a giver…
Oh, but truth is too familiar

"What do you think, kid?" I said. "Grow up here in Meadow Gate with Tia? She'd have you, I'm sure. In a heartbeat. Clean air and honeyberries? Learn to tend bar before you can walk… and then get shipped off to the Infernal Academy before your tenth birthday once they find out you've got the talent."

If he could never be tied to me, then the Academy would actually be one of the safest places in existence for him—a place where he could learn how to use whatever skill in Will he developed, to protect himself.

My son blinked slowly, staring at me from around his bottle, as if everything in the world was shiny and new and couldn't possibly hurt.

"Your mother and father were very selfish to have you," I whispered. "Whichever side you choose, you'll have enemies. Awful young for such nonsense."

No easy answer to this seven-pound problem. He finished the bottle, and I slipped it into a deep pocket of my cloak. I lifted him up against my chest, his tiny head resting just on my shoulder, and supported his neck with my hand. Gently, I patted his back, looking for a burp. I knew little of babies, but I knew enough.

And all I knew was a distant star…
Strung along the roads of gleaming hearts
We stood alone, but we stood for what was ours
Oh, quills did break, and night did fall…

Honey, we were better off apart

And all I knew was a distant star…
Strung along the endless roads of gleaming hearts
We stood together, just a spark within the blaze
And if those damned quills didn't break
and harsh night didn't fall…
Honey, sweet thing, could we go back to the start of it all?

Soft applause greeted Tia throughout her small bar as she played the final chords, and I took that as my cue to leave before she or Ace recognized me under this hood—or by the familiar black cloud of woe and regret hovering above my head. She smiled at the crowd, her cheeks flushed and eyes alight with the music. The scents of the kitchen and the taste of good drink were on the air in an atmosphere of time spent well.

Tia Moreau. Perhaps the only person I knew who had found a way not to play the game and be happy. She was far better off without me in her life. I was pure antithesis to her redemption.

"Come on, kid," I muttered. "We've got work to do."

Another god to kill, the Knights to be appeased… And of course Shadowman—the Hyde to my Jekyll—to be destroyed. Same shit, different day.

First things first, though. I couldn't take my son with me into any of those battles, any more than I could leave him with Tia and dissolve her happiness, so war via True Earth was my road. I needed to phone a friend.

3RD SALVO – I'M NOT ONE TO CRITIQUE A FUNERAL, BUT…

"Love all, trust a few, do wrong to none."

—William Shakespeare, *All's Well That Ends Well*

CHAPTER NINETEEN

Fractured Blackberries

"Declan," Annie Brie said, holding my newborn son in her arms as if he were the most precious thing in all the worlds. "Are you sure about this?"

I nodded and pushed a canvas bag of diapers, bottles, canisters of powdered formula, and a whole bunch of other infant paraphernalia I'd picked up at the 24/7 Pharmacy in Joondalup not an hour ago across my coffee table at her. A stack of pages from my never-finished novel, strewn throughout the writing alcove in my shop, fell to the floor.

Annie held my son still nestled in his mother's blue and bloodstained shawl. I'd bought him some clean blankets, warm and feather-soft, but I wasn't quite ready to remove the shawl. Emily's grace had kept him alive so far…

"There's so much about this I don't understand…" my young detective said in the half-light from the chandeliers overhead. The hour was just after midnight, and outside Riverwood Plaza was quiet. No oily shadows, no madmen with shotguns, just the night. "I never thought you and Emily were ever, you know, together."

"It's a long story," I muttered. "One I'm not sure I understand myself."

"You really don't look well. I mean, I think you may need to go to a hospital."

I was in need of a good long sleep and time to rest my bruised and battered body, but time was running out faster than top shelf booze in an open bar. I still had Shadowman to deal with.

Annie was right, though. I'd glimpsed myself in a mirror, and I looked like death warmed up. My eyes were bloodshot, and big, black suitcases hung under them as if I'd been punched twice. I had a sneaking suspicion—more than a suspicion—that using Myth to get back to True Earth had done that.

The Creation Knife was tainted, dangerous. Using it was killing me.

"I'm just a little frayed around the edges," I told Annie. "Nothing a steak and some hibernation through the winter wouldn't fix."

"And Emily is dead?" she asked tentatively. "I'm sorry—I know you considered her a friend."

I chuckled, as if the idea of Emily as a friend was funny. What the hell *had* we been? Lovers, apparently, although I'd be damned if I understood how that was supposed to work. "Well and truly. I barely escaped with the kid; Emily, I wanted to bury but couldn't; and Oblivion has the Roseblade. You know that proverbial creek without a paddle? Yeah, the Everlasting now have enough firepower to blast that creek into the Void."

"You'll get it back," she said, as if the solution to all my troubles were that obvious.

"Not with him hanging around, I won't," I said, meaning my son. "I can't save the damned day again and worry that someone or something is going to use that kid against me. It would work, you know, in case you were wondering how I felt on the matter. If he were threatened, I'd do considerable… damage to prevent him harm."

"Does he have a name, at least?" Annie asked. "Did Emily…?"

"She did not." And I hadn't even considered naming him yet. *Declan Jr.?* "And perhaps best if I don't, either. He can't stay here. That's why I called you. You know that. Broken quill, better than most, you know that."

"I do. I know the hazards of the life you lead." She sighed. "But what if—"

I took a deep breath and exhaled slowly. "Annie, you know he can't stay with me. Take him to whatever government services will find him a home, get him adopted somewhere far from Perth—the farther, the better. Europe. Norway. Somewhere distant. Never tell me where."

"He's so well behaved," Annie said, cooing down at his tiny face. "Aren't you? Aren't you just? And he has your eyes, but…"

"Kinder?"

Annie smiled a touch sheepishly. "Well, yes."

"And they need to stay that way for as long as we can help it." I felt a surge of something akin to the lust and rage that clawed at me in battle or in war, but more… *righteous.* Every cord of my being wanted to protect my son—and would *melt* worlds, the Story Thread be damned, to guarantee that protection. "Which means he can't have me as a father."

She bit her lip and met my gaze. "Are you sure… Are you sure you're not just taking the easy way out here, Declan? I'm sorry, but… how long have you known this little guy was yours? A day? Less? He could grow on you…"

I should've been angry at her words, at the implication I didn't want the responsibility falling asleep in her arms, but what I *wanted* was far outweighed by what was best for the boy. "There's more at work here than I understand yet, Annie. Emily gave me only glimpses of… of the truth. Enough to make me believe he's my kid, even though we haven't… Broken quill, I sense some fucked-up time travel in my future, and that alone means he shouldn't be with me."

"Can't you run away from all of that? Buy a farm out in the country? Hide?" Annie stood carefully, moved around the coffee table and sat down next to me, close enough that our knees brushed. She smelled of cinnamon and rainfall. A familiar scent. "If he's yours, Declan, couldn't you do that for him?"

I looked down at my son and felt a genuine desire to run—to run and hide from all the Knights, the Renegades, the Everlasting, the Voidlings, the shadows, demons, monsters, and the lions and tigers and bears. To embrace my own final exile.

Kid needs a mother, I thought, and my mind put Annie in that picture—the three of us hidden away together, living and loving a normal life far away from here. Canada, perhaps, or the Swiss Alps. Somewhere with mountains, little rivers, lush forests, and snow in the winter.

I could do anything—be anything.

I could be a blackberry farmer.

I could worry about phone bills and nipping out to the corner shop for milk and bread of a morning.

Little Declan Jr. could learn to walk and talk with his real father, alive and well, and I could teach him how to wear a waistcoat with just the right amount of tragic charm, take him to school in a few years, maybe make him a little sister to look out for, someone to keep him on his toes. He could play a sport—tennis, maybe, or football. I'd attend parent-teacher meetings and have after-work drinks with the neighbors, talking about how well so-and-so is doing, and why yes, Declan Jr. is learning to play the piano. Top of his class, you know—he has his mother's grace…

I could see all of that, as clear in my mind as sunlight on fresh snow, and so much more.

Just living day to day. One morning we could have picnics, my family and I, next to blue glacial lakes. One afternoon my son would be old enough to meet a girl, get in a fight, need to shave. One evening his sister will need help with her homework, and he'll complain, but he'll help.

And then one day the Elder Gods would descend from a blood-red sky in chariots lashed together from bone and flame and take away all my blackberries.

"Everything I've ever loved, Annie," I said slowly, carefully, making sure she heard me and heard me well. "Or even started to love… has been taken from me. My fault, most of the time, I know. It's the Hale family curse. *Everything*, Annie. My father, Clare, Tal, Emily, and so many friends in the Tome Wars." *And you, sweet thing… although you don't know it.* "So I am begging you now, please stand, pick up that bag, and take my son away from me before he's cursed."

I covered my face with my hands, shoulders slumped, and rested my elbows on my knees. I stayed that way, a coward, for the long half-minute Annie didn't move. Then I heard her stand, heard her pick up the bag of supplies, heard her heels grow fainter on the dusty wooden floors, and then I heard the bell above my door chime and the latch click shut behind her.

After she was gone, I reached down over the arm of the couch and retrieved a brown paper bag. The weight of the bag was comfortable, familiar. I unscrewed the cap on something amber and aged and knocked back two fingers' worth in the quiet and the dark.

A hundred days sober, pissed away in a moment.

The sting felt like coming home.

~~*~*

I could've Will-travelled using one of the many books in my shop to get to Ascension City, but all the written paths were too well known, and I had no idea how I'd be received. Did the Knights want my head for the Historian? Had Sophie and Ethan cleared the air for me? I also could have cut a new path with Myth, but I was fairly certain the tainted petals in the blade were exacting a cost in my very soul and life force every time I used the blade, making me weaker and cranky. Using Myth anytime soon was out of the question.

So I instead headed into Perth on the late train, finding myself on Murray Street at two in the morning, hands stuffed into my pockets against a chill in the air out front of McSorley's—my favorite bar in this part of the world, after Paddy's.

But Paddy's didn't exist anymore. Emissary had blown it up to draw me out a few months ago. *Once it's rebuilt, however…*

Old Albert McSorley was a retired Knight, and he kept a portal to the Atlas Lexicon, a grand terminal of trains and shuttles between hundreds of worlds, in his wine cellar. Emissary had blown up the Lexicon, too, not so long ago, but I was willing to bet a few of the routes were operational again.

In case all else failed, I carried a book to Ascension in my waistcoat holster, but I would've rather not had to use it. And Myth, I'd secured back in the cutlery drawer.

'Ware to anyone who stumbled upon that tainted menace.

I strolled through the heavy oak door of McSorley's, trying to stand tall and ignore my various aches and pains. As soon as I stopped to rest for more than an hour, I was going to be as stiff as a bruised board.

The scents of strong wood polish and stale beer hung in the air, a scent that felt like coming home. A row of mahogany stools lined the bar, which held about twenty taps of various specialty beers. Tables and chairs, as worn and old as I felt, were scattered about the dim room, and sawdust coated the floor, to soak up any spills. A grand piano gathered dust in a corner against the back wall. All the light in the place came from a half dozen flickering torches in brass brackets on the wall.

McSorley's was sparsely populated, given the late hour on a weeknight, but one old drunk sat on the stools in front of the polished bar, and the old man himself stood at ease against the liquor shelves, polishing pint glasses with a white rag.

I stepped across the hardwood floors and tapped the bar twice with the tip of my ring finger—a universal signal for the barkeep to pour me a damned drink.

"Thought you'd given it up," Albert McSorley said, as if battered and knackered Knights strolled into his pub all the time, as if he had been expecting me. Chances were good they probably did, that he probably had been. "And put half the bars and liquor stores in Perth out of business."

"I am off the wagon," I said slowly. McSorley shrugged, poured, and I raised a shot glass full of amber liquid. "To your health!"

I knocked the shot back and grimaced, favoring the familiar burn. The drunk at the bar—the other drunk—shuffled on his stool, and I got a good look at his wrinkled face under a thin mop of salt-and-pepper hair.

Aloysius Jade, my old teacher from the Infernal Academy, a man sent to kill me not too long ago—after he spent half a decade in Starhold, the orbital prison above Ascension City—and the man who had instead saved my life, after a fashion.

"Hale," Jade said, once-sharp eyes a little murky. "You look like shit."

"I lost a fight today." I tapped the bar again. *I lost a son today.*

McSorley grunted and poured me another scotch.

"On the tab?" I asked.

"On the house," he said.

Some years before, I'd burned down the bar when fighting an incursion of demonic imps. My 'tab' was somewhere in the region of half a million dollars. I inclined my head in thanks and drank.

I slammed the glass down on the bar. The glass cracked, slicing my ring finger. Blood, hot and red, ran down the back of my hand. "The Immortal Queen is dead."

Jade choked on a sip of his beer, and McSorley sighed, as if he'd been expecting a blow to fall hard and instead it fell cruel. I used a few bar napkins to dab at my bloody finger, already wanting another sip. *Perhaps I could just stay here tonight and get drunk with old Knights and old enemies and forget about Forget.*

Thing about addiction—and I knew this from long years on the sauce—was that I never just wanted one hit. It was either none or ten. If I stayed much longer, I'd be no good to anyone, especially myself.

And the game wasn't over yet.

"That's some sad news," McSorley said. "I saw her once, a century ago. She was… lovely."

"Kind," Jade said. "I remember her as kind. We once spent an afternoon in the Outer Territories, talking peace and signing accords that ensured neutral ground for the war's refugees. How... how did she die?" Jade's voice was like gravel scraped against a chalkboard—ragged.

"The Everlasting Oblivion plunged a weapon of celestial illusion into her heart in the ruins of Old Voraskel." I choked back a bitter laugh. "Oh, and Oblivion has the Roseblade. Won't be long before that fucker tears aside the protective veils around this planet and claims True Earth for the Elder Gods."

McSorley lined up three glasses and, his hand shaking, poured us all another shot of delicious, numbing morning's regret—as if I didn't have enough of those to fill a lifetime. "Last orders, then."

"What's the state of the Lexicon?" I asked, holding the shot but not quite ready to toss it back. Jade dropped his shot into his beer with a dull clink and chugged his impromptu depth charge in four quick swallows.

McSorley took a sip and licked his lips, as if savoring the taste. "Few lines operating. I get a bit of foot traffic every day. Not like it was a few months back, of course. People not quite ready to trust the place again just yet."

"It'll get me to Ascension?"

Jade grunted hard laughter. "Heard you were wanted for kidnapping the Historian. You sure that's the best place to be heading?"

"Wasn't me," I said.

Jade had spent the better part of the last six years in Starhold, the orbital prison above Ascension City. He had been let out, pardoned as a favour to Morpheus Renegade, in order to hunt me down and, well, slit my throat. In the end, he'd done just the opposite and saved my life. Jade had brought me back from the dead. "No? Then who was it?"

"Some shadowy figure in the night," I muttered. "Heard he looks just like me."

"Aye, well, if you go down for it, ask for one of the cells on the outer rings of Starhold. Nice view of the planet at sunset."

"I'll keep that in mind." I raised the shot to my lips, hesitated, ran my tongue along the rim of the glass, and then set it back down on the bar. "Key?" I asked McSorley.

He dug around in his pocket and tossed me a heavy golden key inscribed with sharp-angled Infernal runes—the pass code for the gateway in his wine cellar.

"Cheers." I strolled along the bar and around to the steps leading down to the cellar. I swayed a touch on the first step and gave a quick wave to the barkeep and his lonely patron. "Gentlemen, don't do anything I wouldn't do."

"Good luck, Hale," McSorley said. "Chin up, lad, and give them hell."

"And tell that brother of yours to stop keeping your seat warm," Jade called as I disappeared down into the cellar—a little drunk, a little tired, a little lost.

CHAPTER TWENTY

Stolen

The Atlas Lexicon stood as a testament to the ingenuity and resolve of just one man: Thomas Lucien Atkinson, the original dreamer. He had envisioned a network of rail lines spanning the rough and varied pathways through the Void. They had called him mad at the time, but one by one, he linked the worlds and opened up universal travel to the masses.

The Lexicon was a lifetime's work, a feat of engineering on par with the greatest works ever undertaken by humanity, and I'd managed to destroy most of it in the space of about twenty minutes.

Well, to be fair, Emissary had done most of the damage in dragon form, but he'd only gone there to face me and steal the Creation Knife. Still, entropy was a dark and terrible thing. Everything could die far more easily than it could be born.

I didn't bother to mask or disguise my appearance as I strolled through the somewhat functional stations of the Lexicon. I wasn't hiding or exiled any longer. My grim face as dark and terrible as entropy itself, I was a Knight Infernal—a member of the most revered and feared order in all creation. With a single look, I could wither my enemies. A raised eyebrow could turn fierce negotiations into groveling placations, and a grunt of displeasure could avert wars spanning entire universes.

"No trains until six," the guard in the ticket booth said. "By order of the Knights, you ken. They've got some trouble in Ascension and are only running three services a day."

"I am a Knight," I said, trying not to slur my words on the tail end of that last shot at McSorley's. "And I'm saying I need to get to Ascension. My name is Declan Hale."

The old guard looked up from behind his newspaper at that, gave me a once-over, and chuckled. "You had a few too many, lad?"

"Yes, but that doesn't change who I am or what I need."

He rolled his eyes and slapped his paper against his desk, fixing me with a two-fingered point. "Well, if you're a Knight, then you've got other means of reaching Ascension, don't ya? Don't need our trains."

Entire worlds are spinning into the Void, and I'm delayed by one old man with crumbs in his moustache… "I'd rather not take the easy road. Got a feeling I'll need to pop in and out of a few more worlds before the day is done." I took a deep breath and exhaled slowly. "So that train over there? It's on the track for Ascension?"

He nodded. "Tickets are fourteen gems, and the service will depart at six." He glanced at a timepiece on his desk in the booth. "Three hours and twelve minutes from now. We've got the food court up and running again, if you want to sober up and grab a pint of honeyberry juice."

I thanked the man for his time and wandered off through the sparse, late night–early morning traffic seen in airports and train stations the world over. People sleeping on benches, plugged into earphones and video screens, one old cleaner on his motorized cart sweeping the floors, and a half dozen chain retailers with one token staff member just in case someone wanted a triple-decker deluxe cheeseburger with extra onion at three in the morning. *Actually, that doesn't sound half bad…*

A shame I had somewhere to be.

I ran my hand along the outer carriage of the train, moving down the platform until I reached the driver's compartment. The handle was locked—*good security*, I thought sarcastically—so I melted it with a palm full of hot light and let myself in. A few onlookers stared as I powered up the console. The readings and instruments were not what I was used to, flying cruisers and battleships, but they were close enough that I could puzzle them out.

"Aux power and… navigation." I flicked a switch on the console, and a crystal platform came to life on the dashboard. A codex pod full of sunlight, linking the Lexicon to that jewel—that radiant gem of the Story Thread—Ascension City. "Reality beacons, Tia, remember those?" I muttered.

The track ahead disappeared down a dark tunnel. I knew from past use of the Lexicon that about a half mile down the tunnel was a net, a portal arch, into the Void. So long as the reality beacon onboard was shiny and bright, we'd travel through the Void to the mirror station beneath Ascension City.

"All aboard!" I called, offered the guard just emerging from his booth a wink and a quick salute, and released the brake. The train shuddered forward, quickly picking up speed, and I stole my way across universes, tired and fearing the morning's hangover.

~~*~*

A warship hung in the twilit sky above Ascension City. It was a massive, sleek silver vessel fitted with dual-core cycling fusion engines, enough heavy cannons and firepower to take a sizeable chunk out of the moon, and—unless I missed my guess—a reality matrix, which was kind of like a versatile reality beacon that could latch onto waypoints on a thousand different worlds. I couldn't be sure from just a glance, but I'd be willing to bet the farm I was looking at the next generation of military cruisers—and the flagship of the Cascade Fleet.

Blimey, if I hadn't been exiled… As commander of the fleet during the final months of the Tome Wars, I would've ended up with that ship.

After abandoning my stolen train in the underground, I'd found the station relatively unmanned and empty, given that the next scheduled arrival wasn't for a few hours. No doubt I'd be reprimanded appropriately in the days to come, if I survived, for breaches of the code of conduct—namely, stealing an interdimensional train—but I'd take it on the chin, grin, and do it all again next week.

The air in the city was tense and stank of crystal fuel, like hot electricity or strikes of ionic lightning. Dozens of smaller craft flew in the air around the mighty ship. Cruisers and troop-movers, a few battleships—and their size in comparison to the big *sumabitch* reminded me of pilot fish swimming around a shark for protection.

Only the smaller craft were not in any sort of defensive formation. No, those ships were arrayed *offensively* against the flagship. As if...

"It's not friendly," I said.

And as if to emphasize my point, a burst of red light crackled from the flagship's starboard cannons and *obliterated* one of the smaller craft, dissolving the craft and the dozens of Knights and support staff onboard to less than ash. Nothing remained of the ship, sparing the city a deadly rain of fire and burning metal—for now—but the heat and shockwave from the blast shattered windows and rocked the ground beneath my feet. A collective scream arose from the streets of Ascension City.

I began to run for the palace.

An unhappy surety gripped me and laughed in the back of my mind as I raced through the streets of my old stomping ground, pushing through crowds and throngs of scared people pointing at the sky and screaming of hellfire and doom. The person in command of the flagship, the captain of the *Hellfire*, was no person at all.

Shadowman.

The pieces fit too well and too unfairly for it to be anyone else. He'd used the Historian to predict the future and seized control of one of the Knights' greatest assets. But to what end?

I'd know soon enough. It was the only outcome that made even a vague kind of sense, so I was sure I had the right of it.

He said he wanted to kill Everlasting… and he can see everything through her. Everything except me. The very reason for his existence was also the reason the Historian's unique and dreadful Sight was blind to me. An advantage, of sorts, but he would be expecting me, nevertheless. What had the Historian said, last time we met in the forests surrounding this marvelous city?

"As you are now—without shadow—my Sight passes over you."

She could see future events *around* me, but not the actions I would take to either bring those events about or thwart them and remap the future toward one of the millions of other outcomes burning through her mind. *Broken quill, I'd go mad…*

The crowds grew sparser the closer I jogged to the Fae Palace—and for good reason. A concerted bombardment from that flagship could, conceivably, overwhelm the Infernal defense enchantments and bring the monumental tower crashing down. I could scarcely conceive the effect upon Forget and the Story Thread if that linchpin came undone. Taking out the Fae Palace would be like knocking the first domino down… Entire universes would be cut off, and millions would be left adrift on cold and lonely worlds.

Was Shadowman insane enough to do such a thing?

Did it matter? He was here, and the threat existed. That meant I had to stop him—or die trying.

~~*~*

The Fae Palace was on lockdown and high alert.

I was still four blocks away when I hit the first manned checkpoint restricting access to the palace and grounds. A hastily constructed barrier of stone had been hewn from the cobblestones using Willful enchantment. *Sloppy but effective, right, Clare?*

"Declan Hale," I said, panting hard, to a low-level Guardian Knight who looked about three minutes fresh out of the Academy and probably had to shave once every six months. His too-big gilded armor looked as if it had been slapped together from half a dozen spare chest pieces. More ceremonial than actually combat-ready.

Technically, we were the same rank, given that my reinstatement had been grudging at best. But that was only on paper. I was still the Shadowless Arbiter—and very nearly King Hale of the Knights Infernal. My reputation was a noose around my neck, but a somewhat multipurpose noose. "Looks like you chaps have a bit of a problem. I can fix that."

The young guard gaped, slack-jawed. "You… you're Declan Hale?"

"That's what it says on my Subway Club Card." Back in Perth, I was three subs away from a free six-inch. Would've been closer, but an Emissary-dragon had eaten my wallet not too long back. "What? They tell you I had three heads, mad eyes, and devil horns?"

"No. But yesterday they were telling us it was you who kidnapped the Historian and took control of the *Blade of Spring.* Now it's a skinwalker that looks like you or… something. A double." He shrugged. "Thought you'd be taller."

Sophie and Ethan must have had some good fortune when spreading the word about Shadowman. I clapped the guard on his shoulder and grinned. "It's always about perception, kid. Remember that. Now let me pass or I'm blasting my way through."

The guard wiggled his fingers and muttered a string of Willful invocations. Six feet of stone rippled as if jelly and melted back into the ground, clearing a path through to the palace. "Am I going to be disciplined for letting you through?"

"Not if that ship blows up the palace," I quipped, and his face fell. "Chin up, mate. We're on the same side here."

"Yeah, but the stories they tell about you at the Academy… broken quill! You're *Declan Hale.*"

"And I've eaten the sandwiches to prove it. Stay out of trouble, kid."

I hit two more barriers before reaching the palace, but with a busy, determined look on my face and a skip in my step, I was waved through without so much as a stern glance. On any other day, that might have been worrying, but with the better part of at least two hundred live cannons held to the palace's throat, flaws in security and guard laziness was small potatoes. I would surely be stopped before I actually entered the palace proper. *Or maybe not… if I'm expected.* Had Sophie and Ethan been that convincing?

The main thoroughfare leading down to the palace was often a pleasant walk on mosaic marble, lined with fountains and wildflowers, bordered by grass as green as emeralds and as fragrant as spring air—a wide-open space for Knightly passage, scholarly enlightenment, and even romantic picnics.

All that beauty had been trampled by troop supplies, field command tents, and the heavy boots of hundreds of Knights Infernal, ready to march to war.

I was just one face amongst the somewhat organized rabble, and though I caught one or two startled looks from the corner of my good eye from folk who recognized me, I was left alone.

As I approached the palace, its white walls grew larger, hung with flags and banners of a thousand different worlds. The sun was at my back, so I wasn't in the palace's shadow, but I felt an immense chill regardless. The history of the tower spanned millennia.

I would *not* be responsible, in whole or in part, for its destruction.

I stepped into the cool, quiet foyer of the Fae Palace without question or alarm. I'd breached the inner sanctum, the very seat of power in Forget, and only been waylaid once by a kid wearing armor two sizes too big.

But as was usually the way when it came to physical security, getting through the first and often *easiest* layer made accessing the inner layers a walk in the park. That was why a person with a confident smile and a clipboard could saunter into the cockpit of a 747.

Or ex-exiles and feared three-headed warmongers could amble into the most heavily fortified structure in the known universes.

CHAPTER TWENTY-ONE

Shadow Games

Word spread through the palace like wildfire, as the best gossip always did, and I was quickly ushered by a series of low-level Guardian Knights up through the levels and echelons of command to the War Room. It seemed I was expected, perhaps even overdue. On my previous visits, I'd been graced by the presence of the ruling class in front of the Dragon Throne itself, but with the palace on high alert and the throne far too open to bombardment from on high, Faraday and his motley crew had set up shop in the heart of the palace.

The War Room was a high-tech, modern facility in contrast to the old marble, grand white pillars, and archaic tradition of the rest of the palace. Dozens of staff and knights manned access points, monitors, private world-portal arches, and stocked shelves with tomes enough to unmake empires, if that was what the situation called for. Across the room on the far wall hung a massive monitor the size of a movie theater screen, which depicted a real-time image of the *Blade of Spring*, Shadowman's stolen vessel, overlaid with a display of live-updating military options. Deep within the bowels of the palace, a network of impossibly powerful computers processed hundreds of thousands of data streams and generated strategy.

High Lord and King of the Knights Infernal Jon Faraday stood in front of the screen, his hands clasped behind his back, looking a lot better than he had the last time we met, surrounded by his retinue and listening to reports being rattled off by his advisors.

As I approached, he held up his hand for silence, and the crowd obeyed. "Hello, little brother." He offered me a cunning smile, as if he'd been waiting for me. "You are late."

"Hello, Jon. I was never summoned."

"A contingent was sent to that quaint shop of yours on True Earth not twenty-four hours ago. Imagine our surprise to learn you'd fled worlds—with the Immortal Queen, no less."

Jon Faraday, my half-brother on my father's side, was a man of average height. His shaven head rested on a thick neck, and he wore a resplendent red coat with gold trim to hide a thick layer of corded muscle. A few months before, Jon had been withered and dying, branded by Emissary, and signs of that affliction were still carried in the canyons under his eyes. But other than that, he was the epitome of health and leadership, the bastard.

"Ethan and Sophie?" I asked.

"They were aboard the *Blade* when your darker half seized control of the vessel. We believe he's using the Historian to predict our response pattern."

"That's what I'd do…" I muttered. *That's what you are doing.* All the computing power in the universe couldn't match the Historian's brain and what she could See. "So my friends are his hostages. Who else is aboard?"

"Apart from Sophie Levy, Ethan Reilly, and the Historian," King Faraday said, "no one. The *Blade* is built for minimal crew, operated through a control visor. Your shadow has taken sole command of the deadliest ship in the fleet. He disintegrated a boarding party vessel, killing four Knights."

I rubbed the split skin on my knuckles and couldn't remember when I'd hurt them. Somewhere on Old Voraskel, most likely. Absently I used what meager talent I had in healing to seal the abrasions, buying myself a few moments to think. "That's my ship," I said after I'd spent my few moments. "All things being even, it should have been mine. And I want it back."

"By all means, if you have a recovery option that doesn't end with an aerial bombardment of this palace and the city, we are eager to hear it." Faraday scratched at the stubble on his chin, his eyes piercing me with something that I had once thought was hate. Now I wasn't so sure, given that we seemed to be on something of an even footing. "A weapon of celestial illusion up your sleeve, mayhap?"

"No, I broke one and gave the other to the Everlasting Oblivion."

Faraday's eye twitched, and a vein in his temple seemed to throb to a tango beat. The folk around us all gaped, gasped, or let out strangled whispers.

"Long story," I said. "Ends with the Immortal Queen dying on Old Voraskel…" Thoughts of Emily made me sway. I already missed her something fierce. "But we've more pressing matters at the moment. Order of priorities, yeah? Have we tried talking to the son of a bitch up there?" I gestured with my thumb to the ship on the screen. "Maybe he wants to negotiate."

Faraday took a long moment before replying. "You are one of us again now, Declan," he said, his voice thick with the command of someone used to being the king. "Remember that before handing our enemies weapons of mass destruction. Are you so eager to be branded 'traitor'?"

"Or to be exiled?" I asked, sporting half a smirk. "What you've never been able to swallow, Jon, is that I fall ass backwards into these roles that make me indispensable. You need me; I don't need you. Right now you need me because I'm the only one who can hide from the Historian's sight. Shadowless, I'm not even a blip on her radar. That's what I've got up my sleeve, King Faraday, but first we should have a chat with the bastard."

Faraday nodded. "Hail the *Blade*."

One of the faces seated in front of the giant screen barked a quick "Aye, sir" and pressed a few of the buttons on his station.

The image on the screen blurred as the call was accepted aboard the ship. A bridge of sleek command stations and a view overlooking the palace swept across the massive screen.

"Who… is it?" Shadowman asked, twirling around in a high-backed leather chair to face us. He stopped spinning and leaned closer to the camera, a thin visor over his left eye, and grinned. "Declan? Declan Hale, as I live and breathe! I'd be somewhere else soon, if I were you. That whole palace is going to come a-tumbling down."

"Come on now, handsome," I said. "You're not going to kill me, but keep this up, and I'm coming to kill you."

"You believe you could, don't you?" Shadowman asked, sounding astonished. "You believe you can… that you're capable of such self-destruction." He laughed long and hard and a few miles north of sanity. "But I found one of them, Declan. Yes, yes. With the Historian's help, I have found one of the stinking bastards!"

"Who's he talking about?" Faraday asked.

"The Everlasting." I sighed and ran a hand back through my hair. "It's not Oblivion, is it? Don't be kicking no hornets' nests now." Telling myself off seemed foolish, even if Shadowman did look dead three days.

"This ship will be the spear through their hearts, Declan. I'm doing you all a service. *King* Faraday, sitting atop your stolen throne and trying to keep up with your wayward baby brother." Shadowman spat on the camera, and a globule of saliva ran down the massive screen in the War Room. "You will swear allegiance to me, the Godslayer, before this day is through."

Faraday looked at me askance.

I shrugged. "Godslayer? Subtle, mate. But you've gotta earn it before you get T-shirts made."

Shadowman took a deep breath and exhaled slowly. "Okay. I'm going to go earn it, then. And if you don't want to play, then don't follow me." He shot me a wink, and then the screen changed back to the view of the flagship hanging in the sky. The cannons along the port side of the vessel began to glow…

"Oh, you arrogant bastard," I muttered, gripping the corner of a desk a split second before the cannons on the *Blade* erupted with blistering light. A hundred bolts of focused Willfire rained down upon the palace and the city with enough force to reduce skyscrapers to dust.

"*Defend*!" Faraday cried, but the automated systems were already precious seconds ahead of him.

Salvos fired from dozens of unseen turrets on the palace, and surrounding vessels intercepted as much of the incoming bombardment as possible. Anti-aircraft guns on rooftops all across the city fired sizzling shots of spiraling blue energy. The shots exploded against the bolts from the *Blade* and lit up the darkening sky with a display of booming fireworks, as if it were New Year's Eve in Times Square back on True Earth. The explosion sent shockwaves rippling over the city, and even encased within the palace, the floor still shook underfoot.

"Bring him down!" Faraday cried. "*Attack*!"

Shadowman isn't attacking, not really, I thought as a few bolts struck the palace and gouged boulder-sized chunks from the white stone, shown on the display. *He's using the chaos to disappear.*

Sure enough, the ship had veered away from the palace and taken to the atmosphere, growing smaller and trailed by three dozen Knight-controlled cruisers. The *Blade of Spring* swept through the clouds and vanished. A burst of energy scattered the clouds and revealed a wake of silver and blue, an ion trail stretching up toward the heavens.

Shadowman had engaged the reality drive. He had fled with my ship, my friends, and the Historian—off to kill a god, if he was to be believed.

Even with all that firepower, the Everlasting didn't go down easily. Best I'd ever managed, fighting those bastards, was to wound and force retreat. Astoria, Emily Grace, had fallen, but that had been a ten thousand-year slow death of her own making.

The bombardment over and the threat to the city gone for the time being, Faraday started barking orders and organizing the damage assessment and aid to the damaged buildings far below. He had maintained his cool, his aura of command, which was grating but useful—again, for the time being. I didn't have time for a game of thrones that day.

"We have to go after him. Now. Send *me* after him," I said. "He can't have disabled all the damn locators in that beast of a ship. Give me a cruiser, and I'll follow the ion stream."

Faraday pierced me with a hot near-feral glare. "How do you always find yourself at the heart of these matters, brother?" He shook his head. "It doesn't matter. You're damn right, we're going after him. You'll give chase on the *Argent Shield*, Hale. You will lead a boarding party and recover the ship and the Historian."

Exactly what I wanted to hear—*use and abuse* me, I thought, *because I'm good at this stuff.* I saluted and then clenched my fists.

Damn, but it felt good to be back. This was old-school soldier work—just a simple mission, with none of the Everlasting, Roseblade, or Atlantis nonsense that had torn me asunder and killed all my friends. *And Emily…*

But then, that wasn't worth dwelling on at the moment. I had work to do.

~~*~*

Being back in the Knights' good graces—well, back in good *enough* graces—had its perks. From the War Room, I was taken to the armory for assessment and outfitting. The armory spanned an entire three floors of the palace and stretched off-world through the use of a few reality beacons.

Holy hell, but standing in the assessment foyer for the first time in half a decade, I felt like a kid on Christmas morning. For the past year, I'd been fighting on the outside looking in, driving a beat-up old '87 Astra with a half-million miles on the clock in the Bathurst 1000. Having access to the resources of the Knights again was like being handed the keys to a brand new Ferrari with personalized license plates. I'd been saving the worlds—from Morpheus Renegade, from Scion—with string, buttons, and luck. Hell, I'd been MacGyvering my unhappy work on a wing and a prayer.

No longer would I have to beg for scraps.

The armory was a well-oiled and well-ordered series of cascading stacks and shelves that might as well have been endless. Lower-level Knights (like me, I supposed) and clerical staff zoomed about the vast open space, filling orders on silent hovercraft—flat, circular disks about the size of tractor tires attached to the base of large shopping baskets for transporting the merchandise. The disks were piloted through use of a control display attached to the clerks' wrists. Given the nature of the portals fuelled by the reality beacons, the exact size of the armory was open to interpretation. It physically existed in Ascension City, within the palace, for about a square mile, but the wide-open space I stood in was immeasurably bigger. Off in the distance there was even a touch of dawn light. That part of the facility was off-world but easily accessed.

The shelves and stacks on the various levels contained weapons, armor, tactical gear, enchanted clothing, Infernal blades, and thousands of nameless trinkets and devices sourced from a million books and a million worlds. It would not be unfair to say, amidst the scent of cordite and grease, that the Armory was the largest cache of weaponry and military supplies in known existence.

I stood on an assessment platform in the foyer of the open complex, on a circle of glowing light. In the space of about fifteen minutes, a legion of armory staff had me stripped to my boxers, prodded, measured, and strapped me into a suit of mythril body armor, matte-black and sleek. The material was paper-thin and flexible, and it clung to my arms, legs, and chest like a second skin. For all that, it was strong and enchanted with hundreds of Will protections. I slipped back into my trousers, shirt, and waistcoat. Apart from what showed under my collar and my rolled-up sleeves, an observer wouldn't know I was wearing a suit of priceless battle armor.

If I'd had this during that scuffle with Morpheus Renegade, I wouldn't have died. I snorted. *Coulda, woulda, shoulda…* My death made me think for a moment on Emily and on her last gift to me, which I had given away to Annie. Worlds away, my son was blinking and breathing. *Only way he'll stay that way is the path you're on right now.*

True enough. I placed my arms above my head and stretched, feeling the armor mold around my form as I moved.

"Commander Hale," a familiar voice said from behind me. "Arbiter Vrail Corban, reporting for duty."

I turned and clapped my old friend on the arm. Vrail and I had been through some tough shit during the Tome Wars. He'd also sent me the recipe for those star iron shotgun shells that had saved me on Old Voraskel. Vrail was a tall man, a head above me, who wore his curling, shoulder-length dark hair pulled back in a loose ponytail. His sharp face and clear, intelligent eyes had managed to retain some measure of happiness after the Tome Wars. His shoulders were wrapped in a heavy purple cloak, concealing probably about thirty various weapons hidden about his person.

"Vrail, you old horse thief. Arbiter, is it now? Broken quill, they must be scraping the bottom of the barrel if they assigned you to me on this one," I teased.

Vrail laughed and offered me a wink. "I volunteered, of course. Wild dragons couldn't keep me away."

"Remember you said that." I chuckled wryly. "Given the current state of affairs, the Everlasting popping up like weeds faster than we can stomp them out, dragons aren't out of the question."

Vrail looked me up and down and frowned. "No blade?"

"Just my razor-sharp wit and winning attitude." I shrugged. "Perhaps I'll grab a shotgun—grew partial to the new design you sent through. Thanks for that, by the way. You up to speed on what's happening?"

"Mostly. Although what I have could be outdated. I mean, yesterday we were all after your head yet again. Now it's just someone pretending to be you, or something?"

"Eh… in a way." The mechanics behind Shadowman's existence would take far too long to explain, and we were already a half hour behind him and the *Blade of Spring*. "It's a Void-like creature with my face. It does look like me, but a me that's been dead a few days. Cold, pale. Nothing behind the eyes, you know."

Vrail rubbed his hands together. "Spooky. Capture or kill?"

"The Historian and my friends, Sophie and Ethan, come first and foremost," I said. "This is a rescue mission, not a bit of wet work. Although it will most likely come to that."

"Always seems to," Vrail agreed. "So engagement authorized. I suppose we should also try and recover the *Spring*, yeah?"

"That twelve-cylinder with all the add-ons belongs to me, Vrail. I would very much like my ship back."

He shot off a quick salute. "Roger."

Once outfitted—and after I'd grabbed a shotgun to replace the one lost on Old Voraskel—Vrail and I were escorted from the armory by palace guards to the elevators, down to the ground floor, and back out into the trampled esplanade, militarized to stop Shadowman, out front of the palace. Ahead of us was our destination, a war cruiser about the size of a truck with a semitrailer attached, fuelled and staffed with two other Knights for the mission, according to Faraday. A large crowd seemed far too interested in our ship, mingling around its perimeter. Heads turned to watch our quick march down along the esplanade to the ship.

On any other day, we would have needed to catch a priority shuttle across the city to the shipyards and worldports in the western quadrant. But given that Shadowman had threatened to blast the Fae Palace from existence and stolen the Cascade Fleet's flagship, we were spared the extra miles.

"Is it just me, or are there a lot of people milling about our ride?" I asked Vrail, as a gust of wind set his purple cloak chasing the breeze.

Vrail shifted his cloak so that it covered the Infernal blade strapped to his waist. I noticed he was wearing a chest plate of not-so-subtle silver armor. He smirked. "Word has spread that you're leading the recovery."

"They're here to see me?"

He glanced at me askance. "You know, you should visit more often. You're not nearly as hated as you think."

"Really?"

"Oh, don't get me wrong. Great swaths of the universe would cheer to see your head on a pike out front of the palace, but the Knights—your people—know the good work you've done."

And indeed, as we approached the *Argent Shield*, a slow but sure round of applause rang out from the crowd Eyes that had been watching our approach solemnly, perhaps seeing me for the first time, broke into joyful, bright… *something*, something that may have been hope. A cheer arose in the crowd, and Vrail laughed softly to himself, most likely at my dumbfounded expression.

"Give 'em hell, Hale!" a voice cried out.

"Welcome back, Commander!"

"Nice waistcoat."

And dozens of similar cheers trailed after us, doing no good at all for the headache brewing just behind my eyes, but improving my resolve considerably.

We approached the boarding ramp of the *Argent Shield* and were greeted by the rest of our crew. Two Sentinel Knights that I didn't recognize. Technically they were a rank above me, but I'd been given command through royal decree. Both were old enough to have fought in the Tome Wars, which meant I wasn't dealing with freshly minted recruits, but soldiers who knew what our morbid business was about. "Ship's stocked and ready for departure, Commander Hale," said the one to my right—a young woman, early thirties, blue eyes. Her blond hair was tied back in a no-nonsense braid, tucked into the hood of her silvery cloak. Her molded battle garb complemented her fit figure. "I'm Sentinel Marcia Cotton."

"Ship's not anything flash," said the other Knight—a grizzled, large man who stood a good seven feet tall, more than a head over Vrail. His arms were like tree trunks, under his cloak, and a thick beard covered most of his face below his keen violet eyes. "But she's sturdy and flies true. Sentinel Adam Gough, Commander."

The sleek ship would be fast, given its relatively small size. Next to the *Blade of Spring*, it would be like a small, fluffy Chihuahua nipping at the heels of a Labrador, but that could work in our favor.

I'd like to have a dog one day. Somewhere wide open, green, and quiet. After all my wars are fought… "But then, if I could have that," I muttered, just to myself, "I wouldn't be here at all."

"What was that, Commander?" Marcia asked.

"I said we best be underway. You two pilots?" They nodded. "Then you're driving." I hefted the weapon I'd signed out of the armory onto my shoulder. "I'll ride shotgun."

CHAPTER TWENTY-TWO

Drops of Jupiter

"This could be the start of something, you know," Vrail said. We were seated in the rear compartment of the *Argent Shield*, just after takeoff. Our pilots Marcia and Adam were zeroing in on Shadowman's trail so we could follow him across worlds. "You back in action, I mean. It's been a slow half-decade without you. If you're back for good, we could see about cleaning up the Outer Territories. Piracy's getting worse out on the spiral arm of the Golden Carousel. You leading your own small unit, high-value missions like this… We could get some work done."

Not too long ago Vrail had told me he thought I, not my older half-brother, belonged on the Dragon Throne. What had he said? *"Sentiment in the city may have been twisted against you, Declan, by your brother and his court, but more than a few remember who it was that ended a century of madness and slaughter."* I didn't think I had it in me to seize the Dragon Throne. *"You have a duty, Declan. And that's the last word I'll say on this matter."*

True to his word, he hadn't mentioned the feasibility of committing high treason since. Perhaps he'd soured to the idea of a drunken madman on the throne.

"It's good to be back in the fold," I admitted. The triumphant cheers I'd received upon approaching the *Argent Shield* had been encouraging. Perhaps I wasn't as hated as my exile had led me to believe. Perhaps I had it in me to do a good job at Knightly business again.

A second chance was rare in my line of work, as most first chances failed in death or worse than death. Could I ever be forgiven for the things I'd done? For the Degradation? For desolating Reach City with the Roseblade to thwart the Renegades? For the legions that had died, for me and my insistence that the job get done, no matter the cost?

Broken quill, I didn't deserve a second chance, but perhaps Vrail was right. Perhaps I could find meaning and purpose in my work. If my exile had taught me one thing, it was that life needed purpose, whether you were a Knight or a blackberry farmer. When all was said and done, I was good at being a soldier, if not the best, and I could do some good…

I flexed my arms and stretched the mythril plates under my shirt and across my chest. "I like the sound of that. Better than a civil war for the throne, eh?" I joked. "Let's go see where we're headed."

The *Argent Shield* was a small enough vessel, fast and light, so all that separated the flight deck from the rear compartment was a small galley containing standard rations and an airlock for zero atmosphere or underwater work. The Knights built their ships to be versatile. We entered the flight deck, and I leaned on the headrest of Sentinel Adam's seat.

"How are we looking?" I asked Marcia, who was strapped into the command chair. The flight deck resembled a cockpit of an airliner, save for the crystal beacons and weaponry controls. All seven feet of Adam was squashed into the co-pilot's chair. He monitored a screen that displayed an ion trail through the upper atmosphere—Shadowman's footprints in the sand.

"He's jumped some distance," Marcia said, giving me a glance over her shoulder. "Narrowing the pattern down now."

Smoke rose from a dozen fires far below in Ascension City. At our height, we held a commanding view of the city and the miles upon miles of districts spanning the east and south. I could see right up to the mountains that encased the city to the west and the distant blue sea to the north.

One of the consoles chimed an agreeable bell tone, and I cracked my knuckles. "Right then, where we headed?"

"Oh, you're not going to like it," Adam grunted, squinting at the display. "He's somewhere near…"

"True Earth," Marcia said. "He's in the true universe."

Visions of the *Blade of Spring* hovering in the sky above Perth ran through my mind, and I swallowed hard. Most of the planet remained ignorant about the worlds behind the world. If Shadowman blazed through the atmosphere in that ship, however, he'd start a global panic. We might have already been too late.

"Somewhere *near*?" Vrail asked.

"Best as we can tell," Adam said. "Do we follow?"

I didn't need to think too hard on that one. "Let's get him then, sentinels."

Adam and Marcia set to work, igniting the reality beacon on the console and keying in the coordinates along Shadowman's trail. The ship lurched—Vrail and I grasped handles just above our head—and *jumped* forward into the Void. The world of Ascension City faded away, replaced by a cord of strong golden light surrounded by inky blackness.

The *Argent Shield* shuddered as it leapt across universes, heading back to the start of the Story Thread. The trip lasted only about thirty seconds, yet in that time we covered a distance so inconceivably infinite that the mind couldn't comprehend it.

Reality reasserted itself as we exited the Void, wisps of frost clinging to the outer hull of the ship, and a planet a thousand times the size of True Earth hung just off the starboard engines against a backdrop of about a hundred million stars.

"Is that…?" Vrail asked.

"Jupiter," I said. "Can my new friends please tell me why we're hovering above Jupiter, millions of miles from anything important?"

"Because he's here," Marcia said.

"Confirmed." Adam tapped his screen and stared out at the planet.

"Where?" I asked, glancing through the windscreen and scanning the visible space. "Are we below him?" *The enemy's gate is down…*

"No, he's in the atmosphere," Marcia said, speaking slowly as if I were a child—or something dangerous she wasn't sure would react well to being prodded. "The *Blade of Spring* can take the storms. The *Argent Shield* would be torn apart," she said simply. "We can't follow them any farther, Commander."

"Not with that attitude," I quipped, already pondering how to navigate into a gas supergiant riddled with storms the size of True Earth. *Why the hell is he hiding out here?*

"The bastard must've known he had one of the only ships currently outfitted for planet dives," Adam said.

What was my shadow doing? Ducking into Jupiter's atmosphere was a move I would have made, but only if I were trying to hide.

Shadowman was not trying to hide—he'd bombarded Ascension City, sworn death to the Everlasting. He was loud and bleeding arrogance… but he'd retreated into the storm clouds of Jupiter? What was his game? *But I found one of them, Declan. Yes, yes. With the Historian's help, I have found one of the stinking bastards…*

Out here? Did he think the planet a place I couldn't—wouldn't—follow him?

"Well played, Shadowman…" I wasn't beaten yet. An insane yet alluring idea formed in the back of my mind and shuffled forward, a wicked glint in its eye. "Have any of you read *Prince of Galaxy VII* by Tom… I forget his last name. It's sci-fi, nothing groundbreaking. Just good old-fashioned space opera."

"Was the author Willful?" Vrail asked.

"He most assuredly was," I said. "It's one of the many books I read during my exile—you guys probably wouldn't ever encounter it without five years of empty time on your hands."

"What tricks did you pull from it?" Adam asked, urging me to get to the point.

I clenched and unclenched my fists, staring out of the shielded glass up at the planet. Or down at the planet—direction didn't really apply in a vacuum, so long as you applied propulsion in the correct manner. "So we definitely have a lock on the *Blade,* right? Precise coordinates within the planet?"

"To the inch," Marcia said. "You thinking of firing one of the missiles? The storms will throw it off by hundreds—if not thousands—of miles."

"This is a rescue mission. *Res-cue,*" I emphasized, stretching the word. "He's got high-value hostages aboard. You don't fire a missile at hostages."

Marcia nodded. "Then what?"

I pooled smoky, luminescent Will into my palms. The bright smoke leaked between my fingers and lit the blood in my veins. *It* could *work… But, hell, this will be one for the record books.*

"See that look on his face?" Vrail asked Adam and Marcia. He was grinning. "That's the look that ended the Tome Wars."

~~*~*

Vrail helped me with the enchantments. We'd left the bridge and stood in the corridor just outside the portside airlock, opposite the galley. My skin and clothes were aglow with precise Will weaves and invocations. The mythril armor tingled and made me feel pins and needles in my legs and arms.

"This is stupid," Vrail said. "No, this is reckless."

"No reason it won't work," I said, my voice tight and perhaps betraying the worry seeping into my very bones.

Or was that "worry" coiled excitement? Hard to tell, but I was caring about the stakes in the game again. For the longest time, I'd been drifting in a fugue of indifference. I was back to work. Alive and productive. "Also, I received a pretty big inside tip a day or so ago that I've got at least a few years left in me. And—let's be honest—I've done stupider things."

Vrail considered that for a moment, then smiled wryly. "You know, if it were anyone else, this would be certain death. But how much longer do you think you can keep taking these chances, Hale, before one of them doesn't pay off? You've the luck of a hundred Knights, you ken, but it'll only take one wrong move to put you in the ground."

"Or the cold, endless vacuum of space?"

"Or that."

He had a point—a more than valid one, when all was said and done. I played the game, and I played it well, but at a certain point, didn't the risk have to outweigh the benefit? Not saving the lives of Ethan, Sophie, and the Historian, of course—that was personal—but the risk of playing the game at all. *You're in too deep to ever stop playing*, whispered that deceitful, belittling voice in the back of my head. *You turn away now, and there are a hundred enemies, just waiting to plunge a dagger into your back. Just waiting for you to blink.*

I took a deep breath.

That's why you gave the kid to Annie.

And exhaled slowly.

"Well, I can only play the moves I have," I told Vrail. A subtle but unnerving vibration shook the ship. Marcia and Adam must have steered us a lot closer to the planet than the occupational health and safety manual would recommend. "And right now, this is my *only* move. So let's be about our work."

"I think we must be in position," Vrail said.

Marcia's static-laden voice burst through the intercom on the airlock's hatch. "That's as close as we can get. Any closer will compromise the hull. If you're going to do this mad thing, then do it." She cut off with a string of curses.

"That one wouldn't cry at your funeral." Vrail chuckled.

"Oh, she just hasn't got to know me yet."

A heavy silence fell between us, the kind of silence only possible between two old friends who might've been about to never see each other again. I'd shared far too many of those silences, with far too many lost friends, and the lonely years that followed had been deafening in their silence.

We clapped each other on the shoulder and pressed our foreheads together, then separated.

"Pint at Edgar's when this is all over?" he asked.

I was still nursing a headache from the shots I'd done at McSorley's. "I'll drink you under the table."

"That's the spirit."

After one last check of the enchantments flowing across my skin, I stepped into the airlock, and the door slid closed behind me on near-silent rails. I was trapped in a small compartment about the size of a prison cell, and through the porthole window, I could glimpse nothing save the Earth-sized orange-and-purple storms, surging across the gas giant like bruises blossoming on skin.

"Ready?" Vrail asked through the intercom.

I steeled myself, said my final goodbyes to my son, Annie Brie, and a few others in my head then nodded. "Once I'm gone, head back to Ascension and let them know. Either I'll return with the *Blade* or I won't."

"Long odds," Vrail agreed. "Luck, Commander."

A warning light bathed the white walls orange, and I heard the air start to leak from the compartment. The soft light turned to police siren blue, warning me of decompression. I was relatively safe inside my enchanted suit.

The outer door on the hull silently slid open, exposing me to the pure vacuum of space. Jupiter spun across my vision, and I took a deep breath. *This is going to be spectacular.* I squashed my lingering worry under a wave of devil-may-care excitement.

I felt a gentle tug, as if I were hooked on a loose line from within the atmosphere of the planet, and decided not to drag the moment out any longer.

Taking a leap of faith, I kicked off from the floor of the *Argent Shield*, out into space… and began my dive into the storm clouds of Jupiter.

CHAPTER TWENTY-THREE

Knight Fall

The enchantments coating my skin sealed me in a suit of artificial atmosphere—an invisible spacesuit, complete with a bubble of air—air that tasted like an ashtray, but air nonetheless. To an outside observer, however, I shot toward the planet in nothing save shirt, trousers, and a getup of waistcoat and scuffed black shoes. A lone figure hurtling toward certain death, if he wasn't dead already, equipped with nothing more than a badass eye patch and a whole lot of wasted good intentions. I'd have liked to have brought the shotgun along, but there were limits even to this level of absurdity.

Space was quiet. Empty. Vast.

I didn't feel the cold, but I could hear my own panted breathing and heart pounding. Jupiter filled my field of vision. A great, swirling sentinel of stormy gas and impossible size. Somewhere, in that mess, hid Shadowman and the *Blade of Spring*. The enchantment work Vrail and I had done, engineered from the tricks pulled from that sci-fi novel, *should* have been pulling me straight toward the ship's hull.

All I had to do was grit my teeth, think of Paddy's, and fall.

The *Blade* and I were like two magnets being drawn together. The stronger, more powerful magnet—the ship—was pulling me in. But blimey, if this worked, they'd be studying it in the Academy for centuries to come. If it didn't—well, they'd still be studying it, but as a warning that no matter how much raw talent or power a Knight might have, he could still suffer from a monumental case of the fuckups.

As far as deaths went, though, I could've gone in a lot worse ways than by being pulled apart in the storm clouds of Jupiter. No one would ever say I died boringly.

Or without anyone to carry on your name…

I pushed that thought aside and concentrated on the task at hand.

The ability to pull enchantments out of stories already written was one of the greatest strengths of the Knights Infernal. We had needed to be precise, careful, and clever in devising my invisible protective layers, but because the general idea existed within the pages of a book, the enchantments could adapt and account for a thousand little details that simply wouldn't have occurred to someone not versed in orbital diving. I didn't glance off the atmosphere or shatter my bones into dust, because the enchantments absorbed the impact, pierced the upper atmosphere like a needle through a balloon, and flung me into the tortured sky of the planet.

I hit the storms a few minutes later and stretched the enchantments to their breaking point.

The storm was power.

Raw, untempered, elemental power.

The only thing I'd ever felt that came close to the sheer intensity of the storm raging around me was when I'd wielded the Roseblade to destroy the Reach near the end of the Tome Wars. Not even in Atlantis, where I'd fallen broken and bloody from the tower through a break in time and reality to my death, had I come close to the apocalyptic hurricane of bruised purple and harsh orange tornadoes that battered against my enchantments.

Epic thunderclaps, muffled somewhat by my protections, still rattled my teeth. Violent, acidic winds that would have dissolved me in seconds ran down my arms like slick oil on glass, only to be swept away. I plummeted through the storm, mostly blind and on my own but anticipating contact with the *Blade*—the tug was growing stronger. A half minute later, I struck gold.

Having washed most of my speed off in the storms, I hit the hull of the ship with about as much force as if I'd fallen from ten feet or so. It jarred me for a minute, and I rolled along the sleek, silver hull like a rag doll, but the enchantments soon stuck me down—two magnets, pinned together.

Sweet, broken quill—I made it!

I lay there for a moment, spread-eagled to the outside of the *Blade*, and took a moment to catch my breath. The artificial air bubble had left a weird taste in my mouth, and it seemed so fragile next to the majesty of the storms raging around me, now that I wasn't hurtling through the atmosphere, but I sucked in great gulps of the air, as if I'd been suffocating moments before. Adrenaline pumped through my veins and made the hair on my arms stand to attention.

After a minute or so, I activated my Will and picked at the threads holding all the enchantments together around my body and lessened the one that magnetized me, just enough so I could move about the hull.

Find the nearest airlock. Pint with Vrail when all this is said and done.

I managed to turn over onto my arms and knees, though the pull of the magnetic enchantment wanted to flatten me against the hull again. Slowly, carefully, I began to crawl forward as the storms raged around me. It felt like moving through treacle or tree sap, but I made grudging progress. Although I couldn't feel it thanks to the invisible skin of enchantments keeping me alive, I imagined the hull of the *Blade* would be cold enough to strip the flesh from my bones. Not a happy thought—but then, I wasn't in a happy place.

The storms and the lights on the outside of the ship were enough to show me the path. After about five minutes, I found an airlock. I glanced through the porthole and found it empty.

He was only one pseudo-man, but once I activated the door lock, Shadowman would know I was there. A console up on the bridge would flare to buzzing life.

He may be able to feel you out anyway… You're two halves of the same whole. He may already know you're here. Not that I could sense Shadowman, but I was used to being at a disadvantage in these matters and had to err on the side of caution. *He probably knows you're here.*

True, so instead of clinging to the hull of the ship and wondering, it was time to remove all doubt and board the *Blade of Spring*.

I knocked once and then let myself in.

~~*~*

Inside I pressurized the airlock, undid the half-dozen enchantments that had kept me alive, and wondered if anybody had ever cheated death more often than I had.

The air was warm inside the *Blade*, and more importantly, it didn't have the recycled bland taste of the stuff I'd used to get here.

In the corridor outside, I found the Historian of Future Prospect waiting for me, wearing the same serene smile on her face that I'd only ever seen her wear—even as a child.

She's still a child, seventeen if she's a day.

"Hello, Declan," she said warmly. The Historian had Forgetful eyes, which meant they varied in color—Clare had possessed a pair, and even Annie had shown some talent in changing her eye color. Although she was unaware of it, Annie had a spark—a troubling spark that shouldn't have been, given that she had no Will of her own.

At the moment, the Historian's eyes were a soft sky blue, and her lips were as red as blood. Her silver hair hung in gentle waves over her shoulders, and she wore a net of spun gold, sort of a crown for her station, on the top of her head. Her long blue dress had silver trim, and a white shawl covered her shoulders. A tiny sapphire gemstone glowed on a golden chain around her neck.

"Hello, my dear," I said. "You Saw me coming, huh?"

"My gift can show me a great many things, but to you I am blind. The abomination holding me captive directed me here to greet you." She sighed. "Shadowman, as he calls himself, knew you were coming. Did you just jump from orbit to get here?"

We could take our time, then. No sense being stealthy, if I was expected. "More a precision fall than a jump. Are Sophie and Ethan still alive?"

The Historian nodded. "On the bridge, cuffed in star iron, but mostly unharmed. Oh, they have your *fire*, Declan. You can inspire such terrible loyalty."

I ignored that remark, which felt more like a gibe. "Has he told you what he wants?"

She shrugged and put her hand in mine as we began a slow amble up through the ship. Her fingers were warm against my cold skin. "To kill the Everlasting."

"Which one…" I muttered. The Nine were down to Eight, with Emily's death, which begged the question. "Did you see… Did you know about Emily Grace?"

The Historian gazed at me with eyes far too old to belong to such a young and innocent face. Sky blue flickered to violet and back again. "Fair Astoria sleeps," she said sadly.

She had known.

"Christ, you could've warned me last time we met that she was Everlasting."

The Historian *tsk*ed. "Had you found out too soon, Scion would have killed you and claimed True Earth as his dominion. What I See, Declan, in my mind… It's like cords of light, billions of threads, and the futures that are more likely to happen are brighter, you ken? Some futures blaze like the sun, all but certain to happen, while others are as dark as midnight."

"So not likely to happen?"

"Yes, but also no. All the futures that surround you are dark, because of the bargain struck with Oblivion for your shadow. Shadowless, you turn certainty to shadow, Declan Hale. That's what makes you so dangerous and why I did not risk telling you about Astoria. I've steered you as best I can, but you are not to be steered. Worlds come tumbling down and collide like marbles when someone is foolish enough to try to *steer* you. But when you play with events, you *mask* what may be the true future, the brightest cord, in shadow. That's why… I insisted on your exile six years ago."

I missed a step. *She argued for my banishment?* At the time, she would have been barely eleven years old.

Blimey. "Well, maybe we're better off not knowing the future," I said, a touch bitterly. I had considered the Historian something of an ally. "That way we can at least pretend everything's going to be okay…"

The Historian brushed a loose strand of her hair back behind her ear and smiled wistfully. "If only."

We entered the gravity platform at the end of the corridor, which shot us straight up a dozen levels, toward the bridge of the ship.

The Historian didn't seem to want to let my hand go, which was comforting in a friendly sort of way. A gentle reminder that I wasn't multi-universally hated. *Gosh darn it, Declan, people like you…*

After having crossed half the ship in about half a minute, we stepped off the gravity lift. I was familiar enough with the design of Knights Infernal vessels to recognize that the wide corridor ahead, lit by illuminated wall panels, led to the bridge. We started up it, headed for the bow of the ship.

"Last time we met," I said, "you said I was going to be given a choice—a choice to do something important, something no one has ever done before. Was that choice severing the Infernal Clock in Atlantis? Did I make the right choice?"

In the light, the Historian's silver hair seemed to sparkle under her cap of spun gold, as if a bunch of those hovering snowflake sparks on Old Voraskel nested in her curls. She shook her head, seeming uncertain. "That future… it still hasn't happened yet. Severing the Infernal Clock and unlocking the Everlasting's prison was not… was not as vital as the choice yet to come." She pressed her hand against her forehead, as if some thought pained her. "I'm sorry. I can only See glimpses of the futures you brush against, and even those possibilities, far removed from the worst of your influence, are vague and darkened by your shadow. It is somewhat frustrating."

"But what I did in Atlantis… it's going to start a war. Hell, I've already been fighting that war for half a year! Just waiting for the rest of Forget to catch up." I cursed and sliced my free hand down through the air. "Historian, if plunging the entirety of creation into a war against the Everlasting wasn't the world-ending choice I was supposed to make, then what the hell could it be?"

For some unknown and possibly insane reason, the Historian of Future Prospect smiled. "I do not know." She giggled. "And do you have any idea how rare that is?" She giggled again and a tear of mirth ran from the corner of her eye to the corner of her mouth.

The wide illuminated corridor of smooth and glossy gray floors ended in a pair of pneumatic doors. We were about to enter the demon's lair, and me without a bottle of something to take the edge away.

"Do you have a real name?" I asked, having never thought to ask before now. "Beyond the title, I mean."

A delighted smile lit the Historian's face. "No one ever asks." She giggled once more, like—well, like the young schoolgirl she might have been, if not for her curse. "My name is Amy. Before taking up the mantle of the Historian, I was born Amy Delacroix."

I squeezed her hand in mine. "A pleasure to know you, Amy Delacroix."

We stepped forward, and the doors parted right down the middle and slipped into the walls, revealing the bridge of the *Blade of Spring.*

My dark reflection spun in the commander's chair to greet us. He cocked his thumb and forefinger like a gun and shot me an all-too-friendly grin.

CHAPTER TWENTY-FOUR

The Blade of Spring

"Declan!" Shadowman said, smiling from ear to ear. "Welcome aboard! Rather unorthodox entrance, wasn't it? I admire your—our?—resolve. How far you've travelled since first we met in the cold and the rain outside your bookshop."

"Nice ship," I replied. The bridge was a wide-open space containing banks of monitors, thin screens of computerized glass, and about a dozen chairs for the various command positions, such as navigation and weapons control. A long piece of shielded glass formed a half-circle from one corner to another, and on the other side of the glass churned the bruised storms of Jupiter. "You can fly it all by yourself, huh?"

He stretched his arms out wide and smirked. "Scheduled maintenance aside, she's built to fly on hopes and dreams." He tapped the device that wrapped around his ear and covered his left eye with a small, transparent visor. "Oh, sure, you could outfit her with a regular old crew. But the control column responds to my thoughts. As fast as I can thunk 'em."

I rolled my eyes, the effect doubtless ruined somewhat by the eye patch. "Shit, I'd like to meet the guy who thought that was a good idea." I scanned the bridge and saw some familiar faces sitting in the navigation pods. "Hello, you two. I send you to have a chat, and you end up kidnapped? For shame."

"Hey, boss." Ethan looked weary and drawn, but that would be the star iron, working an enchantment of fatigue as well as blocking his access to Will. "Can you believe this? That's Jupiter out there!"

"Is it? I hadn't noticed, no. Sophie?"

"Did you…" she began carefully. "Did you see Tal?"

I nodded.

"Yes, Declan," Shadowman said. "We'd very much like to find Oblivion. That creature is at the top of my to-kill list. He made me and will die for such folly. But where are my manners… please, would you have a drink with me?" He produced a half-empty bottle of amber scotch from down the side of his chair. Shadowman took a long pull on the sauce and offered it to me, as he had done back at the start of this game in Riverwood Plaza.

"Cheers," I said, taking the bottle this time. The scotch burned down my throat as it always did, and it settled warm in my gut. A little kick in my step and something to calm my nerves after my fall from on high. I put the bottle on the navigation column beside me and rubbed my hands together. "So, give me the ship."

Shadowman snorted and stroked the buttons on his old worn waistcoat. Not only did he look like me, but he had a few of my mannerisms, too. "But now that you're here, we can get underway. I knew you'd follow. Do you know where we are?"

"Jupiter," I said. "Universe One, being bombarded by storms and violent pressure that will, given enough time, tear even this mighty ship asunder."

"Yes, but do you know what's hidden here?"

I shook my head. "I'm going to assume very little worth writing home about. Look at it out there. Nothing could survive for long."

"And yet look at this!" Shadowman blinked, and the entire ship shuddered. We descended through the storm, gases and ugly rain falling across the hull.

Look at what? "What am I supposed to…"

Something came into view. A structure, floating without visible support within the storms—of old stone, parapets, collapsed domes, and cracked cobblestoned walkways that ended in wide, circular platforms. "Is that… is that a temple? It looks vaguely Atlantean."

"It's been there for hundreds of thousands of years," Shadowman said seriously.

"That's… impossible," I said, but the truth of it was staring me in the face. The distance was hard to judge, but the temple looked as if it stretched in a rough diamond about a half a mile long by the same wide.

"I know. I know!" Shadowman laughed. "First of all, it should never have existed in such an environment, let alone survive abandoned for half a million years."

"Okay, you have my attention. What do you think it is? And how did you know it was here?" *Half a million?* If that was accurate, the temple was far older than Atlantis.

"I could *smell* it," Shadowman hissed and tapped the side of his nose. "Smell what's locked away inside it. Oblivion forged me not only from your shadow but from Void essence and old—*old*—magic. I can smell the Everlasting." He snarled. "Broken quill, but they *reek*. That, Declan, floating out there amidst the storms, is a prison for one of them."

"But the prisons, as I understand it, were created about ten thousand years ago. You said this has been here much longer."

Shadowman nodded along with my words. "Yes! So my question is, if whatever is in there can hold something as powerful as one of the Everlasting, that might be something worth having, don't you think? And no harm taking out the Elder God while we're down there."

"A weapon…" I said slowly, stroking my stubbly chin. Shadowman mirrored me. "Against the blight." Damn it all, I was intrigued. More than intrigued—I wanted what my dark reflection wanted. We were on the same page.

"Declan," Sophie said carefully, "this is a bad idea."

"I am inclined to agree," the Historian said.

Ethan yawned and shrugged against the star iron bonds. "You're going to go anyway."

I nodded. "Best bad idea I've had today, though. So which one is it?" I asked Shadowman. "Who are we going to bother?"

Shadowman sniffed the air and growled with distaste. "The stench of Scarred Axis roams like plague rats through that temple."

CHAPTER TWENTY-FIVE

I Still Don't Like Mondays

We used one of the cruisers in the *Blade's* transport bays to travel over to the old temple. Cathedrals of storm clouds battered our tiny cruiser, but she was made to bear the brunt of the weather, just like her mother, and we landed on one of the platforms encircling the temple.

Shadowman cycled down the engine and ran some diagnostics, using the crystal core–powered instruments to scan the environment. "Not surprisingly, there's nothing alive out there. Axis is here, I guarantee you, but he doesn't register as alive. What *is* surprising is the bubble of atmosphere… There's breathable air out there. As if we're expected."

I glanced out through the porthole, at the wild storms lashing the temple, and grunted. The violent climate of Jupiter did seem to be giving the temple a beating, but at the right angle, I could see that the storms glanced off an unseen barrier like stones skipping over the surface of a lake.

"Huh," I said. "We're standing inside a soap bubble being battered by a storm the size of True Earth. We need to be very, very careful." I ran a hand back through my hair and gazed at my dark twin. I jerked a thumb over my shoulder. "The sun's about five hundred million miles thataway, which means my shadow—if I had one—would be hitting the ground before me. You're going first, buddy."

"The science on that seems sound…" Shadowman muttered. He picked up a sword of star iron from against the door, swiped from the armory on the *Blade* before we departed. "Very well. Let's behead a god, find what makes this place so special, and be gone."

Hesitating only a moment, Shadowman pressurized the cruiser to match the fortunate atmosphere outside and lowered the exit ramp. The heavy door slid open, and a wave of foul air rushed into the ship. I tasted dust and the waste of years, a stench of stone so old the rock had petrified. All across the sky rippled bands of untamed lightning. The sound of the storm was strangely muffled, as if it were echoing down a tunnel and around corners.

Shadowman stepped down the ramp, and I followed, half expecting the ground to give way beneath us and the temple to be torn apart by Jupiter's fury. *The temple's a fossil. Old and brittle.*

"It's stood for at least ten millenniums," Shadowman said, doubtless mirroring my thoughts. "No reason for it to fade away now…"

"We're an uncertain element, after ten millenniums," I said, but he already knew that. "Introduce uncertainty, and entropy has a handle to pull a jagged, rusted hook through our lips. I've been here before—not *here*, but in similar situations. Any move we make—particularly against Scarred Axis, since you're so certain that son of a bitch is here—will likely result in conflicting enchantments, cancelling one another out. This temple will crack like an egg, caught in a hurricane. On the positive side, we'll be reduced to atoms faster than we can feel it."

Shadowman chuckled and grasped my shoulder. "You and I are going to do big things."

His touch left a funny taste in my mouth, as if I'd been sucking on a copper penny. When he let go, my shoulder was numb with cold, but I wasn't about to let him know that. I rolled it in the joint a few times to encourage circulation.

The Tomb of the Sleeping Goddess had been a graceful monument to Fair Astoria, strewn with hanging vines, elegant marble, and statues of her beauty, albeit fallen. Of Scarred Axis's temple, all I could say of it was that it was barren. *Scarred is a good word for it, actually.* The ground was uneven, patched together from misshapen, blackened stone. The temple walls seemed to change dimensions, depending on whether I looked at them head-on or out of the corner of my good eye. The dome of the great temple had collapsed, and the entire structure looked one good sneeze away from tumbling down, as if the supports were made of straw. *Scarred*, I thought again. Even Jupiter's atmosphere above it was constantly cutting and sewing itself back together, but the temple was all cut, no repair.

"He's here, he's here…" Shadowman whispered, clutching the hilt of his stolen Infernal blade, a good two feet of pure star iron. It was our only real weapon against the Everlasting, save celestial illusion, but I'd fucked up both of the known celestial blades, so star iron would have to suffice.

"Careless." I tapped my teeth together a few times. I was neither cold nor warm, but I shivered anyway. That place was *wrong*, impossible, and we were damned for being there.

We moved under and climbed over broken keystone archways, the ground sloping toward an entrance entirely devoid of light. Trepidation rose in my gut at what lay ahead, but as always, I swallowed hard, acknowledged the fear, and marched on regardless. *Whatever happens will happen… All I need to do is stay alive for as long as I can.*

I was beginning to see an end to this game of alien shadows, dying gods, and unexpected infants—perhaps an end I could exploit. It had been the better part of a day since Emily's death and Oblivion had seized the Roseblade, and yet the Everlasting had done nothing with the sword. The Knights Infernal would have heard—and *felt*—the blade being used, like the shockwave of a nuclear explosion. That meant Oblivion was biding his time, for whatever reason. *Or maybe he doesn't have a clear move to make…*

"Declan," Shadowman said. "Are you listening?"

I fell out of my thoughts and blinked twice. "Yeah, I'm here. Just thinking on the steak special at Paddy's. Blimey, they cook a good steak at that pub. *Cooked* a good steak, I should say." The destruction of Paddy's was another wrong I had to right.

The archway into the darkened temple loomed before us now, making me think of some giant beast with its maw wide open to swallow us whole. Knightly work had put me in similar situations in the past. Following our mandate to protect the Story Thread, we Knights often found ourselves in places lost to time and memory, places and levels of existence that had been forgotten—quite on purpose, I imagined, and left to rot.

The men and women of Atlantis, all those millenniums ago, had meant well by sealing away the Everlasting, but the evil of the Elder Gods was bubbling up through the cracks once more. Would've been better if the means the Knights of Atlantis had used to accomplish such a feat hadn't been forgotten. But if I were hoping on better days, then better if someone else—someone a lot less inclined to the amber sauce and misery—shouldered the burden.

Well, whether I liked it or not—and, if I were being honest, I kind of liked it—I seemed to always stand at the heart of such earth-shattering events. Hated or loved, I was never bored.

Shadowman and shadowless stepped into the prison of the Everlasting Scarred Axis and were swept into the darkness and cold, lost in a bubble suspended within a planetary maelstrom.

~~*~*

Our journey through the temple had been swift and uneventful.

Given that the dome had collapsed at some point in the distant past, the central chamber of the temple was actually fairly well lit by the gaseous clouds overhead. A dozen bolts of lightning tore across the sky every other second, offering a pulsing bright light in the otherwise dim chamber. The place was barren, empty.

Almost empty, I corrected, my heart leaping into my throat. A quick scan of the central chamber with my one good eye quickly identified the only thing of any real interest.

"Oh…" Shadowman whispered. "Look at that."

Chained to a spike of obsidian in the center of the chamber was a pale creature, thin and wasted, with skin the color of winter snow under moonlight. At least eight feet tall, suspended off the floor, the creature's bulbous head was the size of a watermelon. The heavy chains carried millennia of rust and wear, yet they held the creature to the spike as tight as any bonds I'd ever seen. Its bulbous head slumped over its chest, wide jaw hanging askew, and its eye sockets were sewn shut in scarecrow scars.

Very clearly dead, Scarred Axis had been nailed to the fucking wall and left to… rot… for the better part of ten thousand years.

"Well." I cleared my throat. *This is good, isn't it?* "That's one less of the bastards to worry about."

With Emily… Astoria… dead, too, that reduces their number to seven. Seven Everlasting, with Scion licking his wounds from our last encounter. I didn't know why seven gods seemed more manageable than nine, but it did, and I'd take any sort of motivating news I could grasp.

Something didn't feel right about my count—another of those nagging thoughts digging jagged hooks in the back of my mind—but I couldn't quite taste it on the tip of my tongue.

"We're too late," Shadowman said, disappointed. He let the tip of his sword drag along the stone floors—bad discipline. I'd had wartime instructors at the Academy who would've beaten me sevens shades of shit for such carelessness. "I wonder if there are any old artifacts here…"

The nagging thought slipped another hook in my mind, and I was certain something was amiss. Something I was *missing.*

In my mind's eye, I saw Emily Grace, stabbed and dying in her secret grove, but smiling at me with an ethereal calm.

"All this way," Shadowman said, sauntering across the chamber. The walls were bare, holding no mosaics or stories of long ago, and there was very little space for any old treasure or artifacts to be hiding. "I suppose we should be happy, eh? But I wanted to kill the son of a bitch myself… The Everlasting have taken too much from us, Declan."

That sentiment, I wholeheartedly agreed with. For Tal alone, the Everlasting would be made to bleed.

Never fewer and never more… Emily's words came back to me with all the force of a train hitting a soda can. *Oh, bugger…* "Never more than Nine," I said slowly. "And never fewer. That's what she said."

"What who said?" Shadowman asked.

With a sense of wearied trepidation, I turned back to the spike and beheld Scarred Axis grinning down at me through yellowed teeth and staring into my soul with scar tissue where eyes should've been.

CHAPTER TWENTY-SIX

Voided

Scarred Axis's grin turned cruel, and he screamed in anger.

The unholy soul-crushing scream seemed to suck the air from the chamber and howl in my ears, increasing in pitch until it was like the screeching of a thousand rusty talons on chalkboards. The weight of that noise forced me to my knees.

A long minute passed as I took deep breaths, riding the wave of the scream. We were safe enough, as the Everlasting was bound to the obsidian spike, but I'd be hearing his scream in my nightmares for years to come. The scream felt like a weight around my neck, urging me to bow. Shadowman suffered the same—he'd dropped his sword and clutched the sides of his head as if his skull were about to rupture.

They don't get to put you on your knees…

No, no the Everlasting didn't. I lifted my head and stared into the crisscross scarring over Axis's eyes. The strain on my neck felt liable to snap my spine, but I managed to straighten my back and then forced my left foot flat against the floor.

Every muscle screamed as loud as Axis as I rose to my feet, hunched under the weight, and summoned a pool of smoky Will into my palm.

Axis's scream lessened into rougher bursts, and I realized, with a weary sort of fear, that he wasn't screaming—he was *laughing.*

"Declan Hale," Scarred Axis said slowly, his voice rolling over each syllable. "The Shadowless Arbiter himself. Whispers of your deeds ripple through the ether, and the ether, Declan, is the only source of information that can leak into my prison. I know you."

"I've met a few of your brothers and sisters," I said.

"Yes, and our influence, whether you see it or not, has driven you quite mad." Scarred Axis snorted, but his tone suggested sorrow. "After all, you think all this is a game, do you not?"

That gave me pause. Ever since I'd left Riverwood Plaza, I had been thinking in terms of chess pieces moving on a vast board, but I'd been trained to think in such terms. Strategy and logistics had been hammered into me harder than thousand fold steel, at the Infernal Academy. And that training let me see the game a few moves ahead, now, as pieces of the greater puzzle fell into place. I knew where I could find Oblivion and mayhap recover the Roseblade. *Back to where all this nonsense started, of course.*

"Yes, a game," Axis said, dragging me back to the monster at hand. "You grin, you wink with what little sight you have left, and drink yourself to death between moves. Declan Hale—the immortal Declan Hale, creation's only chance to avert untold catastrophe—

thinks he's playing a game. You see why I laugh—at the *sheer* absurdity of your fate!"

I clenched my fists and scoffed, "All fates aside, I'm not the one chained to a fucking spike, am I?"

"And this," Axis said distastefully, his tongue slapping his parchment-colored lips. "This… pale shadow who bears such striking resemblance. An abomination. Oblivion's work, unless I miss my guess. He never was much for creativity."

Shadowman found his feet and picked up his star iron blade. "I've come to kill you."

"Have you? That would almost be a pleasant change of pace. I suffer in monotony. The Knights who sealed me here all those years ago devised a most perfect prison, oh yes." Axis rolled his massive head around, popping the joints in his neck. "Forgive me. I haven't spoken a word in nearly three thousand years."

"A perfect prison?" I asked, keeping a safe distance between Shadowman and the chained Elder God, forming the tip of a rough triangle between my two adversaries.

"Release me," Scarred Axis commanded. "I was a scholar, in my time, and a great engineer—the greatest. I built vast engines, Declan. Planet-sized constructs that harness the wells of Origin, the very lifeblood of the cosmos. But my machines have been without maintenance for more than ten thousand years. My work is becoming undone, the gears miss their bite, and the belts are unraveling. And Declan, oh, Declan, the gift of Origin—your Will—will fade from all worlds unless I am freed to *work*."

The implications of Axis's words boggled me.

Shadowman didn't seem to share my vexation. "He's lying. We should chop his head off now," he said lightly, as if discussing the matter over a spot of afternoon tea.

"Hold on," I said. *Axis is saying that he constructed some sort of… engine… that allows humans to use Will. Shit. If that's true, and it fails…* I could feel my headache getting worse, forged by more than just my first hangover in three months and the fatigue biting at my very bones.

Do you believe the Everlasting? whispered a voice in the back of my mind—the source of my impending headache, no doubt. *They've deceived you before. Emily did so for years, and let's not even think too long on Oblivion…*

"The watchful will have already seen my machines winding down," Axis said. "Origin occasionally failing to work as intended, or the power—loose sparks from worn gears and cogs, you ken—jumping into humans not born with the predisposition to harness the power. Have you been watchful, Declan?" Axis grinned. "It can usually be seen in the eyes… Wild Origin alters the color in the eyes."

Annie… She wasn't Willful, not a drop of talent in her, and yet once or twice I'd seen her eyes change, usually under moments of high stress and battle. *Broken quill, I think I believe him… which means, if he's not released, Origin will fail—and we'll all be left powerless against the Void, the Orc Mare, and a hundred thousand other threats.*

But to release another of the Everlasting... would I always be their tool, their puppet?

Axis was right to laugh at my blasted fate.

"I won't let you do it." Shadowman had been watching my face and had doubtless guessed my conclusion. "Think of all the Everlasting have taken from us!" He spat. "All the wars fought in their name so long ago. Oceans of blood, Declan. The innocent and the young cut down by their rusted scythes. We need to end it, you and I, before the Story Thread is plunged into a new old war."

Axis grinned and licked his lips. His scar-tissue eyes laughed at me.

"If I want it so badly," Shadowman said, "then you must as well. Embrace that desire, Declan. You've killed before—oceans of our own, yes?—and destroyed creatures far less guilty than the monstrosity chained to this spike of dark stone."

"Well, when you put it like that… give me the sword." *And let me chop your head off…*

Shadowman gripped the hilt and set his jaw in a firm line. "That I cannot do."

"Then we're going to have to scuffle, I'm afraid."

Wisps of Void-light curled around his shoulders, emanating from within his skin. His eyes dulled to a dead pallor, and the fabric of reality surrounding Shadowman dimmed. "The Void will take us all before I let you unleash Scarred Axis." His voice was like a deep, hollow drumbeat. "We're no longer the puppet of these creatures, Declan. I give you one last chance to join me on my great quest to rid creation of these beasts. If you decline, then I will kill you and assume your mantle as my own."

"You're going to steal my ID?" I smirked. "You can take my face, even my name, but I'll be damned if you're getting my Subway card—not when I'm so close to that free sandwich!"

Shadowman glared, and his shoulders slumped. The wisps of Void essence coalesced into small gruesome winged creatures, which dissolved as soon as they broke away from him. "You decline?"

I clicked my fingers. "You sure are pretty, but I've already got a date, this dance."

Scarred Axis laughed.

Shadowman howled, and a flash of wild murder swam across his blackened eyes like lightning on a dark night. He ran at the god, raising his star iron blade up above his head. Freezing waves of raw Void essence bleeding off him made me duck and shield my good eye.

The best defense often included a *helluva* offensive hammer strike, however, so with my free hand I conjured a spinning golf ball-sized sphere and hurled it across the space between Shadowman and Axis. The sphere struck the floor and exploded in a dazzling array of light, splintered stone, and concussive force.

I'd raised a quick shield, a simple static block of air, in front of me to deflect the blast. Shadowman wasn't so quick and found himself hurled head over heels back across the chamber.

Chips of stone peppered Axis, cutting into his wasted chest. The god didn't bleed.

I gained my feet and wished I'd been able to bring the shotgun from the Armory with me down here. The star iron shells would have given Axis cause for consideration—and may have dissuaded Shadowman, as well.

I wasn't entirely without weapons—the book I'd brought from my shop still rested in the custom holster inside my waistcoat. I drew the book now, an old travelogue to a hundred different worlds, and held it up before me, bent at the spine to a random page, as if I were toting a heavy revolver.

The Knights had a unique skill, a terrible power that set them apart from the millions of general Will users. Not only could we use the written word to travel through the Void—we had weaponized it. A Knight could bind a living being to the world described on a page.

My old instructors at the Academy had explained it well. *"This is what makes the Knights and the Renegades so dangerous. Never mind the spells, charms, wards, or enchantments we can learn from the right books; never mind our armies or our fleets of Eternity-class battleships. We can bind our enemies in shackles of words and, with a thought, cast them beyond perdition…"*

I thrust my Will into the pages, and the words shone with a wraithlike, ethereal light.

The words *leapt* from the page.

I didn't know what page, and it didn't matter. I had to stop Shadowman from wounding Axis—from doing any more harm to anyone—and I could think of only one way to trip my evil clone: to send him back to the Void.

I wasn't using my power to cast my enemies "beyond perdition." I was using it for something forbidden.

With enough force, I could tear the canvas of reality and cause a Voidflood.

The very thought made my stomach churn with fear. A Voidflood had destroyed Avalon and doomed Old Voraskel. Hell, a Voidflood had drowned Atlantis and trapped Oblivion for ten millennia. Yet I was all out of moves, and at least Jupiter wasn't inhabited.

The flickering words whipped through the air, chains harder than steel and hotter than a furnace. I coiled them around Shadowman, snaked them up and around the chains that held Scarred Axis and across the god himself. The words marked him with living tattoos, and I took a step back, yanking Shadowman from his feet and Axis forward in his chains, pulling them toward me.

And then I spread the words further, draining the tome and enfolding the old pillars of the temple in unbreakable Will. The entire chamber was alight with cords of shining words and the sharp coppery taste of Will on the air.

"Declan, we can *kill* him!" Shadowman spat, the very essence of the Void frothing from his mouth. "A chance to end his blight! *We must take it!*"

Shadowman was insane—as mad as I was, but without the conscience, good intentions, and five-year cooldown in exile, to keep him in check. Let loose, he would kill with little regard for the laws of the Knights

Infernal. He would kidnap children, hold my friends hostage, and bombard an innocent population with cannon fire.

I offered him a grim smile. “Enough gods have died today.”

I wrenched with all my physical strength and Will on the book in my hands. The spinning cords of words tore at the pillars, at Axis’s chains, and at the very core of Shadowman.

A shudder, the aching yawn of a waking giant, trembled through the chamber, and the temple staggered, as if it were caught in a massive storm. The lashings from the book, the true power of a Knight, pressed against the Void, and I didn’t temper my strength—I let Will flood the pages and pressed harder, harder, against the fabric of reality.

Shadowman squirmed and wriggled like a cat on fire in the bonds, slicing through them as fast as I could wrap him in the words. The control visor for the *Blade of Spring* had melted around his head and fused to his pale skin—the pain didn’t seem to bother him. Axis merely laughed as millennia of stone and dust began to crack overhead and rain down upon the chamber.

The heat and the chains of words bursting from the book ravaged my hands. The pain flared hot and razor-sharp, and then I felt nothing but a numb sort of cold. A quick glance down at my hands revealed a bloody, shredded mess. I glimpsed white bone jutting from a few of my fingers.

Well, that’s going to sting in a minute…

The balance tipped, and a crack in reality gained purchase, spreading like a sheet of paper torn down the middle. The Void cascaded through that crack, a black wave of liquid nothing. Freezing daggers pierced my every breath as the crack widened, spread, and began to absorb the temple.

Axis roared and bucked at his chains, grinning from ear to ear. He didn't have eyes to wink, but I felt him shoot me one anyway.

"*No!*" Shadowman cried, a note of crippling fear in his tone. "I *won't* go back! I won't! I won't!"

The crack was beyond my control now. I dropped the fiery book and fled, stumbling out of the chamber as fast as I could. The pain of my hands was a distant thing, growing closer. I didn't have long to escape—minutes, less—before the Void overwhelmed the entire temple.

Ground shattered underfoot, and tonnes of old stone fell out through the bubble of atmosphere and into the violent storms of Jupiter. I stumbled, scraped my shins and my knees, but kept on the path back to the cruiser. The mythril armor under my clothes prevented any further injury.

I just hope the cruiser's still there, I thought, picturing the small ship falling away as easily as the ground. If that had happened, I was done. *Game over.*

I emerged from the inner chambers of the temple and my heart leapt into my throat—the cruiser was still where we'd parked it, just a few hundred feet away. I ran as fast as my tired legs could carry me and covered the distance as ancient pillars and walls collapsed in my wake, consumed by the Void in half a minute.

Panting and shaking, I stumbled up the ramp and into the cruiser, throwing myself into the pilot's chair and breathing a sigh of near-wailing relief. I fired up the engines and took to the tortured sky only heartbeats before the entire temple was absorbed and overrun by the Voidflood.

CHAPTER TWENTY-SEVEN

All Roads Lead Home

My fingers were broken and bleeding, mangled from the sheer effort needed to force a Voidflood. I had to fly the cruiser back to the *Blade of Spring* using the palms of my hands and a bit of nifty elbow work, dripping blood over the consoles and the crystal reality beacon. Shadows clung to the edge of my vision, and I was in danger of passing out.

Baby, I've been here before…

I docked with the *Blade* and sort of half-stumbled, half-fell onto the hard floor of the docks. I could barely keep my eyes open, glaring at dizzying fuzzy lights high above, and strange thoughts swam through my mind—things I hadn't thought of in twenty years or more, when I was just a child.

"Huh…" I muttered and managed a rough chuckle. "Life flashing before my eyes…"

Ethan and Sophie found me, sweet little 'Phie, and her cooling light repaired my damaged hands. I borrowed a piece of her energy just to stay conscious, lying dirty and beaten on the clean white floors of the immense ship. For some reason, just for a dark moment, I'd never felt more alone and… small.

The moment passed, and I was the all-consuming center of creation again—fit as a fiddle.

"There now," Sophie murmured. Sweat dripped down her brow, and strands of her auburn hair clung to her forehead. "As good as new. You had six fingers on the left hand, didn't you?"

I blinked and looked at my hands. The effort required to focus and actually count to five was embarrassing. "That's not funny," I muttered. "Help me up, Ethan. Let's get back to the bridge and out of this storm."

Ethan half-carried me up to the bridge, but with my hands repaired I felt a bit of vitality seep back into my body. I'd more than overdone it, using a tome to summon the Void like that, but I'd seen no other option. Opening reality to the Void was ridiculously stupid and actually a crime punishable by death under the laws of the Knights Infernal. I'd been damned lucky to survive.

"I'm running on empty here," I said once we reached the bridge. The Historian greeted us there and offered me an encouraging shoulder squeeze. "Less than fumes. So I'm going to raid the galley, eat some rations, and then find a bunk for an hour before we do anything else today."

A resounding alarm echoed up from the console in front of Sophie, and a dozen red lights flared to life on the panel. Sophie glanced at the screen, and her face fell. "Oh, you're going to love this."

I used a bit of Will light to clear the blood from my hands. "What we got now?"

"It's a distress call," she said, as if the harsh alarm hadn't given that away. "Look at the coordinates…" She spun the screen to face me, and I gave it a quick look, but I'd already figured out the final few moves of the game and knew where the call was coming from.

"Where is that?" Ethan asked.

"You've been there before," I said wearily. "If only briefly, but you've been there. The Plains of Perdition. Looks like the Knights guarding the ruins of Atlantis are under attack."

"There's a video burst, too," Sophie said. She tapped a few buttons, and the stream ran from the console and took over one of the wide screens on the bridge's front window shields.

The footage was shaky, desperate, and showed squadrons of bloodied Knights engaged in battle with battalions of ragged Orc Mare. Bursts of Willfire rocketed across the Plains of Perdition, vibrant green fields, and glimpsed in the distance were the spires and ancient ruins of Atlantis. Thousands of Orc Mare swarmed up the hill toward the city—the Knights would be overrun.

A monumental spire of white fire shot across the battlefield and cut through swaths of Orc Mare and Knights alike. Familiar razor-sharp and white-hot laser beams, a good half-mile long, swung through the battling forces and slaughtered hundreds in less time than it took to draw a breath.

Sophie gasped, and Ethan cried out. The Historian crossed herself and muttered a string of rather impressive curses under her breath. Young and feisty was Amy Delacroix.

The video stream died.

I sat myself down in the command chair and rubbed at my temple. The inevitable headache was in full swing now.

"Declan, what was that?" Sophie whispered.

I held my eye closed for a long moment before I could bring myself to look into hers. "That, my dear, was the Roseblade."

~~*~*

With no time for respite—no time to even update Vrail, Adam, and Marcia on my successful rescue—I manually entered the coordinates for the Plains of Perdition and activated the *Blade's* extraordinary reality drive. The ship shuffled forward and slipped across the Void as easily as silk on smooth skin. Without the control visor, lost with Shadowman, we wouldn't be able to maneuver the ship to any great degree or even activate and target the cannons, but I was expected back in Atlantis, Oblivion had sent out a fiery calling card across the Plains of Perdition, and all the ship was good for now was transport.

We burst into the skies above the Plains of Perdition and found them roasting—charnel pits of Knights and whole fists of Orc Mare. Blackened, snapped bones and laughing skulls were all the external cameras on the *Blade* could piece together through the smoke and the dying embers of hot rock.

Carnage.

"Broken quill," Sophie cursed. "Oblivion did this… in Tal?"

"Yes. Yes, he did." I saw no sense keeping the terrible truth from Tal's baby sister any longer. Our time on Voraskel had confirmed what I'd suspected since facing Oblivion atop the tower in Atlantis. "Tal's alive,

'Phie. She's trapped but alive—Oblivion kept her under his possession all these years."

She recoiled as if struck, raised her hand to strike *me*, and then burst into tears. Ethan was there, young and hopeless, and Sophie buried her face in his shoulder.

"We'll take one of the cruisers into the city," I said. "You two, your mission is to recover the Roseblade—nothing else matters, you hear me?"

"Sure, boss," Ethan said. "What about you?"

"Oblivion's come back here for a reason." I stared at the slaughter fields below, making sure I committed the cost to memory. "I'm going to take that reason from him."

Sophie sniffed and rubbed at her eyes. "Atlantis is massive—miles across. How are you going to find him?"

"Only one place he'll be."

Ethan had to ask. "Where?"

"The Infernal Clock, of course." I rubbed my hands together and my shoulders slumped. "Where Tal and I bargained for the end of the Tome Wars, where she was taken and my shadow was spun into the Void. The very top of the tallest tower… Where just six months ago I killed Morpheus Renegade and was killed by Emily Grace in return. The small plateau where all this began—where I uncovered the Roseblade and attracted the ire of the gods."

Amy, the Historian, cleared her throat. "I can't enter that city," she said. "The residual energy and the infinite number of possible futures converging on Atlantis will turn my brain to mush."

I shrugged. "Consider yourself rescued, then. We'll activate the retrieval beacon, but I'm sure the Knights will be along soon, regardless, in force and mightily pissed."

"Thank you, Declan," she said. "When you return, you and I need to talk about what Scarred Axis said to you."

I blinked. "You could see that? I thought—"

"I saw nothing, but I can tell something has you… terrified."

Plunging Axis into the Void likely wouldn't have killed the Elder God, but had it been enough to free him from his bonds? I had believed him, scarecrow eyes and all, when he claimed to be responsible for creating some vast engine that fuelled Origin, the power of Will, in humanity. And when he claimed that the engines were overdue for a service. *Annie is proof…* Without Will, the Story Thread would be overrun. Humanity would be left unprotected. The dead would choke the living inside six months.

"We will talk," I told the Historian. "You won't like what I've got to say, but broken quill, we'll talk."

~~*~*

Sophie, Ethan, and my good self abandoned the *Blade of Spring* to the Historian and piloted a fresh cruiser—not the one I had bled all over—out over the Plains of Perdition and toward the western horizon.

We flew over the vast, ruined fields strewn with smoking bones and rose toward the crest of two valleys on the edge of a ring of mountains. The tips of the ancient skyscrapers of Atlantis rested between the break in the valleys, and after weaseling through a network of canyons, our cruiser delivered us along the edge of a long-dead sea.

From the flight deck, we held a commanding view of the Lost City of Atlantis.

Ever since the Degradation had come down, the Knights had been plundering the city for its ancient wonders, but I doubted they'd explored more than a small percentage of the whole. Atlantis was massive, built in and around the monumental mountains and barriers of natural rock. Ruined buildings that looked far beyond their time had, until recently, still flickered with crystal light, even after ten thousand years without care. Towers scraped the sky, high above our cruiser, connected by clear walkways and glass bridges.

Atlantis had been powered by the eternal energy of the Infernal Clock. I'd severed that power source and plunged the city into a final darkness. Only some neon-blue light remained, clinging to the outer shell of the tower at the center of the city.

The dark tower was cut from the same obsidian stone as the Fae Palace, an unbroken citadel eclipsing the height of all the other structures. I flew the ship through the city streets, past old statues a hundred feet high of lords and kings long dead. As I had before, I sensed their gazes and their disapproval.

"This is fucking wonderful," Ethan whispered, crude and to the point.

"Yes, it is," I said. "And the start of all my problems ten years ago, when I first found it. Whatever happens here, we must stop Oblivion from achieving his goals."

"Oh, Declan," Sophie said, as if saying my name pained her greatly. "All you've done, all the games you've won and lost… I want to ask you a favor. I feel like you owe me at least one."

"I owe you more than I could ever repay," I said softly, keeping my eye on the road ahead, gliding softly through the metal and glass canyons of Atlantis. The tower in the heart of the city, much like the Fae Palace back in Ascension, stood miles above the streets and cast a long shadow. That tower was our destination.

"Whatever the cost," Sophie said. "I'm begging you, Declan, whatever the cost… If you see a chance to save Tal, please take it."

"Sophie, of course—"

She leaned over and placed her finger on my lips. "Just this once, listen to me, please. Damn the greater good. In the past you've been such a… such a *slave* to doing the right thing. Or what looked like the right thing. And it's gotten *so* many of us killed." Tears ran down her cheeks, and she swatted them away. "But now there's a real chance to… to maybe save one. Just one. Not whole worlds or universes. Just one. Be selfish—you loved her once, and I think you still do. Be selfish, and damn the cost of saving her."

Nothing I could say would have done any good, so I nodded and piloted the cruiser up out of the street canyons and circled the mighty tower in the city's heart, spiraling around the tower, higher and higher above the city. More than once—twice, in fact—I'd climbed this tower on foot. Both times had ended poorly.

It seemed like cheating, taking the cruiser. An express elevator to hell.

At the summit of the tower, a clear mile above the streets below, was the open courtyard that had sheltered the Infernal Clock. Four pillars, once at each point of the compass, marked the edge of the courtyard and the long drop to the city streets. I set the cruiser to hover in place and extended the exit ramp down onto the hard stone, just to the left to the spiraling staircase that led down into the tower. Given how long I'd been awake, and how weary I felt, I don't think I'd have managed more than a handful of those steps.

I exited the cruiser first. Sophie and Ethan followed just behind me, silent and fearful.

The plateau was abandoned. The shards of the Infernal Clock protruded from the ground. Its crystal rose stem was dark and withered. The roots from that once-living miracle had hardened into black diamond all across the plateau.

I'd killed the Clock to unmake the Degradation, and by doing so had released the Everlasting from their prisons, allowing the Elder Gods to touch the worlds again. I would be responsible for every death in the coming war.

I'd made a choice for *the greater good*, lost Clare Valentine to have the *chance* to make a choice, and in the end, I'd done more harm than good. Story of my life, more harm than good.

And my friends suffered the worst. Sophie had driven that nail into my heart.

Rusty red stains from where I'd started bleeding to death after destroying Morpheus Renegade had dried into the marble floor. Dead cherry blossom petals from the storm during my last visit gathered in the corners, shriveled. *Tal always loved the cherry blossoms…* The sky overhead was peaceful, blue, and yet I felt unnerved.

"I don't like this," Sophie said. "It's one of those 'too quiet' moments…"

Nothing. Just an old bloodstain and a dead rose in the heart of a smooth, circular dais. I sighed and took a few steps forward, flicking my eye across the courtyard. The patterned walls and the pillared mosaics felt old. Something caught my eye, and I swung my head around to view the ruins of the Infernal Clock, just behind the crystal stem."Oh, bother," I said—and felt the bear trap spring closed around my ankle.

CHAPTER TWENTY-EIGHT

The Gambler

Resting on the dais, as if the sword had been cast aside as useless or a cheap novelty prize, was the Roseblade.

The *Roseblade*!

I took an urgent step forward and then faltered, common sense catching up with my desire to recover the sword and behead one or two uppity gods with it.

Shadowman had been right about my desire to kill the Everlasting. Simple, petty revenge drove that desire. They had wronged me, and I wanted to wrong them back before they gained a foothold in the Story Thread and plunged us all into war. But this was too easy.

It's a trap—has to be. A snare set to snap my bloody neck…

I cast a quick subtle net of sensory enchantment with a few muttered words and a wave of my hand. The net shuddered across the plateau, invisible to the eye, searching for life or any unseen invocations. When I pulled the net back in, the amount of raw data cast through my mind as bright sparks of light and energy almost forced me to my knees.

I swayed as if drunk. Atlantis brimmed and damn near shrieked with feral energy—something I should have expected, really. *Enough to blend the Historian's unique mind.* Bands of Will, of hidden Origin, swam through the ether, coursing swift and unstoppable like a river turned to flood. The very stonework, glass, and marble, *thrummed* with Will.

The city was a powerful reactor, layered with untold years of energy that had only grown stronger and *wild* in the ten millennia since Atlantis was lost.

I severed my sensory net, broke the enchantment, and chuckled. No telling what retrieving the Roseblade would do. But only a few pieces were left on the board now. The game was all but over, and as was par for the course round these parts, those left standing would make their final moves in the city where the sordid mess began—for me, at least. There were not a lot of players left, either, which made those of us playing for keeps all the more dangerous.

Oblivion was watching, of that I could be damn sure.

Tal… Blimey, I should've just stayed in that memory with Clare, I thought, a touch wryly and only half joking.

Sophie stepped up behind me and grasped my arm. "Is that what I think it is?" she whispered.

"The Roseblade!" Ethan, on my other side, gaped. "We should—"

"Don't move," I snapped. "Don't take another step. This is a trap. Oh good grief, if ever I've seen one… You don't leave something that priceless lying around. Particularly when you know that I'm coming after it. We're expected."

Pick it up, whispered the insane voice in my mind. *Trap or not, you hold that blade and* nothing *can stop you.*

I took a few steps forward, skirting around my bloodstains in the stonework, and glanced from pillar to pillar, dais to the empty space over the edge of the plateau, and finally to the shattered stem of the Infernal Clock. *Where did you hide the rest of those petals, Emily? I could've brought you back, if you'd kept just one of those nearby.*

"Coulda, woulda, shoulda…" I muttered.

I spiraled closer to the Roseblade, and the sky failed to fall. Nothing erupted in cascading sheets of liquid flame, and no Elder Gods made an appearance.

Another step and I was on the dais, gazing down at the withered stem of the Infernal Clock. When I'd severed the Clock and shattered the rose, the stem had burst outward in thin strands of fragile crystal. A dark slot about the length of my hand and as wide as my thumb disappeared down into the heart of the stem. *Curious*… I looked past the Clock and at the sword of celestial illusion.

The Roseblade had been tainted.

"Shit." I knelt down on my haunches above the blade, about as close as I dared, and sighed heavily. The petals within the crystal sword had blackened, just like the ones in Myth. Oblivion had passed on his taint to both known weapons of celestial illusion. The Roseblade looked *sick*, broken, and I feared what using its power would do to me if I picked it up.

"A strange hesitance in you, Declan Hale," Lord Oblivion of the Everlasting said. "Times were, you'd have claimed that sword and wiped a few cities off the map before the sun was halfway across the sky."

I licked my lips, bared my teeth, and stood. Oblivion sat atop one of the four pillars that were at each corner of the courtyard. Tal's legs dangled, and he swung them back and forth against the obsidian stonework.

"Oh, Tal…" Sophie whispered.

"You didn't need to slaughter the Knights on the Plains of Perdition," I said.

Oblivion grinned and clapped Tal's hands together. "I needed your attention, Declan."

"You've never lost it. One day you'll regret that." I crossed my arms over my chest. "Scarred Axis sends his regards."

"Ah, I'd felt ripples in the ether… Another of us, set loose from his prison. And at your hand, no less, Declan! What is it you always say? Oh, yes. You're a sad song stuck on repeat, baby." The last he said using Tal's voice, unblemished by the gravelly tone of his own. Sophie choked back a sob. "How is my clever brother?"

"I sent him into the Void." That wiped the smile from Tal's face. "Did he really construct some sort of Will-driven engine?"

"Yes," Oblivion hissed. "He stole the fire of the gods and gave it to humanity. Traitor, I branded him, to our Family and our Father. The Origin Matrix gave your people *teeth*, Declan. All that you have achieved or ever will, you owe to the Everlasting Scarred Axis."

Axis was telling the truth… which means Will is failing. Annie's eyes, violet and afraid, were just the start of something catastrophic. "Well, you got me here," I said. "What is it you want?"

"Fitting that we've come full circle to where we first met, Declan." Oblivion gestured to the remains of the Infernal Clock. "Where you and Miss Levy bargained for the Degradation. I'm going to kill you and your companions today, Declan."

"Oh?"

Oblivion smiled. "Unless you pick up the Roseblade."

The corrupted sword pulled at the corner of my eye. "You want me to have the sword?"

"It's a trick," Ethan said. "Has to be."

"Speak again, and I'll rip your heart from your chest," Oblivion said, picking at loose strands on Tal's blouse.

I gave Ethan a warning glance, and in that moment when I looked away from Oblivion, the Everlasting *blurred* through the air and stood between my friends and me.

He winked at me again and then slammed Tal's hand into Ethan. I *felt* his ribs crack. He was hurled backwards, six feet into the air and out *over the edge of the tower.*

Sophie did something quick, clever, and—I imagine—purely instinctual. Her palms blazed white, and a lasso of power whipped through the air and wrapped around Ethan's waist like a belt. None too gently, she pulled him back onto the plateau before gravity could end his life.

Oblivion snarled and used Sophie's distraction to grab her around the neck. As Ethan hit the floor, the Everlasting drove Tal's fingernails into Sophie's neck, squeezing hard enough to choke her, and drawing blood in five little crescents. Sophie gagged and clawed at Tal's arm, but Oblivion's grip was unbreakable.

Oblivion turned to face me, holding Sophie in front of him like a shield—or a lamb for the slaughter. "Pick up the sword."

I glanced at the Roseblade but made no move toward the sword.

"One squeeze, and I'll crush her throat." Oblivion licked Tal's lips and lifted Sophie off her feet. Her white sneakers kicked uselessly in the air as she struggled for breath. "I will tear her head from her neck, Declan, unless you *pick up that sword*!"

"Boss…" Ethan gasped, cradling his broken ribs. He looked wildly between Sophie and me. "Please."

"What's the end game here?" I asked, feeling Sophie's pain as if it were my own. *They always*—always—*suffer for your games…*

"The *Atlanteans*"—Oblivion spat—"sealed away more than just my brothers and sisters when they created the Infernal Clock. Our armies, our armadas and great weapons—vast resources garnered over centuries—were suspended in time, locked by the Clock. The Roseblade is the key, Declan, but only the blood of a *willing* Knight can turn the key in the lock. You see the recess before you?"

I looked down at the ruins of the Infernal Clock. The Roseblade would fit quite nicely in the slot I'd noticed earlier in the stem. *Shit.*

With a weary trepidation, I grasped the hilt of the Roseblade and raised the sword. As always, the crystal blade felt far too light for its size. Through the handle ran jarring shocks, singing the same old song of unfathomable power, but on a piano out of key.

"Declan Hale, Shadowless," Oblivion said. "You will unleash the Peace Arsenal, or I will snap this whelp's neck."

The Peace Arsenal? "I… don't think I'll be doing that."

Oblivion growled. "You'd let her die?"

A ball of fear rose from my gut to my throat. I swallowed hard. *No.* "Yes."

I was stalling, searching for a way out. But in my heart, I knew…

"You have been groomed for this, Hale," Oblivion said. "From the moment you were born, the Everlasting have tied you to this path. You think it coincidence you've met *four* of us, while the masses think us nothing but myth? I *own* you, boy. You live only at my sufferance."

He cut Tal's hand down through the air and snarled. "Now dance, puppet. You severed the Infernal Clock and shattered the bars on our prison. Finish the job and use that cursed blade to unleash the Peace Arsenal!"

Dumbest fucking name... I held the sword at the ready and didn't know which choice I was about to take.

Sophie stared at me. Ethan looked grim and offered me an uncertain shoulder shrug. Tal, hidden behind eyes of blood, could give me nothing. But then, did I really need their guidance at this point?

A puppet, was I? Bound to this course because I'd always sacrifice my friends and the people I loved for the greater good? *The greater greed…*

"Perhaps you don't know me as well as you think you do, my lord Oblivion," I said carefully. For the sake of my sanity, there was only one choice to be made that day. And, really, it wasn't much of a choice.

Oblivion squeezed Sophie's throat. Her eyes bulged, and she choked, bucking in his unnaturally strong grip. "I will break her, Hale. And then I will make her sister drink her heart's blood."

"No doubt," I said. "You're the big bad. You're the nightmare and the thing under the bed. Shit, we've all been so afraid of you for over ten thousand years. Dark thoughts of you exist in every culture across the millions of worlds dangling from the Story Thread. And yet…"

"And yet what?" Oblivion snarled, turning Tal's beautiful face ugly.

"And yet I'm not afraid of you." I laughed and took a seat on the edge of the dais. I used the Roseblade for support, tip digging into the marble and ethereal crystal glowing softly in the half-light. "Perhaps you had my number years ago, even as far back as my birth, but your plans and machinations cut both ways, asshole. After all I've done and all I've seen, you think I care about one more death?"

Ethan swore. "Declan, no…"

Sophie's nerve broke, and she wept.

"Oh yes, I'm afraid so." I pointed a finger at Oblivion. "So listen closely, because I'm through being a pawn. You need me, do you hear? You've always needed me. I don't know why it *had* to be me, but okay, I can take it. Luck of the draw, you ken? Someone had to be the universe's favorite fuck-up." I ran a hand through my hair and sighed. "So as I see it, I've got something to sell—and honey, it ain't going to be cheap."

Oblivion absorbed my words, and given the look on Tal's face, he didn't find their taste to his liking. I could see him weighing his options—the mind of a god, painted clear on the face of a young girl. My girl.

After a long moment, he asked, "What… is your price?" His voice was low, dangerous.

I swallowed hard and steeled my resolve, but for the first time, I could feel the true ire of the creature inside Tal. It wasn't a lie when I said I didn't give a fuck. After so long and the stakes always so high, I was just tired—and there were miles to go before I could sleep. But that low voice, the crimson glare… I was trying to outfox the Devil, and he knew it.

I stood, walked around the dais to the recess in the Infernal Clock, and rested the tip of the blade against it. "My friends go free in the cruiser. Your word, which I know better than most and from the old accords, is *binding*. I'll have your word that you will not harm them so long as I unleash this… arsenal."

Oblivion stared at me, licked Tal's lips, and I knew his eternal mind was searching for a loophole or a hidden snare. "Agreed."

Was that a note of eagerness in his tone?

"And one more thing," I said. "Just a little thing, really. You will give Tal back to me—her mind, body, and soul. I would bargain with you, Lord Oblivion, for Tal Levy. An arsenal for just one girl and the lives of my friends. Hell, I'll even throw in a coupon for a bottle of house wine at Paddy's with any full-price meal to sweeten the deal."

"You do not have enough to bargain for both," Oblivion said. "Choose—your friends or your lover."

"How about I throw in seventy-five percent of a free Subway sandwich?" I spat at the ground and swiped the Roseblade down through the air. A reverberating *thrum* echoed across the courtyard and out into the open air. "Never in life. That meatball sub is mine, and my bargain is for *both*, Oblivion—or I swear *by the Everlasting* that I will use this sword to cast Atlantis into the Void."

"I will find another host," he said. "You condemn someone else to this fate. Do you think this woman will love you for that? She, who knows best my touch?"

"I don't care if she loves me," I lied. "I've always loved her—and I'm willing to hand over an armada of warships and god knows what else to my enemies for that love. Like I said, I don't give a fuck about the game anymore. I'm tired of playing. I want… I want the little things to matter again. I don't want to gamble with the *fate of the fucking cosmos* hanging in the balance."

"The contract will only bind me so long as you keep your word," Oblivion rasped. "You fail to unlock the Peace Arsenal, and she is mine forever. And I will make her *suffer* for your broken promise, Hale."

"You'll have your weapons," I said. "Honestly, I couldn't care less after all these years. Just give her back, give me that—a victory, however selfish or small when weighed against the damage you'll do… I just want to win, for once."

Oblivion used Tal's mouth to smile, her eye to wink. "Then enjoy your victory, Shadowless. From what I have seen of your future, it will not last long. You have my word—your friends are awarded safe passage and I will abandon my host. Our bargain is struck."

I didn't expect fireworks, thunder, or lightning and I didn't get them. An invisible weight seemed to fall around my shoulders, however. Another shackle to my soul. *Nothing for it…*

With no more moves left to make, I plunged the Roseblade into the recess and unleashed the Everlasting's Peace Arsenal.

CHAPTER TWENTY-NINE

The Future Soon

The blade sank into the stem of the Infernal Clock as if it had been made for that purpose. The handle of the weapon splintered and a metal barb exploded through my palm and out the back of my hand, pinning me to the sword.

No stranger to injury, I grunted and bit back on the pain, but I couldn't have released the sword now even if I wanted to. My blood flowed down the sword, mingling with the crystal, and strange light shone up from the remains of the Infernal Clock.

For a long moment, nothing happened.

And then the tower shook to its foundations, and wind howled across the plateau, buffeting me like a sail in a storm. I gritted my teeth and bore the gale as the corrupted petals in the blade began to shine with a sickly black light.

Oblivion smiled through Tal and spread her arms wide, casting Sophie aside. She rolled across the plateau, her neck bruised and bleeding. Ethan swooped in and grabbed his girlfriend, pulling her close and hunching himself against the wind. *He's a good kid…*

Tal's head snapped back toward the sky, and a slick oily mist, crackling with energy, bled from her mouth, nostrils, and eyes. *Bargain struck…* The essence of Lord Oblivion abandoned Tal, and after hanging in the air for a moment, dispersed into the ether with a thunderclap of power.

Oblivion was gone.

Tal moaned, clutching her head, and fell to her knees as the whole wide world started to tear apart at the seams.

The great parapets encircling the plateau splintered and fell away, nearly crashing into the hovering cruiser, as great cracks ran like spider webs through the old stone floor. The tower was coming down—*and I couldn't release the blade.*

"Take Tal and run!" I cried above the wind and the oncoming devastation. "Back to the cruiser! Leave me!"

Sophie crawled across the courtyard toward her sister. Tal had fallen to the floor, rocking back and forth, and she flinched and looked up when Sophie's hand came down on her shoulder. Their eyes met—so much was said in a glance—and they embraced. Blood gushing down the Roseblade from my punctured hand, I still managed to smile.

That alone has made my choices worth it…

Ethan appeared and pulled Sophie to her feet. "We have to go."

"Help me carry her," Sophie said, grasping Tal under her arms. Tal looked disorientated, pained, and she glanced over me as if I were a stranger. Ethan grabbed her other arm, and together he and Sophie helped Tal gain her feet.

"Declan," he said. "Come on!"

I tried to release the sword and was driven to my knees by some unseen weight on my shoulders. The blade protested, its ugly petals shining with dead, Voidish light and shooting bolts of pure agony through my body.

I couldn't let go. As Oblivion had said, the blade needed the blood of a Knight to unleash the Peace Arsenal.

"You have to go now," I told my friends. "You have to leave me."

Ethan cut his hand down through the air, struggling to support Tal against the wind. "Fuck that."

Tal frowned, blinked hard as if dazed, and stumbled to keep her footing.

"I can't let go, and this tower is going to come crashing down!" I said. "Ethan, Sophie—you will do as I ask and leave."

Tears streamed down Sophie's face. "But we can't…"

I fixed them with my sternest, most Knightly glare. "You asked me for this. Broken quill, you told me to be selfish. I saved her from Oblivion but not without cost. I'm that cost, and it's a price I'm more than happy to pay. So you will do as I ask now—you will both be selfish and save yourselves. Leave."

Ethan took a step toward me. I sent a blast of Willfire to scatter at his feet, keeping him away.

Chunks of stone began to collapse under our feet. The ramp up to the hovering cruiser would not be accessible much longer.

So I smiled at my friends, gave them a wink, and made them a promise I had no idea if I would keep. "I'll see you again. You think this, of all things, could end me?" I scoffed at the idea. "Now go. I won't be far behind."

The power in the sword was building, and the whole dais started to glow. The liquid light flowed along invisible tracks, forming archaic runes, and the blade grew hot in my grip. A breeze rushed up from the slot in the Clock stem, tossing my waistcoat back. I didn't know what was about to happen—and I was afraid.

At least my friends would be safe.

"Thank you, Declan," Sophie said, with such sincerity that my resolve almost broke. She knew—oh, they both knew—what leaving me meant.

Sophie and Ethan fled, stumbling a little with Tal dangling between them.

The tower split down the middle just as my friends reached the cruiser ramp. *Go on…* They ascended the ramp and were just about to enter the cruiser when Tal bucked in their grip, throwing herself back. She rolled back down the ramp and landed on her knees and elbows.

Her honey-brown hair whipped in the breeze, and she looked up—right at me—a fierce smile and a mask of determination on her face.

"Tal!" Sophie cried. "No, *Tal*!"

Tal leapt to her feet, and just as the courtyard broke away entirely and a monumental piece of the tower collapsed on the ruined city below, she closed the distance between us and *jumped* across the gap, landing on the dais before the remains of the Infernal Clock. The wind whipped up strands of her long hair into my face, tickling my chin.

Sophie made to run after her sister, but Ethan grabbed her around the waist and pulled her into the cruiser. A good thing, too, as the ramp now ended with a mile of open sky. The last I saw of my friends was Sophie *clawing* at Ethan to release her…

And then the Roseblade exploded.

A blinding burst of heat and light overwhelmed me, and I shielded my good eye against the brightness. The world shook underfoot, and when I chanced a look, I saw that the dais was aglow with a rainbow of glyphs and runes, spinning across the diameter of the stone faster than the eye could follow.

The Roseblade melted in my grip, hot and fierce, releasing my wounded and bloodied palm, and I ran across to Tal and put my arms around her as the dais was swept out of Atlantis and sent tumbling into the Void. Thunderous wailing and even harsher coils of air forced me to my knees, cradling Tal against the storm as the encroaching darkness absorbed everything but the ten feet of glowing stone beneath us.

Blackened petals from the melted blade stuck to the dais. The sword had been destroyed, but just *what* in all creation had I unlocked?

We're going to die… Just when I've got her back, in my arms, we're going to die.

Tal looked up into my eye, and a thousand words were said in a heartbeat. We both knew it was the end—together again, only briefly. She had abandoned Sophie and Ethan to die with me.

I gasped, and something hot and warm rolled down my cheek.

Tears fell from my eye and into Tal's hair. I was *weeping.* And the odds against that were a long fool's bet, so much so that I laughed, honest and true, and pulled Tal closer.

If I was to die young, then so be it. Fuck the causality; at least I'd freed Tal from Oblivion's grip. One good act before the end. Time and the Story Thread could sort itself out regarding Emily and my son, given that we had never done the deed, so to speak, to conceive him in the first place. If I were to die here, then bring on the darkness, because I was done and dusted a long time ago.

Death seemed like a fair price to pay for what I'd achieved.

Blimey, if anything, I'd gotten off light. Death was easy—I'd done it before and felt nothing but relief. The sheer cost of my life up until that point was overwhelming. The people who had died for me, because of me… the numbers were staggering. Lives I had ended, cut short, sheared as white roses in the rain. Lives that just *weren't* anymore. It was too easy to attach some cause or purpose to why the dead were dead. To end the Tome Wars, to stop the Everlasting, to prevent a Voidflood…

All the reasons I had acted. All the reasons why the weight of a million souls—and a million more—sat heavy on my shoulders.

Easier to make the choices than to live with the dire cost.

That's the rub, you know. The unseen but all-too-well-known consequence to playing the game. I could make all the right choices, checkmate in two moves, and still carry the infernal weight of those I had damned.

It would be better, easier, if I were crueler.

Better if I were a lot of things. Knight, exile, renegade, ghost, shadowless… father.

The dais struck something hard, and we were knocked off-balance, out of each other's arms, and bright reality reasserted itself. Like paint spilled from a tin against a blank canvas, an azure sky spread across the heavens, bleeding over a true horizon under a golden sun. Scents of cool air, of wildflowers on the wind, and the sounds of a bustling city far below appeared on the canvas, drawn by some unseen hand.

We'd fallen out of the Void—*alive.*

When and where… I looked around, taking in my surroundings, and fell off my feet with a strangled cry. It seemed we hadn't moved at all, at least in space, but the courtyard and the scattered crystal petals burnt into the floor… I landed on my injured hand, and a spike of pain shooting up my arm forced me onto my back. A bird, an eagle or seahawk, flew across the cloudless sky.

Somewhere nearby, I heard shuffling and a soft gasp.

"I don't know if I should've done that," I said to the shuffling. "Unleashing the Arsenal… it was selfish." The shuffling stopped. "When all is said and done, Oblivion is going to do far more harm than good."

"So you'd rather I had stayed his leash?" Shuffling whispered.

"I'd rather a lot of things, you know. Rather I'd been born to some other role and left alone to enjoy the simple things—sandy beaches, blue oceans, tall mountains, and fresh snowfall." Blackberry jam. "I love you," I said, cradling my wounded hand in my lap as I sat up. "Even when we were kids and didn't know what that meant, I loved you."

Tal Levy sat on the dais next to me and hefted me up into a sitting position. She placed her small arm across my shoulders, pulling me in close. "Love you, too. Please look at me, Declan."

I looked at the scattered rose petals instead, dispersed from the Roseblade and fused to the dais. A profound relief, to have destroyed that sword, and another ounce of victory I could scrape from the bottom of the barrel.

The world around us felt familiar, like a comfortable pair of boots, and a terrifying idea of just where we had ended up gripped me and wouldn't let go. I couldn't say how far the blade had pulled us through the Void—certainly a good distance, but we were exactly where we had started: the tower in Atlantis.

Only here it still stood, whole and hearty. The tower looked *new*.

We were alive. I could guess where I was, but *when* I was…

I feared I was dead and this—and Tal—was a cruel dream.

But Tal felt real. Her warm breath, her olive skin, and the quiet strength in her arm across my shoulders. At the Tomb of the Sleeping Goddess she had been *real* only in the sense that she was a mouthpiece for the Everlasting. She had been torn asunder then and for the last six years, but now… a bargain struck and another death cheated.

Please look at me, Declan, she had said.

"I'm afraid you'll disappear," I whispered. After all the years and all the worlds, how would I even know what was a dream or not? Did it matter?

We lived in a universe full of horrors, and we strolled through worlds that were once dreams in the minds of madmen. And I guessed you had to be a little mad to not only dream but to actually try to create that dream. Put the words on the page, so to speak. Forget and the Story Thread, at their heart, were nothing more than a dream within a dream, imposing themselves on pure reality.

After everything, it would surprise me little if I woke up in a padded cell wearing a straitjacket. Although I would be disappointed.

Strange shuttles and speeding craft surrounded the tower. Cannons and sharp weaponry zeroed in on me and Tal. Footsteps echoed up from within the tower, and a single guard, garbed in resplendent armor and toting an honest-to-god blunderbuss, emerged on the plateau.

"*Ji'to, nah*!" he barked, gesturing with his weapon.

I didn't recognize the language but the meaning was universal. Tal and I rose to our knees and put our hands above our heads. My left hand, impaled and mostly cauterized by the Roseblade, still bled a little, tricking down my arm. Tal slipped her left hand into my right. Her fingers were warm, alive, and I couldn't help but *laugh*.

Here we were—young, battle-torn, once dead, and alive—the pair of us… and unless I missed my guess, thrust back in time at least ten thousand years at the cost of an Everlasting armada and God knew how much war and carnage to come back home.

But after all was said and done, the last six years and the odds against us, there we were, together again. I'd won for once.

And that was hilarious.

"*Al'do… sadwe*!" barked the Atlantean guard, his ancient blunderbuss pointed square between my eyes. "*Na-hoc one sulari!*"

"I think he wants your number," I said to Tal, as soldiers descended on flat spheres of energy from the hovering shuttles. *We must have tripped an alarm…*

She chuckled, low and soft. "Your eye patch?"

"Yeah?"

"Looks good."

"Oh, by the Everlasting, not even half as good as you, songbird."

Tal squeezed my fingers. "I love that name. Shoes are scuffed, and the waistcoat seems a little worse for wear, though."

"*Hala-du'sad we*!" The guard gestured upward with his weapon. Another universal sign, if ever there was one. Tal and I stood, our hands still clasped together above our heads.

Far too long since I've held her hand…

"There's this little bar," I said. "Quiet, out of the way, only blown up once, and well on its way to being rebuilt… Paddy's Pub in Joondalup on True Earth. You, me, and the Wednesday steak special make three?"

Tal giggled—a sound so pure I doubt she had uttered the same in over six years. "Are you asking me out on a date, Mister Hale?"

"I'd never presume, Miss Levy."

"Maybe you should, just this once…"

"I'm sorry for getting you killed. Mind, body, and soul."

"Don't be. I chose it." Tal sighed. "And we'll always have Atlantis…"

The guard scowled. "*Altantias*? *Suur… Nae Infernius lo dalis grewn*!"

"I think we've pissed him off." I was good at that. Some would say a touch too good. Paddy's would have to wait about ten millenniums, unless my math was off. "Would you ever want to be the wife of a blackberry farmer?"

Tal hummed over the question for a moment. "Would this farmer of mine wear a devastatingly handsome eye patch and a ragged waistcoat?"

"I fear he would insist. But I'd make you queen of my jam empire…"

Tal looked me in the eye. I almost had to look away from her gaze, from eyes that had seen through me since we had first met—such a short time ago in the grand scheme of things. "Okay, one date at this pub of yours."

The soldiers swooped in behind us, pulled our hands apart, and produced sparkling manacles of star iron. I winced a bit as my wounded hand was pulled behind my back and the cuffs snapped shut around my wrists.

Before they pulled us away, I leaned in close and caught Tal's lips with my own, nothing more than a brush of a kiss and soon ended. It was the best in my life. "Got you," I said.

Tal laughed, clear and *free*. "Oh, Declan, you had me from the start."

THE END OF
BOOK THREE!
☺

Bonus Story!

A sneak peek at the first installment of Joe Ducie's zombie apocalypse novel!

Z-APOC

I – BABY, I'VE BEEN HERE BEFORE

For John Allen, the end of the world began with a slutty pumpkin.

Looking back a year to the day, he found it almost prophetically funny that he'd been dressed as one of the dead that Halloween night.

As a walker.

The soulless.

A biter.

Call them what you will, John had been dressed to impress. His zombie makeup, torn clothes, and yellow contact lenses had swept Holly Beckett, the slutty pumpkin from some sitcom, off her feet and into the backseat of his '87 Astra. The logistics of the pumpkin costume had almost foiled any foreplay, but John had persevered, as lads thinking with their dick are wont to do.

That's the last good thing that happened to me, John thought, shifting into third on the Pacific Highway, as dawn crept over the horizon a few hundred clicks north of what had once been Sydney.

He smiled as he thought of Holly, her orange face dashed with pumpkin-seed freckles and a green leafed hat atop her head. As cute as they come, only just sixteen, and a year below him back at Ocean Bay High School. They had laughed, they had fucked, and they had drunk cheap children's booze, *Chateau Cardboard*, as Bowie's Greatest Hits blasted out of the radio.

"You're a sweet thing, John Allen," she had whispered, her breath hot against his neck.

A zombie had eaten Holly's freckled face a day later, as the whole country—and, as far as Haven knew, the world—had torn itself asunder. John, alone and afraid, had buried her under the cherry blossoms south of Dunsborough. Holly clawed her way out of her shallow grave later that night, as he slept nearby in the Astra, and John had killed his first Z—with a tyre iron.

You always remember your first. He snorted, veered around an overturned sheep carrier full of bones, kicked up orange dust in the emergency lane, and jumped up into fourth gear. The road ahead was clear.

John had kept pretty close to the coast this trip to the mainland. The survival business was always touch and go, and what worked for one didn't always work for another, but he'd found some supplies and encountered very little in the way of hordes near the coast on past trips. Suburbia and the city itself would be a different game entirely, but a year on since the end of the world—*and I feel fine*—and most outlying towns had zilch in the way of supplies.

These days survivors of Z-Apoc had to suck it up and scavenge nearer to what had once been mass-population centres.

Every ten minutes or so John flicked the stereo in his purple Jeep Cherokee from the CD player over to the AM/FM bands, scanning for a signal. Casey Tully, the comms girl back on Haven, had a theory that if there were still any government or military in New South Wales, they'd be pinging emergency messages off the radio towers in and around Sydney. So far John had heard nothing.

He didn't expect to hear anything. Mainland belonged to the Z's.

John flicked back to the Chili Peppers and tapped his hands against the wheel, keeping the beat. He had been driving for near-on seven hours, down from the docks at Port Macquarie, making a wide berth around the charred pit of grinning skulls that had been Newcastle, and heading for Sydney. Almost time for a rest stop, and perhaps a power nap. Dangerous to sleep alone, but locked doors usually provided enough time for a quick getaway.

The roads had been disturbingly quiet—free of Z's.

Pleased with the time he was making, John allowed himself a rare treat. He popped the tab on a can of warm Coca-Cola and savoured that fizzy first sip.

"Oh sweet gravy, baby."

He finished the can and tossed it over his shoulder into the backseat, next to a small chest of assorted weaponry. One pistol—never used—garden shears, a hammer, and a six-inch hunting blade. His tried and true favourite weapon, the crowd pleaser—a cricket bat he'd affectionately dubbed 'Thumper'—rested on the passenger seat within arm's reach.

The list of Haven's sorely needed supplies was taped to the dashboard. Food was on the list, but not the priority. Medical supplies first and foremost, followed swiftly by motor oil, batteries, and any sort of combustible fuel. John's contribution to the island community of Haven, known as Hamilton Island before the outbreak, was these supply runs. He, and a dozen other men and women, braved the mainland once a month, travelling down by boat to Port Macquarie, bypassing Brisbane entirely. Most of the land north of Brisbane had been picked dry. This was his sixth and, so far, least productive trip.

A second, unofficial list was folded in his pocket. Special requests from some of Haven's two hundred and fifty residents—mostly liquor and cigarettes. A pack of cigarettes could be worth as much as a week's rations, and the Haven Council had expressly forbid their use as currency, which made them the perfect item to scavenge in exchange for favours back on the island. Jack Trask, a horticulturist before the end of the world and Haven's crop supervisor, was rumoured to be growing a tobacco patch somewhere on the island. If the rumours were true, Jack would soon be the world's first post-apocalyptic millionaire.

Which was bad for business, as far as John was concerned, but he had Trask in his pocket, for now. The old man needed a steady supply of eye drops for his glaucoma.

John rounded a curve in the highway, squinting against the bright mirage of heat waves dancing on the hot asphalt. Down to the east, the land dropped away to coastal plains. The ocean glittered like a band of diamonds. Ahead, bauxite-rich orange sand had blown over most of the road. Not in the mood for an invisible pothole, he slowed to a crawl and glimpsed a fallen road sign lying in the scrub. As good a place as any to stop for a leak.

Pulled up onto the shoulder, John sat idle for a few minutes, and scanned his surroundings. Z's were attracted by noise, even the dull roar of an idling engine. He couldn't see any of the bastards, but that didn't mean they weren't there. He reached into the back, holstered his pistol, strapped on the knife, and lifted Thumper up over his head as he exited the Cherokee.

A wave of dry heat almost knocked him back into the jeep. The air carried a taste of salt and the heady aroma of native bottlebrush.

John unzipped and relieved himself on the fallen road sign. He washed away some of the dust coating the green, reflective distance marker and saw something encouraging.

WYONG	**30**
BEROWRA	**86**
SYDNEY	**123**

Almost to Wyong—one of a scant number of towns still likely to have something in the way of supplies, given its relative remoteness. At least according to Casey, who was often right about these things. The land between

Sydney and Brisbane, two major cities, fell hard and fast to the Z's. With any luck, John could gather what he needed there and avoid circling any closer to Sydney. He'd yet to see any of the infected this trip, but that luck couldn't hold forever.

Something else was written underneath the sand on the sign. John swung his stream that'a'way and washed the muck clear. Someone had scrawled a crude message in ugly, red paint. The sun had faded it to crimson reminiscent of old, rusty blood.

DEAD AHEAD!
☹

Not so encouraging, but the sad face was a nice touch.

He got back into the Cherokee, locked the doors, and went to sleep for an hour.

When he awoke just after nine, the air in the jeep was stifling. Aussie summer—brutal and unforgiving. And it didn't bother the dead one godforsaken bit. The virus, or whatever it was, had thrived in last year's heat. It hadn't affected everyone—a slim few, like John, were immune. Casey had crunched some very loose numbers, based mostly on her own observations and stories from other survivors, and tentatively suggested that one in every two thousand had been naturally immune to what had become known as Z-Apoc—*zaypoc*—the end of the world disease.

And of those immune, a bite from the infected was still a short drop and a quick stop. Fever followed by rage followed by death... followed by *not*-death. For that reason, John wore shin guards under his jeans, two pair front and back, a thick leather jacket even in the heat, and kept a hockey helmet in his emergency gear. *But*, he reasoned, *if you were at the stage where the helmet was necessary, then you were most likely fucked six ways from Sunday anyway.* And not by a slutty pumpkin.

With a quarter-tank left in the Cherokee, John made the distance to Wyong in good time. He'd had to stop twice in the night and pump fuel manually from servo reservoirs, and would have to do so again before he left Wyong. Good thing about these country towns was an abundance of petrol stations. The roads were a little busier with dead cars closer to town, and he had to weave his way down the highway for the last few kilometres, getting out once or twice to smash windows and release the handbrakes on a few vehicles, nudging them gently out of the way with his mighty jeep.

Wyong was as silent as the grave.

As expected, great swaths of the town had burnt—months ago, if not the full year since Z-Apoc—and there wasn't a soul, living or dead, in sight.

"I know you're here, you bastards..." John whispered, and pulled into the lot of an abandoned 7/11 just off the main strip. Spider webs of cracks splintered the windows and the shelves looked bare from the car park, but a quick expedition might scrounge a few tins.

John suited up again, stepped out of the jeep, and stretched his legs before slinging an empty backpack over one shoulder. He gripped the worn rubber handle on Thumper hard enough to turn his knuckles white, and then relaxed.

The lot was quiet and the noise from his engine should have had any of the dead stumbling out of the minimart. *Conduct an environmental risk assessment,* Sergeant Charles Cook, Haven's security chief whispered in the back of John's mind. *Identify, Assess, Evaluate, Check, Review.*

John assessed, checked with his gut, then nodded. This was as safe as it got, and the supplies weren't going to come to him. Broken glass and sand crunched underfoot as he stepped inside. The air was stale but didn't stink of death or decay. The aisles had been ransacked months ago, toppled and discarded, but it looked like whoever had been through here had been in a hurry. They'd missed a diamond the size of his fist. He found an unopened packet of Mi-Goreng noodles on the top shelf. That alone made the 850 kilometres he'd travelled since midnight worth it. The rest of the shelves were bare. What hadn't been taken had turned rancid and dried in the heat. Nothing else to be had here.

John saddled up and circled the outskirts of the town in his Cherokee. He drove down Main Street, eyes peeled, and pulled up in front of Friendly's Chemist. Medical supplies were in dire need back on Haven. He had a good feeling about this place—but if there was nothing here, he'd have to brave Berowra or, worse, Sydney. That felt a little too much like suicide, but there was still the supposed distribution centre around here somewhere...

Most of the shelves were barren inside the chemist. A few packets of allergy meds and over-the-counter aspirin were all that remained. Not too shabby, but not worth the time and the risk. Moving quietly, John walked around the pharmacist's counter toward the prescription cabinets—the good stuff.

The cabinets had been sealed, even with the power out, and sometime in the last year the batteries or whatever protecting the drugs had failed. John, feeling giddy, kicked open the metal grate and began to stuff his pack with anything and everything.

Antibiotics—mostly penicillin. Some Tramadol and Maxalt. He found a stash of doxycycline, enough to last months, at the back of the first cabinet and cleared it out. He raided the second cabinet and stuffed his bag fit to burst. John returned the pack to the car, full of the good stuff, and retrieved another empty sack. He found some ciprofloxacin, excellent for infections. Doc Harvey had trained all the supply runners on how to separate the gold from the silt. Prednisone—steroids—was on his list. John filled half a satchel. Empty IV drip bags, syringes, and rubber tubing for blood transfusions were next.

In boxes next to the failed safety cabinets, John

found rubbing alcohol, betadine, and about a hundred triangular bandages. He loaded it all into the Cherokee. This was the best haul he'd ever stumbled across, and the day was still young.

Before moving on, John took a swig of water from his filtered store in the trunk and wiped the sweat from his brow. The day was going to be a scorcher, probably pushing mid-forties. He was sweating like a pig in his leather jacket and jeans, so he got in the car and cranked the A/C. Sweat began to dry cool and uncomfortable down his back.

"Okay..." He scratched a few of the key items off his supply list. Already this trip could be called a success, but he wanted to see if he could find the rumoured distribution centre. He had to check it out, at least to cross the town off the list as a viable source of supplies, if it had already been scavenged. "I need a map."

Well, Google was out, and GPS had become unreliable nine months ago.

John drove further down Main Street and pulled up in the town centre. He found an information board, cracked and warped after a year without maintenance, but the map of Wyong and surrounds was still readable. Marked on the map were a bunch of nearby tourist destinations—Burbank Nurseries, Little Creek Cheese Factory, and Muirs Lookout, just to name a few—and after a few minutes of study, John found what he was looking for.

Woolworth's Distribution Centre. A spot on the map about five kilometres out of town along Jilliby Road. *I drove past that road on the way in, I think—*

A high-pitched shriek cut through the silent, stagnant air like a knife and John almost jumped out of his skin. He turned on the spot, survival instincts kicking in, and dived back into the Cherokee, slamming the door shut and locking it fast.

The car still running, he made to flee, when a woman

hobbled out from around the dilapidated Subway across from the town centre, about thirty metres from John and the jeep. Even from that distance, John could see her face was a mask of fear. Only one thing, these days, could cause such distress.

The Z's came one at a time. Staggering and stumbling around the back of the Subway after the woman. First one, then two, and then all at once a group at least twenty strong and growing. *Shit, a horde!*

In varying states of decay and rot, what had once been men, women, and children gave chase to the poor women. John hesitated with his hand over the jeep's horn. If he could get her attention... but that would bring the horde, too. He froze, gripped with indecision. A hot shot of nerves shivered up his spine and forced goose bumps to ripple up and down his arms.

The Z's stumbled after the woman—not quite running, but moving at a brisk enough clip on rotten legs. Lifeless eyes glared from sunken and hollow sockets, jaws hung askew and bloody, and the low, deep-throated moan from the creatures rose and fell in eerie waves.

The woman ran across the town green—wild, weedy brown grass—favouring her left leg. She limped with every step, dragging her right ankle. The pack of Z's closed in, like sharks scenting blood in the water. Her head snapped toward the sound of John's engine, and her eyes widened when she saw him sitting behind the wheel of the Cherokee. She changed directions, just as a Z caught her hair in its hands and yanked her head back. The woman screamed and pulled herself free, almost fell, but recovered and limped toward John.

He moved his hand from the horn over to the automatic door lock.

He hesitated again. The Z's were too close. She'd never make it inside.

The woman slammed her hands desperately on the driver's window, tried the door and found it locked, and moved to the rear door. That was locked, too, of course. She stared at John, eyes wild and pleading. His finger had frozen above the unlock...

John and the woman shared a brief look and then the horde washed over her and tore her to pieces. She died screaming, as the Cherokee rocked back and forth under the surge of mindless, hungry Z's.

Taking a deep, shuddering breath, John shifted into reverse and clenched the wheel hard as the undead stumbled and moaned against the windows, leaving bloody smears as they clawed to get inside. He reversed slowly, carefully, taking his time and staying calm, knocking a few of the Z's to the road and driving over them. A trail of distorted, rotten flesh spewed out in disgusting patterns from the front of the jeep.

"Nothing I could've done," he muttered.

He put the woman's terrified face from his mind. *What were you even doing out here on your own?*

II — THUMPER'S LAST STAND

On his way out of Wyong to Jilliby Road, back up on the highway, John stopped at a Caltex Service Station to fill-up. A small place with only four pumps and broken windows, but it was quiet, with few places for Z's to hide. As usual, he sat idling for a few minutes, seeing if his presence attracted anything less than fresh, then got out of the jeep.

Working fast, he used his kit in the trunk to pry the cap off the pipe and breach the underground tanks. Having been syphoning fuel for a year now, the process was old hat. He unfurled his manual pump, stuck one end down the dark hole and the other in the jeep's tank. He had to prime the pump, turning the crank a few dozen times, before the fuel began to flow up from the reservoir. Through the clear tubes, the fuel looked clean, but he wouldn't really know until he was back on the road.

Some risks were unavoidable.

Hot and bothered from the pump, John sat on the rim of the jeep's trunk and knocked back a half-litre of water, resting Thumper on his knees. He watched, amused, as a troop of kangaroos bounced across the highway, disappearing into the scrub and trees. After the tank was full, John filled his two ten litre jerry cans. All things being even, he'd only need to stop once on the drive back to the dock at Port Macquarie.

As he loaded his gear and closed the trunk, a figure emerged from within the darkened interior of the petrol station, crunching glass underfoot and moving slowly.

"Hello," she said, brandishing a tyre iron like a club.

John waved away a few buzzing flies and regarded the woman. She was older than he was, but then at eighteen, a lot of folk were. Not *old* old, though. Mid- to late-twenties, closing in on thirty, perhaps. Her skin was a healthy tan, and her eyes shone like dark sapphires in the heat of the hazy day. A head of frazzled auburn hair clung to her brow. She wore a pair of dirty-white sneakers, khaki shorts, and a blue tank top stained navy with patches of sweat. Over her shoulder, she carried a tartan Burberry bag. John recognised the design. His mother had owned a matching scarf.

"Happy Halloween," he said, and moved around to the front of the jeep, cricket bat in hand. "You look like you haven't slept in days."

"I..." She hesitated, and tried for a smile. "Jeez, that's just what a girl wants to hear. I was travelling with a friend. She went into town this morning, to see about a car or a bike..."

"Young? Brunette? Jeans and a Wallabies jersey?"

She nodded.

"Ah." John kept his eyes away from the gore caked onto the jeep's bumper. "I'm sorry. I saw her go down in the town centre. I... There was nothing I could do."

The woman nodded again and wiped a quick tear from her cheek. She threw the tyre iron to the ground and fought back a sob. "I knew... when she didn't come back. I knew... Oh, Annie. I'm so sorry."

"Wasn't your fault," John said. "Z's got her."

"No..." The woman rubbed her hand on her shorts and offered to shake. "I'm Sarah. Doctor Sarah Bell, Canberra."

John considered, and then nodded. He took her hand. "John Allen. Perth."

"Perth? You've come a long way from home. You don't fear the dead?"

As soon as she said the words, two Z's stumbled around the side of the servo as if summoned, dressed in ragged overalls and stinking like a year's worth of decay. They caught sight of John, standing out in the open, and moaned low in their throats.

With a curse, John stepped in front of Sarah and readied Thumper. The Z's staggered toward him, the world's worst drunks, and as the first one got within arm's reach, John swung. His bat connected with the side of the creature's head and made a resounding, sickening thud.

The Z's may have been lifeless, reanimated corpses, carrying infection in every bite, but they had one weakness—they were rotting, however slowly. A good swing with the cricket bat popped most of their skulls like grapes, and John, a year into surviving the end of the world, was good with his swing.

"No, I don't fear the dead." John swung Thumper again, cracking the other Z's head like an egg. *Two sixes over the fence, and it's back to the pavilion for lunch.* Blood and gore, flecked with bone, splashed the road. He took a deep breath. "I fear the living, Sarah. What we became, after Z-Apoc took a hold. At least with the dead, you know what to expect. With the living…" John used the cuff of his shirt to gently wipe some blood splatter from Sarah's cheek. "Stranger danger, I'm afraid. We've all had to do terrible things to survive."

"You… you don't seem too bad."

John smiled. "According to the laws of where I'm from, a place we call Haven, I'm supposed to leave you out here alone now." He shrugged. "And if you try to follow me, I'm supposed to kill you."

Want to read more?

Check out joeducie.net *for the full story*

Z-APOC: Part 1 – When John Met Sarah

ABOUT THE AUTHOR

Joe Ducie (1987-) is a writer from Perth, Western Australia. By day, he charges a toll to cross a bridge he doesn't own. Yet by night, in a haze of scotch-fuelled insanity, he works tirelessly on an array of stories both short and long. Joe possesses a fierce love of a smooth finish. Under no circumstances should you ask him just what that means.

Joe was born in Barrow-in-Furness, Cumbria in November 1987, and currently resides in Perth, Western Australia. He is primarily an author of urban fantasy and science fiction aimed at young adults. His current stories include *Distant Star, The Rig* (winner of the 2012 Young Writers Prize), *Red vs. Blue*, *Z-Apoc* and *The Forgetful Library.*

Joe attended Edith Cowan University and graduated in 2010 with a Degree of Counterterrorism, Security and Intelligence. He went back, the idiot, and completed post-graduate studies in Security Science in 2011. Joe has also studied Creative and Professional Writing at Curtin University.

When not talking about himself in the third person, Joe enjoys devouring books at an absurdly disgusting rate and sampling fine scotch.

Contact Joe:
email: joe.ducie@gmail.com
Website: joeducie.net
Twitter: @joeducie
Facebook: /jducie

6393869R00167

Printed in Great Britain
by Amazon.co.uk, Ltd.,
Marston Gate.